BETH BOLDEN

To my husband.

Thank you for all the chores you do and the way you never fail to be my biggest cheerleader, but most of all, thank you for letting me borrow your nickname :)

Chapter One

Will Johnson ignored the ache in the small of his back, the inevitable pinch in his most comfortable sneakers, the sticky smear of half-congealed milkshake on his arm, and smiled at the customer in front of him.

Maybe it should've been hard, but actually, it was the easiest thing in the world. He loved this town, this new life, and most of all, the fact that it was *his* name above the door, his name printed on the napkins and on the menu, and that he controlled all of it. *Finally.*

Of course, *this* particular customer strained some of that happiness, but it was still easier than he'd ever imagined to smile at her and mean it.

"Welcome to Cherry's," he said. "What can I get you?"

"Oh, Will," Giana Moretti said, shooting him her family's trademark charming smile, "I forget how beautiful the store is and then I walk in and I'm just blown away all over again."

It was practically a crime not to smile at Giana when she smiled at you, especially like that. But by now he knew a smile was only the beginning.

Out of the corner of his eye he could see Kate, his manager and one of his three employees, wincing, as Giana reached out and put a hand on his arm.

The arm smeared with milkshake, no less.

But that didn't deter her, because in the two months Cherry's had been open, Will had learned that almost nothing deterred Giana Moretti.

"Thanks," he said. "What can I get you today, Giana?" Hoping that maybe this visit would be more straightforward than the last two. Like maybe Giana would order an ice cream cone or a sundae or a milkshake and then give him that big Moretti smile right before she walked back out of his door.

But if he'd been a betting man, he'd have lost.

"Oh, Will, you know exactly what you can get me," she said, a knowing light brightening her dark eyes. "And it's not some of your delicious ice cream."

"Unfortunately that's all that's on the menu today," he said, softening the blow with one of his own smiles.

I'm not on the menu.

Will could acknowledge that he'd had some overly flirtatious customers through his many years working in food service, but he'd never had one who wanted what Giana wanted.

Not a date for her. But for her *son.*

"Oh, what can it hurt?" she questioned. "You just text him—you kids are always texting, Luca tries to tell me why but I don't listen." She waved her hand, like she was dismissing her nephew's explanation in real time. "Enzo's such a nice boy, Will. Handsome and so smart. A wonderful painter."

Will struggled to keep a straight face. "I'm sure he is," he said. "But you know how busy I am getting this place going." *And this very handsome and smart son, who's a wonderful painter, isn't even* here *in Indigo Bay.*

Not that he'd been tempted to take the number anyway. It was too weird and he was not desperate enough for a date to let Giana Moretti deploy her matchmaking tactics on him.

She still claimed that she'd been instrumental in pairing Luca, her nephew, up with the town baker, Oliver Billings. Of course, Luca and Oliver had something *else* to say about how their relationship had begun.

"Life is not work, Will," Giana said very seriously. "I tell Enzo this all the time. He works too hard." She brightened. "Something else you have in common!"

Will had lost count of how many things he and Enzo apparently shared.

This was only the last one in a long line.

"Ah, well. That's . . .uh . . .good."

"You know my nephew?" Giana asked archly.

Will definitely knew Luca Moretti. He owned two businesses in this town and shared another with his husband, Oliver.

Maybe Will had only been here in town for six months, but he liked to think they'd become his friends, too.

Her voice dropped and she leaned in. Will wished someone else would come in and actually order something, so he could pawn her off. But the door stayed stubbornly closed. "You know how handsome Luca is. Enzo is *even more* handsome."

Will lost the fight with himself and winced, too. "He is," he agreed, even though he very much wanted to lie and say no, nobody would ever look twice at Luca Moretti.

"Then I will give you Enzo's number and you will text him. Tell him to come home to his momma and her cooking—but most important-ly, for a date with you," she said, already decided as she whipped a piece of paper out of her purse.

Will stared at it.

She'd doodled a little heart next to the number.

"I'm sorry, Giana, really. Really sorry. But I really can't." *How many reallys are required to convince her, Will? You think you've hit the magic number, yet?* He tacked on another, for good measure. "Really."

Giana shot him a look full of disappointment, and Will ignored the pulse of guilt.

"Really?"

Nope. You didn't hit it yet.

"Really," Will said, with emphasis.

But then that Moretti smile bloomed across her face—and she was still beautiful; honestly she didn't look old enough to have a grown-up son, but Will wasn't going to tell her that, because if he did, he'd have to hear just how handsome Enzo Moretti was again.

"Oh, you will change your mind someday," she said knowingly. "He is *such* a delightful boy."

"I'm sure he is," Will said weakly. "You know, I'm just not really in the market for . . .uh . . .anything. Serious or otherwise."

He'd made the mistake last time of telling her he wasn't in the market for a relationship, and she'd gone on a long tangent about 'hookups' that could lead to more, and by the time she'd finished, he'd been bright red and something beyond embarrassed.

"I understand," Giana said, patting him on the arm again. "You've got this beautiful new business. But someday . . ." There was that smile again. It was potent, Will could give her that.

And he wondered, before he could stop himself, if Enzo Moretti could smile like that, too.

"Maybe someday," Will said firmly. "Are you sure I can't get you something? A nice treat?"

He almost told her if she could actually *get* Enzo into town, he'd consider it more seriously, but if he did, Will had a feeling she'd fly to wherever Enzo was and drag him home by the hair.

She inclined her head. "A scoop of cherry pie, please, Will, darling."

Five minutes and an ice cream dish full of his cherry pie ice cream later, she was gone, *finally*.

"I told you she wasn't going to give up," Kate said, leaning on the counter as they watched Giana's back disappear out of the shop, the door closing behind her.

"I should've listened to you." The last time Giana had come in, he'd been so sure that was the end of it. Frankly, he'd been sure the *first* time he'd told her no, he didn't want her to set him up with her son, she'd give up.

But Giana was nothing if not persistent.

"You should've," Kate agreed.

He turned to her, when Giana had passed by his last window, finally out of sight. "What's the deal with Enzo Moretti?" he finally asked. He'd *very* specifically refused to give in to his curiosity, either in front of Giana or after she'd disappeared, because God only knew what kind of magical matchmaking powers she possessed.

Kate raised an eyebrow. "Don't tell me Giana's actually convinced you that you're interested?"

"How can I be interested in a man I've never met, who's apparently not been back here in almost a year?"

"Fair." Kate considered his question as she straightened a tower of glass banana split dishes. "Well, he's Giana's son, of course. No dad. They moved here when he was seven. And she started the deli. You know about Luca's family, of course."

Will nodded. That had been one of the first bits of gossip he'd heard when he'd moved to Indigo Bay. About Luca Moretti and his whole chain of Italian restaurants on the west coast, in the Napa Valley, but how he'd moved here instead.

To marry Oliver Billings, who owned the local bakery.

Six months later, Luca had bought the deli from Giana, and she'd effectively retired, and apparently, soon after that, Enzo had left town.

"He went to San Francisco for art school, I think. Or maybe Los Angeles? Anyway, before he left town, he was kind of a hot mess."

"A Moretti? I'm surprised they allowed it," Will joked.

"Oh, it was a problem. He tried to date Oliver."

"He dated *Oliver*?" Will hadn't heard *this* piece of gossip. And it stopped him in the middle of restocking the preserved cherries that topped every one of his ice cream creations.

"One date, supposedly. And it didn't go well. But he sulked about that *forever*. Then you know, Luca came to town and met Oliver, himself, and they fell in love and that went over even worse."

"I can imagine," Will said dryly. Kate was going to be a great manager—smart and strategic and personable—but she was also a fantastic source of local gossip.

"Anyway, I guess the problem wasn't so much Oliver, but that Enzo wanted to be an artist, and Giana wouldn't let him go away for school. But pretty much the moment Luca moved here, off he went. He hasn't been back much, not since then, but every time he *does* come back, he seems more and more normal. Way less petulant. So that's a plus in the *yes, you should listen to Giana and text him.*"

Will ignored her teasing jest.

"Doesn't sound like how Giana described him." Giana had described him as a combination of Apollo and Harry Styles and Luca.

"That woman does *not* have a firm grasp on what her son's really like," Kate said.

"So that's why he needs his mother to get him dates," Will theorized.

"Well, I don't know about that," Kate hedged. "But she certainly believes in the best version of him. He *is* successful, apparently a really successful mural painter. Like the big ones, like whole sides of buildings." Her expression became knowing. "He's got an Instagram, you know."

"Everyone has an Instagram," Will said.

"Yeah, but you could check him out. See what he looks like."

"Does he really look like a combination of Luca and Jesus?"

Kate laughed. "I guess so. I don't know. You know he isn't my type."

"Men aren't your type," Will retorted.

"Exactly. But he'd be *your* type. He's definitely Moretti issue. And you know they're all attractive."

In the six months he'd been here, Will had met a variety of Morettis. Luca and Giana, obviously, but also several of Luca's brothers and sisters, who came here every so often to visit him. Then there was Rocco, another cousin, who was in town to work for Oliver and Luca and save up money for his own business someday. And yep—they were all attractive. Every single one of them.

"I don't want to date someone just because they're hot," Will complained.

"And Enzo *is* well . . .Enzo."

Will shot her a knowing look.

"If I'd known Giana was going to hyper-fixate on you as a possible mate for her son, I'd have told you to keep your queerness under your hat."

Will rolled his eyes. "I think I told Luca the first day I was here. It wasn't going to stay a secret. I didn't even want it to. She'll . . .well, she'll just have to get over it."

"Giana Moretti doesn't just move on from things," Kate reminded him. "You know you could just text him. It might not even kill you."

"No," Will said stubbornly. "I'm not going to let her bully me into dating her son."

"You say that now," Kate said, laughing.

Chapter Two

Enzo Moretti was just about to get up on the scaffolding rising against the enormous brick wall when his phone rang.

He glanced at the screen, calculating the time he'd lose by taking the call versus the pain he'd suffer if he declined it.

He pressed accept and set it on the old desk he'd found on the side of the road and dragged over to use as a temporary workstation while he worked on this mural.

"Hi, Mom," he said into the speaker.

"Oh, darling, I'm so happy I caught you," Giana said.

"Just in time," Enzo said. She wasn't here so she couldn't see his eye roll. He loved his mother—for forever it had just been him and her against the whole world, but she'd responded to that by hanging on to him far too tightly, and even being three thousand miles away hadn't really felt far enough from Indigo Bay.

"Are you working?" she asked.

Enzo tried not to let it drive him nuts that she didn't understand what he did. That she seemed to have some misplaced, misguided idea that he just fucked around with paints all day.

When in reality, he was covering hundreds of square feet with artistic creations that could be seen blocks away.

When in reality, it was *work*. Work he loved, too, but hard work nonetheless.

"Yes," he said. Keeping it short and simple. Trying to not be—or *feel*—defensive.

"I thought you'd be almost done with that one, by now," she said. *Don't do it, don't do it.*

"Mom, it's a five-story building."

In his mind's eye, Enzo could see her waving her hand. Dismissing what was actually an enormous expanse of brick to cover. "You know, we have buildings here, too, in Indigo Bay. Buildings you could paint."

He stifled his sigh. It was inevitable.

"I know," he said. "But I've been so busy, Mom." *Thought you'd be happier about that.*

She was proud of him. Always telling him about how she talked to her friends about his accomplishments. Always blown away when he sent pictures of what he was working on.

She certainly seemed to appreciate how solid their financial situation was, compared to years ago, when the deli was struggling, before Luca had ever shown up.

Enzo gazed up at the nearly finished star system sprawled over the brick above him, the dappled blues and grays and purples, dotted with stars. A whole galaxy that he'd painted, on the side of this building that had once been a warehouse but was now going to be a children's museum.

Could use some more lavender on the edges of that black hole.

Considered the problem as she kept talking.

"You've missed so much, already, this year," she said. "Thanksgiving. Christmas. The spring wine dinner Oliver and Luca hosted, the Memorial Day picnic, and of course, the *Festival*."

"Oh, yeah, the Festival."

Ugh, the Sweethearts Festival. Even if he'd been free, Enzo wouldn't have come home for that. It made him feel weird and uncomfortable, surrounded by so much love and romance, when he was alone. *Preferred* to be alone, traveling on his own, making friends where he went, living out of a bag, moving to a new city every six to eight weeks.

It confused the hell out of Giana, but *he* loved it. And wasn't he the person he needed to please? For most of his teenage years and early adulthood, he'd never gotten to. Was it any wonder he was so fanatically dedicated to doing it now?

"I'm just saying, you've missed so much. You should come home. You know, like I said, *we* have buildings here. Buildings that could use murals."

"You've said." *More than once.*

He wasn't against painting a mural in Indigo Bay. He was against going back to Indigo Bay.

Whenever he went back, the town seemed to close around him, reminding him every time he turned a corner of the boy he'd used to be. The boy he'd exorcised, but who somehow rose from the dead every time he crossed the town line.

"We just miss you, darling," Giana said in a small, soft voice, and there it was, like clockwork. The guilt.

"I'll think about it," Enzo said. He pulled out a large empty plastic container, already stained with a half-dozen colors he'd already mixed up and used on the mural. He squirted blue in and added red, then white, mixing and mixing with a wooden stake until the color was exactly what he wanted.

"You will?" She sounded thrilled.

"I said I would," Enzo promised.

"What is your schedule like?" she asked, all official now. "Can we get on it? There's a *perfect* wall here, you know the old hardware store . . ." She laughed. "Of course you do. It's been remodeled inside, and the brick restored, and *oh*, you'd love it. The perfect place for you to paint a mural in Indigo Bay."

He probably would love it. It probably *would* be perfect.

That was the problem with his mother. She knew him too well and knew exactly what kind of treat to lay in the trap.

"Uh . . ."

Enzo had a feeling he knew where this was going.

An inevitable kind of feeling.

Who'd spilled the beans? Luca? Or Oliver?

The other day when they'd talked, he'd told Luca about the suddenly empty slot in his schedule. A building had been delayed in the construction phase, and as a result, the mural he'd been supposed to paint had fallen through. Truthfully he hadn't decided *what* he was going to do about those empty weeks, yet, but he'd toyed with the idea of going and staying with Chiara and Ilaria, Luca's sisters in San Francisco, but he hadn't yet decided. That was the beauty of his schedule. It was up to him.

Of course, Luca might not have been the one to tell Giana. It could very well have been Oliver, who seemed to share Luca's brain, these days.

"I heard about that project that fell through. Luca mentioned it." If Giana had demanded he come home or acted like it was an inevitability, it would've been so easy to turn her down.

To tell her something else had come up, even if it hadn't.

But the hope in her voice made it impossible to do that.

"It just happened, and I haven't had time to think about what it means." All true. The schedule change had happened when he'd been right in the middle of this mural, lost to it the way he was always lost to his best pieces.

All he'd had time to do during the thick of it was paint and fall into bed, after.

"I could send you pictures of the wall," Giana said excitedly.

Enzo rationalized with himself that he'd been meaning to come home, anyway, one of these days. And wouldn't it be nice to spend the summer in a place where he wasn't fighting the cloud cover and the drizzling rain, like he'd been in Seattle?

More than nice to enjoy the kind of blazingly hot summer he'd grown up with. Spend a few days at the beach, soaking in the salt water and the sun?

If the old hardware store really had been restored, Giana wasn't wrong. It *would* be a great spot for a mural.

Enzo knew he could be stubborn, but he wasn't blindly stupid.

"Send the pictures," he said, resigning himself, while also reminding himself that it wouldn't be all bad to go back to Indigo Bay. He'd see Luca and Oliver again.

She must've known that would be his first request, because his phone beeped immediately.

"Not wasting any time, huh?" he teased.

"You're a very important man now. It's not every day you have an unexpected opening on your schedule," she teased right back, and for a second, Enzo felt swamped with love and something deeper and more binding. All the history they shared.

The history that kept tugging him back, when he'd been sure he'd cut the cord.

"Let me look," Enzo said, pulling up the pictures. And she hadn't lied. It was a gorgeous building. Not very big, easily completed in the empty slot in his schedule. He would have plenty of time to relax, too. The brick was nice and clean, not much damage, and whoever had re-modeled the old hardware store had cleared out the ugly, broken-down dumpster that had become more of neighborhood trash heap and then scrubbed the sidewalk, removing even the most stubborn of the stains.

It boded well, and Enzo felt that little artistic tingle he always got when he began to get excited about a project.

"I told you, it's perfect," Giana said as he flicked through the pic-tures she'd sent.

He wanted to argue and say it wasn't, but she'd planned this well. It *was* perfect, and she knew it.

"I'll do it," Enzo said. "I'll even waive my normal fee."

Not that the town collectively couldn't afford it, but if he did this mural for free, it would give him some wiggle room and the kind of flexibility he *normally* enjoyed on a project, but that he knew his mother and her friends wouldn't concede easily the way his typical clients did.

"Oh, Enzo, that is *wonderful*," she said. "I'll scrub out the guest room."

"Mom," he warned.

"Oh, fine, you can stay in the apartment over the garage. I do know you're a grown man and want your space."

"I need my space," Enzo reminded her.

When he'd turned eighteen, he'd insisted on spending his weekends and evenings turning the loft over the little garage next to his mom's house into his own place.

It had given him just enough space that he didn't scream the town down. Especially after she'd hemmed and hawed and ultimately convinced him that he didn't need to go to art school.

That he'd be happy, settling for running the deli.

But he'd never have been happy. He knew that now.

"Right, of course. I'll clean out the loft. Make sure it's all set for you," Giana promised. "You'll let me know when you'll be home? I'll come to Charleston and pick you up."

But if he didn't start the visit the way he meant to live it, it would be a disaster. He'd learned this very early on.

"No, Luca's always flying places. I'll text him, and time my flight with one of his."

She sighed.

"If you're sure."

"I'm sure," Enzo said.

He'd learned after the first few times he'd returned to Indigo Bay he *needed* to be protective of his space, or else he and Giana would end up fighting, and that was *not* the kind of vacation he had in mind.

"Alright." She didn't sound that disappointed, and he counted that as his first win.

"I've got to get to work, Mom," he said.

"Just . . ." Her voice softened, full of pure joy. "Just happy you're coming home, darling."

"I know, Mom." He hesitated. Staring at the lavender paint in his hand. "Me, too."

It wasn't even a lie.

The moment she hung up, he texted Luca.

You flying home any time in the next two weeks? he asked.

Luca's answer came through almost immediately. **In a week. Why? She didn't, did she?**

Hey, I wasn't the one who told her.

Sorry.

You're not.

No. Not really. There's living your own life, Enzo, and then there's avoiding your old one.

You're such a smug asshole.

But Enzo was laughing out loud, enjoying this, because despite what he'd once believed, he now considered Luca the brother he'd never had.

His phone rang again.

"I really don't have time but I'll make time for you," Enzo teased after he answered.

"And you call *me* a smug asshole," Luca said, sounding equally amused.

"Takes one to know one."

Luca chuckled. "It sure does. So how did she convince you?"

"It wasn't actually that hard." Enzo sighed with resignation. "She wants me to paint a mural."

"Oh, on Will's building? Yeah, I can see that."

"Who's Will?" Enzo asked absently.

"A new guy in town. You'll like him. And his ice cream."

"Guess you didn't open that gelateria you'd been talking about," Enzo said.

"You know how busy we are, how were we gonna do *that* justice? It wasn't going to happen. And then Will showed up with all these plans, and you know, Oliver said it best. Why would we try to do something when he's such an expert at it, already?"

"You're a huge sap."

"Guilty as charged."

There'd been a time when Enzo hadn't exactly been thrilled that his smug asshole of a cousin had met, fallen in love, and then married his old teenage crush. But that was water *long* under the bridge.

He and Oliver would've been a disaster.

Had been a disaster. The worst first date both of them had probably ever been on.

"Let me guess," Luca said, "you're trying to avoid Giana driving into Charleston to pick you up."

"If I let her, she'll stop by every antique mall between there and Indigo Bay, and you know how I feel about antiquing."

"It's baffling to me why Giana moved back to Indigo Bay when she was so into the antique scene in Charleston."

"You know it was too big for her. Not enough room to be her natural busybody self," Enzo joked.

Luca laughed again. "You know her well."

"Better than anybody else," Enzo agreed. "So I'll catch a ride back with you. Text me your flight info."

His phone dinged again. "Done," Luca said. "And if for some reason that doesn't work for you, either Oliver or I can come into town and pick you up. No problem. Consider it karmic justice."

"Done," Enzo said.

"Ugh, that's exactly what you intended, wasn't it?"

"A happy accident," Enzo suggested instead, and Luca scoffed.

"Sure," he said, but he still sounded amused. "I *am* happy you'll be home for a little while, karmic justice and all. I'm sure Oliver will be, too. And you know our cousin Rocco's in Indigo Bay for the summer, yeah?"

"Rocco?"

"I'm sure you've met him before. At Chiara and Ilaria's place, maybe? He's a . . .second cousin? Third cousin? Anyway, Oliver's teaching him everything he knows about the bakery, and he's working at our place sometimes, and down the street at Rudy's. Saving up."

"Oh, yeah. Rocco." He remembered the guy now. A real chip off the Moretti block. A fun, cheerful guy with a big smile that seemed to permanently reside on his face. "What's he saving for?"

"Wants to buy his own place. Coffee shop slash bakery of some kind, somewhere."

"He'll be good at that."

"He's already good at that," Luca said wryly. "I said Oliver was teaching him, but I think they're teaching *each other*."

"Aw, feeling a little left out?" Enzo asked knowingly.

"Maybe I'm *not* happy you're coming home, after all."

But Enzo knew he was, and he realized, again, that he hadn't been lying to his mom, when he'd told her he was happy, too.

This was going to be good. He could reconnect with Luca and Oliver. Hang out with Rocco. Paint a mural. Indigo Bay *should* have an Enzo Moretti mural. It only made sense.

Yes, the deli had the interior mural he'd done, before he'd even gone to school, but this one would be for the whole town, in a spot everyone could enjoy it.

"Liar," Enzo said jokingly.

"Smug asshole," Luca retorted fondly.

"Just a Moretti."

Luca laughed.

"See you in a few weeks, cousin," he said.

❧ ⚘ ☙

"Uh-oh," Kate said under her breath to Will as she scooped ice cream into a banana split dish.

"What?" He was distracted. He had two ice cream cones to scoop, a sundae to build, and a milkshake to blend. Cherry's was busy, maybe busier than they'd been since they opened, full of customers enjoying his ice cream and his frozen concoctions. It was only about an hour til closing, but the weather, warming up every week since he'd been open, had finally started to draw the town in like insects towards a lamp.

"Giana's here."

Will glanced up and sure enough she was winding her way through the shop, between the bright white spindly chairs and the magenta enameled tables, shoes clicking purposefully on the black and white checkerboard tile.

"I gotta finish this order," he hissed.

"She's not gonna want to talk to me," Kate retorted as she sliced open a banana and nestled each half on either side of the ice cream.

"She might," Will theorized. But sure enough, he could see out of the corner of his eye that she was heading right in his direction, bypassing the line of customers, Mari, his newest employee, was taking care of.

"Will! Will!" Giana said excitedly, trying to get his attention loudly.

She hadn't had to shout. He was right there, just on the other side of the long ice cream case.

He looked up, bowing to the inevitable. "Sorry, Giana, we're slammed," he said apologetically, giving her one of his best "customer service" smiles. "It might be a while before Mari can get to you."

"Oh no, I'm not here for ice cream." She beamed, and if Will thought he'd been treated to a Moretti smile before, he was floored by the one she was wearing now. "I'm here for *you*! To tell you Enzo will be home soon. For weeks!"

"That's great. I'm really happy for you," Will said, meaning it. Clearly she loved her son a lot, and considering he'd been in town for six months and hadn't met him yet, Enzo didn't come home much.

"I am too. And of course, happy for *you*, because you will finally meet him."

"Giana," Will warned. He scooped ice cream into the aluminum milkshake tin and added milk from a carton he grabbed from the mini fridge below the counter.

"I know, I know, you are too busy to date. But the first time I saw you, I *knew*. You were perfect for my Enzo. Big and strong and handsome, and you work hard. You made this place beautiful, when it was a dump before. Only someone with a little bit of art in their soul could do that."

Or someone who was desperate to carve something out for *himself*, Will thought rebelliously.

It had taken a *lot* of long, hard hours to turn the dirty, dusty, partly dilapidated old hardware store into the bright, shiny white and cherry pink ice cream parlor with its white lacy-backed chairs, magenta-topped tables, and long soda counter with a curved glass ice cream case punctuating the middle, stretching the entire length of the big room.

Then there was the meticulously laid out, sparkling clean commercial kitchen in the back. He'd spared no expense, because he'd wanted a place he loved coming to work every day, and Cherry's had become all of that and more.

"I don't know about that," Will said. He set a hand on his hip. "I just know I'm super busy. But of course, you'll have to tell him to stop by for some ice cream."

"Oh, I will," Giana said and her eyes were glimmering with mischief and promise.

He supposed he should've been more afraid of that look of hers but he had two more sundaes to make, and the line in front of Mari was nearly to the door now.

"See you around," Will said, turning away and whipping up his milkshake. He spooned it carefully into one of the clear fluted glasses that he'd already prepped with a caramel drizzle and then topped it with a beautiful swirl of whipped cream and more caramel. He nestled a snickerdoodle in and a bunch of his signature cherries next to it.

He was just pulling out two more dishes for sundaes when Kate wondered, "Gonna stop by for ice cream, is he? Or maybe something else?"

Glancing up, Will rolled his eyes. "I was trying to be nice. Friendly. Welcoming."

"You gotta be careful," she said. "You're too friendly. Giana's gonna take that as a positive sign and never give up. She *wants* you."

"At least it's not for herself?" Giana was still beautiful, sure, but she was definitely at least twenty-five years older than Will, and the wrong kind of sex for him to be interested in.

"It might be easier to dissuade her if that was her end goal," Will continued with a reluctant sigh. "But hopefully Enzo is just as weirded out by his mom's matchmaking as I am."

"I'm sure he's gonna be thrilled to find out that she's been coming around, pimping him out," Kate said with a grin. "Or maybe he'll *actually* be glad. You never know. Maybe he has trouble getting dates, just like you said."

"Maybe." But Will wasn't convinced. He was sure the first time he met Enzo Moretti, the two of them would share an awkward and uncomfortable moment, hopefully be able to laugh about it directly after, and then move on.

Chapter Three

IT HAD BEEN ANOTHER *very* long day.

Will was torn between being glad that Cherry's had really caught on with the locals and with the tourists filtering into town for the summer, and wishing that maybe they were a little *less* eager.

Maybe then his feet and the small of his back wouldn't be aching like this.

"Flip the sign," Will said to Mari.

She was currently wiping up tables, streaked with smears of chocolate and cherry pie filling and God only knew what else, but she skirted around one of them and flicked the switch that turned the curly-lettered *open* sign, executed in bright cherry pink, to off.

"We're gonna have to hire someone else. And consider staying open later, in the summer. Seven PM might not be late enough to take care of the crowds," Kate suggested as Will leaned against the counter and wondered if it was better or worse if his toes had gone numb. At least they'd stopped hurting for a second?

"Yeah." Will dragged a hand over his face.

Kate wasn't wrong, but that was a problem for Tomorrow Will.

"Especially," Mari chimed in as she went back to scrubbing a particularly stubborn stain off one of the tables, "on nights when there's events at the high school. They're all gonna want to come here. There's only the little diner at the edge of town that's open late enough for that crowd."

"Good point," Kate agreed with a nod. She turned to Will. "Boss?"

Will sighed. "I'll look into it tomorrow."

She gave him a bit of a shove. "You were here even earlier than me. You're exhausted. Go get some fresh air. I'll work on cleaning up back here."

Will almost asked her if she was sure, but he heard his mom's voice echoing in his head, *if you hired her, why can't you trust her?* It was even more annoying because he knew she was right.

"Alright, but I'll be back in a few, to help you guys finish up," Will said.

He pushed open the door. "Lock this behind me, yeah?" he said, motioning towards Mari, and she nodded.

It was still warm outside—Kate wasn't wrong, either; they *needed* to start staying open later, to take full advantage of the summer and its crowds—even though it was dusk now, bordering on full dark, stars emerging overhead, the streets mostly abandoned at this hour.

Will turned the corner and stopped in his tracks.

There was a man there.

Not just *any* man.

His back was to Will, as he stood, staring at the side of Will's building, wearing jeans and a T-shirt that fit him like a glove, hugging his long slender lines.

Will must've made a noise, because he turned around.

The front view was even better than the back. Tousled, curly dark hair that was a little too long matched the scruff on his jaw. Dusk had fallen, making it impossible to see the color of his eyes, but Will imagined they were just as dark brown as his hair. A deep, chocolate brown he could willingly drown in.

"Hey," Will said, wishing that he hadn't been working for the last twelve hours and probably *smelled* like it. Or that he didn't have at least half a banana split smeared across his white T-shirt.

Kate had teased him that he'd picked white for the Cherry's shirts because he looked hot in them, because they were terribly impractical otherwise.

But from the way the guy's gaze drifted across the white fabric, stained yes, but also stretched tight across his pecs and his biceps and hugging his stomach, Will decided it hadn't been such a bad idea, after all.

Then Will's eyes caught on what was behind the guy. A bag full of stuff. And he'd *done* something to Will's wall. There were paint marks on the wall he'd so meticulously cleaned up, scrubbing every bit of ugly graffiti off. Making sure each and every brick was restored. It had been hard, long, back-breaking work, and now this hot guy was doing what . . .painting some kind of bullshit back on it?

He could be hot, but Will wasn't going to let him get away with it.

He straightened up. "What are you doing?" he demanded.

"Excuse me?" the guy retorted. With anger flashing in those dark eyes, he was even hotter.

Will ignored the pull of him, the pulse of desire in his belly.

It had just been way too long since he'd been attracted to any-one—and even longer since he'd done something about it.

"I said, *what are you doing?* You have paint in that bag. I can see it. I can see it on the wall. Are you really gonna graffiti my building right in front of me?"

"Graffiti?" The guy's jaw dropped in surprise. "I don't paint *graffi-ti*."

"Well, what the hell are you doing then?" Will crossed his arms over his chest, because he knew how intimidating that could look.

"It doesn't concern you."

Except it did. Because what Will *thought* what he was doing really freaking pissed him off.

"Somehow, that doesn't make me feel any better," Will said. "I spent *days* in all kinds of shitty weather scrubbing every last bit of paint off this wall. Do you have any idea how long that takes? How much elbow grease I wasted on this? Because I didn't want to pretend that the inside was all that counted."

Will craned his head as the hot guy stared at him, confusion pleating the skin between his dark eyebrows. Realized that he hadn't caught the guy before he'd done it, he'd caught him in the *middle* of defacing Will's building.

Anger surged inside him. "I don't care how hot you are," he said, "but you can't just come here and do this to my building."

"*Your* building?"

Will gave him a sharp nod. "Yes, this is *my* building, and I'll be damned if you paint all over it again, just for me to have to sweat out in the heat of summer to clean your bullshit off."

"My *bullshit*?"

Will couldn't decide what was more annoying; that this asshole had begun to paint all over his building, or that he wouldn't actually admit it.

Especially when evidence was clear behind him. And not even anything *interesting*. Just a few swipes of different colors.

What was the point of that? Will decided he didn't give a crap; he just wanted it gone, and this guy was gonna be the one to remove it.

"Are you just gonna keep repeating every word I say or are you gonna clean this up?" Will asked archly.

The guy's shrug was mechanical and okay, he looked a little puzzled, too. Which confused Will.

Had he not realized what he was doing?

"I think there's been a misunderstanding," the guy said.

"You better believe it," Will said. His temper was maybe a little shorter than it might've been otherwise, but he was exhausted, and this *asshole* was defacing his building. The idea of having to come back here in the morning and not only find another employee and *train* them but figure out how to open even more hours, on top of scrubbing that paint off his building for the *second fucking time,* unwound all his niceness.

"What I mean," the guy said more gently, "is that the town's hired me to paint this wall. It's my job."

"Excuse me?"

The guy gave a short, humorless laugh. "I'm supposed to be here, painting your wall. I was checking some of my paints, seeing how the brick absorbed them, because sometimes brick's been sealed and I need to scrub it off first, before re-sealing it after the mural's done."

Something teased the back of Will's mind. "The mural?"

"Now it's your turn to look confused," the guy said. "I told you, there's been a big misunderstanding. I'm—"

"Enzo Moretti. You're Enzo Moretti." Will could see it now. The hair. The eyes. The handsome face, echoes of Giana and Luca and all those fabulous Moretti genes. He wasn't as built as Luca, shoulders narrower, but Will hadn't missed the hint of muscle under his clothes.

Kate was right; he *was* hot.

"That's me," Enzo said. Not sounding particularly pleased that it had taken Will all this time to catch up. "And you own this building?"

Will nodded sharply. "I sure do. And I didn't give permission for *anyone* to paint it, even the town's most famous son."

Only one thought was echoing through his head, repeating over and over. *If this is Enzo Moretti, he sure doesn't need his mom's help getting dates.*

That particular realization made him a little stupid, and more than a little slow.

"Well, at least you've heard of me." Enzo cracked a smile.

"Oh, I've heard of you." Will considered telling him how Giana had practically *thrown* him at Will, over and over again, but he didn't, because he was still stuck on the fact that apparently they'd hired Enzo Moretti to paint his building and yet *nobody had fucking asked him.*

"Great." Enzo shifted from one foot to the other. "So, we're all good then?"

"Just like that? We're all good then? No, you're not painting my building. In fact, you're going to take the paint you've *already* smeared all over my wall and remove it."

Enzo gaped at him. "Are you fucking kidding me?"

"No," Will said.

He thought Enzo might take more than a moment to recover from his clear shock, but no, he recovered almost instantly. The guy was not only hot, he was quick.

"You do realize that people are clamoring for me to paint their buildings in all fifty states, right? That I agreed to do this *as a favor*? That I'm even waiving my fifty-thousand-dollar fee?"

The man made *that much* for every mural he did? Will might've been impressed, but he was too annoyed.

"I don't care if you're going to paint my wall in solid freaking gold," he said. "It's *my* wall and I worked hard to make it look that good and you're not ruining it."

"Ruining it?" Enzo's voice edged upwards, dangerously. His eyes flashed and he crossed *his* arms over *his* chest, and maybe he wasn't quite as broad as Will, but it was a damn fine look, all the same.

Yep, he was definitely even hotter when he was mad.

That doesn't matter. It doesn't matter if he's appealing, he's kind of an egotistical jerk. Looks or not, maybe his mom really does have to pimp him out to get dates.

"You're cleaning this up. Tonight. Or tomorrow. Take your pick." Will turned around and with that threat hanging in the air, marched back to sanity. Fumbled for his keys, but unlocked the front door to Cherry's and locked it behind him.

Knew he was trembling with fury. The freaking *audacity* of that guy.

To act like Will shouldn't be mad that nobody had even asked him. To act like he was doing Will a *favor* by painting a wall he didn't even want painted!

"You alright?" Kate asked. She eyed him up and down as he pushed the pass-through that let him behind the counter. "You don't look very relaxed."

"I just ran into Enzo Moretti," Will said through clenched teeth.

"Oh, so Giana was wrong. She's going to cry about that. Probably a lot."

"He's hot, she wasn't wrong about that. But he's also an egotistical jerk. He thought he could just waltz into town and decide because he's Enzo freaking Moretti and apparently people pay him way too much to paint pretty pictures on walls that he could paint *my* wall without even asking me. Without even *consulting* me."

"What?" Kate looked surprised. "Are you sure?"

"Pretty damn sure." Will clenched his fists and then tried to relax them. Keyword: *tried*.

"Huh. Are you sure this isn't another one of Giana's tricks?"

The moment Kate said it, Will knew she was probably right. And okay, yes, he had lost his temper, a little. He didn't do that normally, but he'd been so tired when he'd walked out there and the whole conversation had started out on totally the wrong foot when he'd assumed that Enzo was here to graffiti the wall he'd spent so much dang energy cleaning up in the first place.

"Ugh, probably," Will conceded.

Though it wasn't like Enzo, after they'd figured out the misunderstanding, had been particularly apologetic about it. He'd been smug and very sure of his own worth, positive that Will was going to fall all over himself to apologize and smooth the way.

But it was *Will's wall.* He didn't care who Enzo was, or how much he freaking charged to paint a goddamn mural. If he wanted his wall to be blank, that was his right. The deed in his safe in the back proved it.

"So you guys got into it. Lots of clenched teeth and straining muscles and barely concealed angry flirting, huh?" Kate said pointedly, shooting him a knowing grin.

"Something like that," Will muttered. He walked past her into the back, into the little office he'd carved out of the kitchen space. It was a cubbyhole, basically, just big enough for a desk big enough for his laptop and a charger for his phone. He took a deep breath and then another, trying to huff his way through the surge of frustration and anger he'd felt.

Because he could recognize now that he'd overreacted. A little. Only a little, though.

Enzo had been infuriating *and* provoking. He'd asked for at least some of Will's grievances by being so smug about him and his talent.

He picked up his phone from the desk and did the thing he'd told himself he would not do, every single time after Giana appeared, like the matchmaker from hell, and tried to give him her son's phone number.

He looked Enzo Moretti up on Instagram.

And felt the rest of his anger leave him in an unsteady rush.

The murals on his Instagram were stunning. Huge gorgeous things, evocative and colorful and full of details and emotion that Will wanted to dive right into.

It would've been a hell of a lot easier if he hadn't been as talented as he'd claimed, but if anything, he'd actually downplayed his skill.

Will didn't know whether he was more annoyed at himself or Enzo.

After scrolling through a dozen or so of Enzo's murals, he opened his texts and sent one to Luca.

Is it possible that your aunt suggested to your cousin that they paint the side of my building while he's here?

Luca didn't take long to respond. **Don't tell me she didn't ask you—or even mention it to you?**

Will let out another long sigh. His legs gave out and he collapsed onto the chair. **Would that really surprise you?**

No. Not as much as I hoped it might. I'm sorry, Will. We'll figure this out.

For a minute, Will almost wanted to let Luca handle it. After all, Luca was the de facto head of the Morettis, not only here in Indigo Bay, but all Morettis, *everywhere*. A responsibility that Will knew he didn't take lightly, because Oliver had mentioned, more than once, that it still weighed on him, sometimes.

No need. I've got it handled, Will sent back. This wasn't Luca's job, to rein in his aunt. Will owned this building. It would be *his* responsibility to take care of this.

Chapter Four

Enzo's temper was still hot when he walked into Luca and Oliver's house for dinner.

When he'd first turned around and seen the guy, he'd felt an immediate jolt.

First, attraction. That much was easy to understand. The guy was freaking gorgeous—built big and brawny, with messy blond hair a few weeks past needing a cut, piercing blue eyes, and a tan that tight white shirt accentuated to perfection.

Then, annoyance.

How could anyone believe that *he*, Enzo freaking Moretti, was painting graffiti? Enzo still didn't understand how that misunderstanding had happened.

"You've been quiet all night," Oliver said, nudging him.

Enzo had a feeling Oliver had been waiting to bring up his crap mood until his mom had ducked out for a Fourth of July planning meeting at Joy Billings' B&B. Then Luca had followed, claiming he needed to deal with a problem at the restaurant.

"Yeah, you have," Rocco agreed, as he leaned back in one of the teal blue Adirondack chairs dotting Luca and Oliver's patio. "You kept glaring at the chicken piccata like it did something to insult you."

"I just . . ."

"Hate being back here?" Oliver inserted with a raised eyebrow. "I know." He gave Enzo a commiserating glance.

It was *almost* funny to remember a time when he'd had the world's stupidest crush on Oliver Billings.

He'd been an ass back then. A mess of hormones and frustration with no outlet and then the one chance Oliver had given him had gone terribly and he hadn't taken *that* well, either.

When Luca had come to town and he and Oliver had fallen in love, Enzo had begun to understand just how much all of that was *his* fault, and before he'd left for San Francisco, he'd apologized and began to mend the rift between them.

It hadn't been easy or quick but slowly, they'd become friends.

Oliver would've been impossible to avoid as his cousin's husband, especially after he and Luca had become close, but Enzo liked to think he and Oliver had a friendship entirely their own, in-law status notwithstanding.

"It's not being back here, actually," Enzo said. "I've been here less than twenty-four hours. Hard to be miserable, already."

"Then what's up?" Rocco asked, a frown creasing his tanned forehead. "It's not Auntie, is it?"

Giana was not Rocco's aunt, but he liked to call her that, and to Enzo's surprise, Giana actually liked it, and even kept harassing Luca to join in. But Luca would only shoot Giana a look and pretend he hadn't heard her teasing entreaties.

"No." Enzo huffed out a frustrated sigh. "You two don't know anything about the guy who owns the old hardware store, do you? I think it's called Cherry's?"

He'd wanted to ask his mother, because she was the one who'd arranged the mural in the first place, but Enzo knew her well enough to understand, even through his frustration and anger, that there had to be a reason why she hadn't decided to inform—or even *ask*—Will about the mural. He wasn't going to head into that particular conversation without being forearmed with at least a guess why.

"You mean Will? Will Johnson?" Oliver looked confused. "Of course we know Will. He's a great guy."

"Hot, too," Rocco teased.

Oliver shot his young cousin a fond glare. "He's not interested, Rocco. You know that."

"Doesn't mean I can't fantasize," Rocco insisted.

Oliver rolled his eyes.

Enzo didn't need his cousin to tell him how hot Will Johnson was.

"Is it possible that neither of you know that Giana arranged for me to paint a mural on the side of his building?"

Enzo got his answer when Oliver looked surprised and Rocco downright shocked. "I know Luca mentioned it," Oliver said slowly. "Not that you were painting *Will's* building, but that you were going to paint one while you were here. I thought the location was still up in the air."

"It's not," Enzo said. Though maybe after Will's reaction—and then *his* reaction to Will's reaction—it was now.

"Well, that's surprising," Oliver said bluntly. "I saw Will the other day and he didn't say anything about it."

"Because I don't think Giana told him," Enzo said.

Rocco laughed.

Maybe Enzo would've found it equally funny if he hadn't been all butt hurt about Will's graffiti accusations and then reverted back to his teenage form. Acting way too much like the stuck-up prick that he'd been before he'd ever left Indigo Bay.

"Ouch," Oliver said softly. "Let me guess, you found out that info—both of you found out that info—in the worst possible way."

Enzo nodded. "I knew on my way here for dinner I'd pass the building, so I thought I'd take a look at it. Test some paint on the brick. He caught me. Accused me of painting his building with graffiti."

"Ouch," Rocco said this time. "Were you your normal charming self?"

Enzo winced and figured that was enough of an answer.

"I know how hard he worked to get all the old graffiti off that building," Oliver said slowly. "It took him a solid week. I told him it was a waste of time, but he refused to listen. Said he wasn't going to let some punk kids win."

"And then he thought you were one of those punk kids," Rocco said, chuckling.

"Yeah."

"Ouch," Oliver said for the third time and when Enzo made a face, Oliver shot him an apologetic look. "I know I keep saying it, but it applies. Will's really nice."

"And hot, too," Rocco added, again.

Enzo had been trying not to think about that particular fact, but it was hard when Rocco kept bringing it up.

"But I can see how that probably hit him the wrong way," Oliver continued, only shooting Rocco a quick glare over his interruption.

"I bet you were pissed because you showed up all big shot artist and he accused you of vandalism," Rocco said.

"It . . .it could've gone better," Enzo agreed.

"What could've gone better?" Luca asked, pushing open the glass door between the house and the patio.

"Everything okay?" Oliver asked his husband as he leaned in, dropping a kiss on the top of his head.

"Yeah, I just had to grab another three-gallon bucket of vanilla bean from Oliver. *Someone* left it too close to the freezer door—you know the spot—and it got weird and crystallized. Thawed and then re-froze a few times." Then Luca grinned, soft and earnest in a way he'd never been when he'd first come here. "But the good news was I got Will to give us a few pints for dessert." He set a paper bag, white and striped with the same bright cherry pink as the new awning over the old hardware store, on the table between their chairs.

"Speaking of Will," Oliver said, "Enzo met him tonight."

"Oh?" Luca opened the bag and began passing out little cardboard pints, all printed in that same distinctive pink and white stripe.

"You know how Giana told you Enzo's painting a mural while he's here? Apparently it's Will's building and she didn't bother to ask him."

Luca glanced over at Enzo as he handed him a container and a spoon. "I'd heard that," he said carefully. "From Will himself. Ouch."

"Can everyone stop saying that?" Enzo complained.

"And Will totally thought Enzo was painting graffiti on the side of his building," Rocco added.

"Ouch," Luca repeated, shooting Enzo an apologetic smile.

"Clearly I'm gonna have to apologize." He didn't sound happy about it, because he wasn't happy about it.

"I kinda think that should be Auntie," Rocco said.

"Oh, she will," Enzo promised darkly. "But I will, too. I just want to know before I talk to her—before I talk to *Will*—why would she do that?"

Oliver shot him a commiserating glance as he popped the lid off his ice cream and made a satisfied noise. "Rocco already told you why," Oliver said, then turned to Luca. "You got me the tuxedo," he said, giving him the kind of gooey smile that would've made Enzo crazy with jealousy five years ago, but only made him glad his cousin had found someone so good to love now.

"Of course I did. The rest of us got a flavor Will says he's trying out. Cherry Brown Butter Brickle. So feedback's welcome."

The cardboard was slippery and cold against his hand, but Enzo didn't open it yet. "What do you mean?" he asked Oliver.

"He's gorgeous," Oliver said, words muffled by ice cream. "Don't tell me you didn't notice while he was about to have you hauled off for vandalism and you got all up in your ego about it?"

"I noticed," Enzo huffed.

"Right. Well. Think of why your mother might've neglected to inform both of you of your soon-to-be-cozy circumstances."

Enzo groaned. "She's trying to pair me up with Will."

"From the moment she met him. She's been salivating at the possibility of big, built blond grandchildren," Luca said with a dark chuckle.

"I didn't think I needed to explain how babies work to you, Luca," Rocco inserted with a teasing glance towards Oliver.

"You know what I mean," Luca said, waving away his cousin's joke. "She wants Will for you, and you for Will. That's the best guess I've got why she didn't tell *you*. Why she didn't tell Will? No idea."

"Kate mentioned she'd been in a few times to the ice cream parlor, talking about Enzo to Will. Who, of course, had no idea what the fuck to make of her pushiness. She was probably worried he'd move out of town if he realized what she'd done. Or maybe she was thinking she'd spring you on him like a gift, or something."

"Or something," Enzo said morosely. "She was really doing that?"

"You can't be *that* surprised," Luca said. He gestured towards the softening cardboard in his hand. "Eat your ice cream. It'll make you feel better."

"I don't know that it will." He was not only annoyed now, he was embarrassed.

"Will's ice cream solves all problems," Rocco promised.

Enzo almost said, *if it was anyone but Will's ice cream, it might,* but he opened the container anyway and dug his spoon in.

The ice cream looked normal, like ice cream did. Under the strings of lights crisscrossing the patio, it shone a beautiful pale yellow, with bright red streaks through it. The cherries, Enzo assumed.

But when he put that first spoonful in his mouth, he understood that everything he'd ever believed about ice cream was wrong.

That had been flavored skim milk, with emphasis on *skim*, and not on *flavor*.

This was what ice cream really was. Deep and rich, with the fattiness of the butter and the cream on his tongue. It was sweet, but not too sweet, but also shockingly nutty, the sweet-sour of the cherry brickle breaking up the richness.

Enzo might've moaned.

"See?" Rocco said knowingly.

"Damn," Enzo said. "I might marry him for this ice cream."

Rocco laughed. "Don't you dare let Auntie hear you say that."

"Remember when you brought me that bittersweet chocolate with Valencia orange peel home?" Luca's voice went wistful. "And then you insisted I share it?"

"Even after I'd eaten half a pint of coconut macaron? Oh, I remember it."

"It's less than ten minutes' walk from Cherry's to your house. How did you eat half a pint of ice cream?" Enzo asked. Though he was beginning to comprehend the magic of Will's ice cream.

"If you'd ever eaten the coconut macaron, you'd understand," Oliver said.

"What I still don't understand is why I'm supposed to share *mine*, but you have your own?" Luca joked.

Oliver shot Enzo a conspiratorial glance. "That's marriage for you. What's his is mine. And what's mine is mine."

Luca made a frustrated noise, but Enzo thought that even if that was actually true of their marriage, he had a feeling Luca would still commit to it one hundred out of one hundred times.

"And everyone's surprised why I'm not eager to settle down." Enzo believed Luca and Oliver were meant for each other, but that didn't mean he wanted that kind of life-changing love for himself. He was very happy with his life now, thank you very much.

And *God*, the idea that Will believed that he needed his *mother* to get him dates?

A fresh wave of humiliation washed over Enzo.

Especially because, as Rocco had been so eager to volunteer more than once, Will was no-question-about-it, undeniably hot.

"Nobody expects you to settle down. You're making bank and living such an exciting life, a new city every few months," Oliver said, patting his arm.

"Just Giana," Luca said dryly. "You know that was part of Will's attraction. He's *here*."

"I'm not moving back home," Enzo said firmly.

"We know that," Oliver said gently. "But Giana might be still holding out hope."

"Maybe I need to come back here more often," Enzo theorized.

Rocco shot him a look. "If you did that, Auntie might lock you in a closet with Will."

"Listen, I'll talk to her," Luca said.

It was just like Luca to want to intervene. To use his position as de facto head of the Morettis to take care of Enzo's problem. Luca had been taking care of everyone's problems forever. Enzo thought in some kind of sick way, he actually *enjoyed* doing it.

But Enzo shook his head. He was a grown adult now. He didn't need Luca's help. "No. No. I'll talk to her, and I'll talk to Will."

"In which order?" Rocco teased.

Oliver smacked him. "Let your cousin alone. It's bad enough that his own mother is making his life harder. You don't need to add to it, too."

"Fine, fine," Rocco said, with a resigned expression crossing his face. "I'll leave them alone."

"Good."

"I would like to paint the mural, still," Enzo said. "Giana wasn't wrong about the location or the building. It's an ideal spot. But I guess I'll have to convince Will now."

"Maybe smooth it over with him first and then yell at Giana," Luca suggested. "That way she can't . . .well, interfere *worse*."

That was Enzo's plan. "Then maybe she won't imagine me 'smoothing it over' means something else."

"Don't tell me you didn't consider it, even for a minute," Rocco said. "She could've been doing you a favor. Laying some important groundwork."

"Rocco," Oliver warned.

Even though Enzo wouldn't admit it, and definitely not to Rocco, who'd never let him forget it, he *had* thought about it. For the split second after he'd turned around. When Will had been standing there, dazzling in the dusk, lit by a streetlight. Before he'd accused Enzo of vandalism and before Enzo had decided he'd been horribly insulted by even the insinuation that what he created was the same as defacing someone's building.

Yeah, in that moment, he'd thought it. Had thought Will was freaking gorgeous, and even wondered why he'd wasted so much time not coming home when there was someone who looked like him in Indigo Bay.

"Maybe Will's not Enzo's type," Luca said.

"Are you kidding? Will's *everyone's* type. All you need is eyes." Rocco stood, stretching out his long, lean body. He was another chip off the Moretti block, and Enzo could see shades of his own face and also Luca's in Rocco's sculpted cheekbones and dark eyes. "But don't worry, cousin," he said, leaning down and giving Enzo a quick hug. "I'm not gonna move in on your guy. Oliver's right. He's not right for me. I just like looking. Now, I'm gotta take off. I've got an early shift at the bakery."

Oliver nodded absently. He was holding hands with Luca, and Luca was leaning over, murmuring something in his ear.

Enzo almost begged Rocco to stay. That he didn't want to be left alone with all this love in the air. That he was afraid it might be catching.

But that would be ridiculous.

He could spend some time with his cousin and his husband without wanting to crawl out of his skin.

Or without thinking about Will.

Or about Giana's plans for Will.

Chapter Five

Turning the corner to Main Street, Will gave up even trying to stifle his third neck-cracking yawn of the morning.

He'd known, of course, that running his own business without the benefit of the Johnson last name would be hard. Worthwhile, but hard.

He'd still underestimated how much it sucked to be the *only* one who he felt completely comfortable relying on in a pinch. Kate was wonderful, and he knew she'd grow into a great manager, but she was still new enough that he didn't feel like he could call her at all hours.

Like he'd been called last night, by Luca.

So he'd dragged himself out of bed—a bed he'd *just* collapsed into, gratefully—and gone back down to the shop, opening it up and grabbing another few gallons of Tahitian vanilla bean for Luca and the restaurant he ran with Oliver.

He wished he'd grabbed another cup of coffee from Joy, pouring it into one of her to-go cups, before he'd left the Inn. But he'd stubbornly believed that he'd only needed the one.

Will yawned again, and it was why he missed the figure stepping out from the morning shadows underneath the white and bright pink striped awning over the Cherry's door.

His first reaction was, *Oh yes please.* Because in the bright morning light, Enzo Moretti was gorgeous. Even prettier now than he'd been in the dusk, last night. His second was, *What the hell does he want now?*

Maybe he could have been more diplomatic last night, but it wasn't like he was any less tired or any less cranky this morning. He'd woken to his alarm blaring, body aching from a long day of work and the long workout he'd indulged in after, and cock aching from the dry spell of a century. He didn't want to play nice with Enzo.

For the first and the second. Because the first made him want to tell him to fuck off. And the second made him want to tell Enzo to fuck *him*.

"Hey," Enzo said. He pulled away from the brick wall he'd been leaning on.

Will ignored that he was carrying two cups of coffee. Because of course he was. Was there anything more gorgeous in the morning than a man in jean shorts and a T-shirt that hugged all his curves, carrying coffee?

"What do you want now?" Will knew his tone was short, but it was the best he could do, all things considered.

It was so unfair that Enzo was going to rub his attractiveness and smug assholeness in this morning.

He extended the coffee towards Will, who didn't take it. Offering a blinding smile, along with the caffeine.

"I think we might've gotten off on the wrong foot yesterday," Enzo said. Enzo being persuasive was even hotter than Enzo being a jerk.

Unfortunately.

"I can't imagine what you mean. I found you painting on my building. *My* building," Will dryly, still ignoring the coffee, even though he really wanted to take it—and more. He was going to blame this momentary weakness on exhaustion. He unlocked the door and stepped through it, not holding it for Enzo. Hoping that would be enough to dissuade him from following.

It did not.

"I know. And I'm really sorry about that. I didn't realize you hadn't been told about the mural." Another charming smile. Will didn't know how he hadn't recognized the man immediately, from the first moment. Because Luca and Giana also smiled like that, and the effect never failed to captivate anyone within a mile radius.

"Clearly." Will had realized that too, when he'd calmed down enough to think about it.

He flipped lights on, heading behind the counter. He didn't think Enzo would be ballsy enough to continue following him, but sure enough, there he came, coffee still in hand.

"Then let me apologize. For me. And for my interfering mother," Enzo said persuasively, stopping just where Will did, short of the door to the back kitchen. He lifted the coffee again. "Come on, take my peace offering. You look tired."

Will made a face and gave in. Grabbed the cardboard coffee cup, making sure not to touch Enzo while he was at it.

No point in making things worse.

"Isn't it rude to tell someone they look tired?" Will grumbled, sipping the coffee. He'd expected it to be too sweet and prepared totally wrong. But it was perfect, exactly the way he liked it.

Glancing at the cup again, he couldn't miss either the Sweetie Pie's logo—Oliver's bakery—or the large black *W* scrawled on the side.

Enzo shrugged. "It's the truth."

"How did you know how I liked my coffee?" Will asked, changing the subject. To something safer than how he looked. Before he lost his head and asked Enzo if he liked looking, as much as *he* liked looking back.

"This is Indigo Bay. It's a really freaking small town. I could find out anything about anyone, easy as breathing," Enzo said, waving the question away. "Do you like it? Is it right? Rocco said it would be."

"Weirdly, yes," Will said, taking another long sip. "Thanks."

Enzo finished his coffee. Tossed it in one of the large square trashcans behind the counter. "Am I forgiven then?"

"Is that why you're here?"

Will was sure he was here to apologize *and* to convince Will to let him paint the mural.

On his way back to the Inn after closing, he'd stopped by the wall. Found the paint gone. No evidence that Enzo had even been there.

The moment he'd finished cleaning the wall, Will had loved it exactly the way it was. But he'd looked at it last night and had thought, just for a second, that maybe it was a little too big and too blank.

He'd intended to tell Enzo *no*, firmly and definitely.

But now he wasn't quite sure.

"You know why I'm here." There was no question Enzo knew how to charm. The same way he knew how to lean against the back counter, that gorgeous body on display, as he flashed another of those devastating smiles.

Maybe it shouldn't have but it made Will grumpier.

You didn't enjoy being hungry while forced to stare at something delicious—especially when you couldn't possibly take a bite out of it.

"You want to paint the mural," Will stated. He didn't want to mess around.

Okay. He *did*, but he wasn't going to. Enzo wasn't staying, and that was enough, without all the other Giana-shaped considerations.

"I didn't, actually. That was all my mom's idea. But then I saw your wall, and I hate to tell you, but it's perfect."

"It should be. I spent a whole freaking week cleaning shit off it."

"I bet you did," Enzo said. "I usually have to do that work. But you've already done it."

"What are you going to paint on it?" Will asked.

"Uh." Enzo hesitated. "I don't know actually. My clients . . .that's usually something they concede to *me*."

Will stared at him. "Let me get this straight. They pay you to paint a mural on their building, but you get to decide what it is."

Enzo winced. "Yeah. I . . .well, I've learned that's the best way for me to work. And the demand is there, so it made sense for me to make it a requirement."

It was beginning to make more sense why Will's graffiti accusation had bothered Enzo so much. Of course, Will had already begun to see why. Last night, when he'd opened Enzo's Instagram, and not only had the follower number taken him aback, but the undeniable artistry of his work.

You should just let him do it.

But what if he ended up with something he hated?

Will was so proud of Cherry's, of finally having something he could claim as his, something he had worked so hard to carve out.

He wasn't about to cede any part of it to someone else.

"No," Will said.

"No?" Enzo lifted a dark eyebrow.

"No, you don't get to decide what you're painting on my wall."

"Oh." Enzo had the nerve to look disappointed. He straightened. "I . . .I do hope you change your mind, honestly. It's a beautiful building now."

"And what, your mural would make it look even better?" Will asked archly.

Enzo flushed. "Something like that."

"Well, I'll think about it," Will said. That wasn't just lip service, because he was already beginning to think he'd made a mistake.

Stay strong. You don't need to tangle yourself up with Enzo Moretti.

But he wanted to.

"Don't wait too long," Enzo said, flashing him one final smile as he headed towards the door. "I'm not going to be around forever."

But he hadn't had to say it, because Will already knew it.

It didn't surprise Enzo much, but his mom was avoiding him.

She'd had dinner with them last night, but then she'd had a "meeting" and then this morning when he'd walked into her kitchen, it had been empty already.

Clearly she'd discovered that *he* knew the truth about the mural, and she didn't want him to yell at her.

Killing two birds with one stone, he swung by Sweetie Pie's, Oliver's bakery and coffee shop, to pick up apology coffee for Will but when he asked Marjorie if she'd seen his mother, she'd shaken her head no.

Then after talking to Will, he headed to the deli, but Luca was there by himself, and he said he hadn't seen her.

Frustration mounted as he stepped back onto the sidewalk.

He'd needed to make it clear what she'd done was completely inappropriate, nevermind unprofessional, and that was before he'd found out that Will might be charmed into forgiving him, but he wasn't interested in discussing the mural.

Enzo had told himself that was fine. He could simply take a vacation and rest and enjoy himself. But then he'd walked by the wall again, and damnit, he wanted to paint it as badly as he'd wanted to paint anything, ever.

Grabbing his phone he texted Rocco. **You seen my mother?** he asked.

Rocco answered almost immediately. **Yeah. She's at Oliver's. Figured she was safe from your wrath because you'd already been by.**

That was even worse. He wondered who'd given her a heads-up that he'd found out.

Enzo walked back down to Sweetie Pie's, and *yep*, there she was, sitting by the big window at one of the small tables that dotted the bright, cheery space, enjoying a cappuccino.

"There you are," he said, taking the seat opposite her.

Giana pasted on an innocent-looking expression, but he knew her too well to believe it was true. "Oh, were you looking for me?"

"Who told you?" Enzo was grumpy and he didn't even want to hide it.

Not only had she probably ruined his chance at painting that gorgeous blank wall, she'd been advertising to Will—hot, delectable Will—that he couldn't get a date on his own.

"I don't know what you mean," she claimed.

"Come off it, I know what you did. You didn't even *bother* to ask Will about the mural. You do realize we need his permission to paint *his* wall, right?"

"I thought he'd be honored," Giana said with a sniff.

"You're kidding, right?" Enzo made a face. "It really wasn't cool. And it *really* wasn't cool for you to be soliciting dates for me. I can get my own dates."

"Can you?"

Enzo groaned. "Mom, I'm not interested in Will, no matter what you think. I'm busy. I'm going places. I'm crazy busy right now. I don't need to settle down, or whatever it is you've decided I should be doing."

"You don't even have a *home*. You're living out of a suitcase." She leveled an experienced Moretti stare at him.

"And?"

"And it's sad. I want more for you, darling, than just an empty hotel room and a duffel bag full of clothes."

"I have more than that," Enzo said between clenched teeth. "In any case *please* stop trying to throw me at Will. It's embarrassing."

"Because you like him! Because you think he's cute! Oh, he *is* cute, isn't he? I thought so the moment I saw him. And then Luca told me he was gay, and I knew he was perfect for you."

"He's not anything for me," Enzo repeated as patiently as he could. "And because you interfered, now he's pissed at me and doesn't want me to paint the mural. That's not only disappointing, but it makes me look unprofessional, Mom. And I *am* a professional."

"Oh, of course you *are a* professional, darling! You're so good at your job. Brilliant, really." Giana made a face. "I'm sorry. I just thought it would be such a lovely surprise."

"The mural? Or Will?" Enzo asked dryly.

"Well, *both*," she retorted fondly. "Did you not think he was cute?"

Enzo had no intention of telling her how cute Will really was. At least if Giana was attempting matchmaking in earnest now, she had good taste.

"That's not the point," Enzo said. "You've got to stop doing this stuff. I'm my own man now."

Her face fell a little, and that guilt he was far too familiar with swamped him yet again. "I know," she said in a quiet voice. "I suppose I should have talked to him about it."

"Asked his permission," Enzo stressed. "And I should have asked more questions. Made it a more formal proposal. Now I'm not going to get to do it, and that's disappointing."

Giana looked as disappointed as he felt. Maybe she'd been harboring some secret hope that even if her overt matchmaking didn't work out, Enzo painting Will's building might lead to more.

"I'm sorry," she said softly. "I didn't know. I didn't realize."

Enzo resolutely shoved the guilt to the side. "Yes, you did. But it's okay." He reached out and took her hand. "I get it. You just want me to be happy. But I *am* happy."

She didn't look convinced. Enzo didn't know if it was because she didn't understand what did truly make him happy or because he wasn't quite convincing enough.

He *was* happy. Though maybe he did wonder, just a little, whenever he saw his cousin and his husband together what it would be like to have a partner like that. A *love* like that.

But then he remembered that falling in love that way would mean nailing him down to a single spot, and he couldn't deal with that.

Couldn't live like that again.

"Alright, darling," she said. "Do you want me to talk to him?"

"No, *no.* You've done enough damage, already."

"You don't think I'd make it worse, do you?" she asked with surprise as she set her cup onto its saucer.

"Oh, of course not. You'd just try to convince him to date me again," Enzo grumbled.

"He should *want* to date you."

"Well, it's not happening. He's . . ." *Gorgeous. And even cuter when he's annoyed with me, which he is now, thanks to you.* "He lives here, Mom. And I don't." He tried to say it with as much gentleness as he could, but she still frowned.

"I understand," she said and stood. "I've got to meet Joy. We're going to Charleston to find some antiques for the expansion of the Inn."

Enzo didn't remember his mother being quite so close to Joy Billings. Eighteen-year-old Enzo would've been thrilled at this development, but twenty-seven-year-old Enzo was just confused why he'd missed this happening.

"I didn't know the two of you were so close," he said casually as she wrapped him up in a quick hug.

"Oh, since I moved back to town, yes. She's a delightful person, Enzo."

"Just like her son, I'm sure." But there was no heat in his voice. He'd gotten over Oliver ages ago.

"Are you going to stay here?"

"Yeah, I'll have another cappuccino. Maybe sketch some." What he wanted to do was sketch some ideas for the mural—but he wasn't convinced Will would change his mind.

Maybe he should go back to Cherry's and deploy some additional Moretti charm to persuade him.

"Are you sure you don't want me to talk to him?" Giana asked. And Enzo knew exactly who she was referring to. "Maybe if I apologized, smoothed things over, he'd see things differently."

He might. But Enzo couldn't risk her pimping him out again.

"No, it's fine," Enzo said. "I have other work I can play around with. And maybe I can convince Rocco to play hooky."

He pulled out a pencil and his sketchpad from his back pocket.

"You shouldn't," Giana said but she was smiling.

"I'll see you later," Enzo said. "Have fun with Joy."

But before she could walk out the door, it was opening and there was Will standing there, in another of his tight white T-shirts, two cherries with their stems intertwined embroidered on the pocket.

"Oh, Will," Giana said excitedly, beckoning him over and Enzo had to clamp his lips together so he didn't groan out loud.

"I'm so glad I ran into you," she continued, and Enzo was relieved that at least she'd pasted on her most contrite expression. "I wanted to apologize for the misunderstanding."

Will raised an eyebrow. He didn't look convinced by her show of remorse.

"It must've just slipped your mind to tell me," Will said.

"Yes, exactly," Giana said, giving him one of her brightest smiles.

Enzo recognized that smile and didn't think Will would be able to resist it, and sure enough, he didn't. He melted. Only a little, but it was enough.

"Well, no harm, no foul," Will said, and then he turned to Enzo. "I was hoping I'd catch you here. I want to talk to you."

Giana's expression turned rapturous.

Enzo internally winced.

"About the *mural*," Will added, with emphasis.

"Don't you have somewhere you need to be?" Enzo asked his mother.

"Well . . ." She trailed off.

"Go meet Joy. Let me take care of this," Enzo said.

She smiled and gave him a nod. "Alright. Enjoy yourselves. A *lot*."

Even after she disappeared out of the front door, Will didn't sit down. Just stood there, shifting his weight from foot to foot. "I was thinking," he said. "What if I gave you a general subject for the mural and you took it from there?"

I've got him.

But Enzo had a feeling if he got cocky again, he'd scare him away again. "That's not usually the way it works," he reminded him. "But I promise, I'm not going to paint something completely ridiculous on your building."

"I know," Will said.

Enzo gestured towards the seat across from him. "Come on, sit down. Let's talk about this." When Will continued to hesitate, he added, "I promise, I don't believe that if we sit together and share a conversation that we're gonna fall wildly in love and get married."

Will flushed but did finally sit down. "I didn't imagine you would," he said. "But Giana might."

"She might," Enzo agreed. It was best, he'd decided, to face this horrible awkwardness head-on. "I heard she was talking about me. But I . . .that's not me. She doesn't speak for me."

"I get it," Will said. "She just wants what's best for you."

"And who's being egotistical now?" Enzo teased. "'Cause how else could you be so sure *you're* what's best for me?"

Will's face went even redder, under his tan. "Uh, no, I just mean . . .you know what I meant."

"I did," Enzo agreed. But he'd liked making Will blush anyway. Liked flirting with him.

It was a hell of a lot more fun than Will angrily accusing him of vandalizing his building.

"We can . . .uh . . .pretend she didn't get involved," Will said. "I'd prefer that, in fact."

Enzo wanted to tell Will that Giana was more determined than that, but he'd discover the truth after a while, so there was no point in scaring him away now. Especially not when he'd come to Enzo, only a few hours after claiming that he couldn't paint his wall.

"So that was your best offer?" Enzo said. "You give me a subject and I give you a mural?"

Will shrugged awkwardly. "It's a good idea, though Kate was actually the one who suggested it."

"You got an idea?" Enzo found himself curious as to what subject Will wanted him to paint.

Curious. Nothing more.

"You could always paint the town story."

Enzo made a face.

"What? What's wrong with that?" Will asked, confused. "It's such a beautiful story. I love hearing it. Especially when Joy tells it."

"Of course you love it," Enzo complained.

There were many things he didn't like about Indigo Bay, but the story was one of the worst, ultimately so saccharine and fake sounding. Like that could *really* happen in real life. Nobody waited years and years for someone to come home, especially someone who was almost certainly dead. Those stories never had those picture-perfect happy endings, the way this one did.

"What's wrong with it?"

What was wrong with it? *Everything*, as far as Enzo was concerned. "It's like the worst version of a Hallmark holiday. It probably didn't even happen that way."

Will looked surprised. "You really don't like it. I think you're the only person I've met who feels that way. Even Luca enjoys it."

"Luca enjoys the business it brings," Enzo said. And yes, maybe that was a very prosaic way to see it, but that was his cousin through and through.

"I don't believe that's all," Will said slowly. "It's a story about hope, about never giving up. A beautiful love story. Don't tell me you don't believe in love?"

Enzo didn't *not* believe in love. "I just don't believe that real life works out that way."

"What about your cousin and Oliver?"

He waved a hand. "I guess *sometimes* it does. But for most of us? Not so much."

Will smiled. "That's a pretty depressing way to look at things. I like to see the opportunities, not the disappointments." He paused. "Don't you dare say *of course you do.*"

The laugh was startled right out of Enzo. "Unfair," he claimed. But it was very fair.

"Have you ever listened to Joy tell the story?"

Joy was not only the woman who ran the biggest B&B in town, the Sweetheart Inn, but she was also Oliver's mom, and a romance novelist of some renown. Enzo knew her first book had been a retelling of *the story*. He'd grown up hearing her tell it, every single time under duress.

First because he'd been a kid, and love was gross. Then because he'd been unlucky in love himself, pining after a man who not only didn't want him, but who he wasn't really suited to, at all.

Then he'd left town and mercifully had been saved any further retellings.

"It's a stupid question, I know. I know she tells it every year at the Festival," Will continued, a sheepish expression on his face. "I just thought, maybe if she told it, and you really listened to it, you'd . . .I don't know . . .hear what I hear, every time. But that's stupid."

"It's not stupid," Enzo said firmly, even though maybe he might've believed that, before. He didn't know Will, but he'd already learned he didn't like to see that shadow of disappointment in his light blue eyes. They should always be happy.

Enzo knew that was kind of an impossibility. It wasn't even his responsibility to *make* Will happy. But he wanted to make sure, anyway.

"So you'll consider it?" Will said, and there it was, the joy lighting him up like he'd just been plugged in, and Enzo was only a man. That look was difficult to ignore.

Even harder to reject.

He nodded. "I'll consider it."

"You *have* to listen to Joy tell it," Will insisted. "I'll text her, ask her to come around to Cherry's tonight. Do you have plans?"

"It's Indigo Bay." Enzo rolled his eyes. "You live here. You know I don't have any plans."

"Well, come to Cherry's tonight. Listen to Joy."

"You gonna bribe me with some more of your delicious ice cream?"

Will looked disappointed, then, which was confusing. Enzo *had* said it was delicious.

"I didn't realize you'd tried it already. Oh—of course. Luca took those samples back to his house. You must've been over."

"Whatever the new thing is you were trying, keep doing it," Enzo said.

"Yeah?" There was that glow again.

"Oh, yeah. And if you bribe me with more, I'll be there tonight, no matter who's gonna talk to me."

"Okay." Will smiled and stood. "I'll see you then, tonight? About seven thirty?"

"Don't you close at eight?"

"Yeah, but that way maybe the crowd will have cleared out some." Will looked sheepish. "Then maybe I can crash and listen in, too."

"You really do love the story," Enzo said. Which, of course he did. He'd just said so, hadn't he? Enzo felt like he must be losing his touch.

But Will was still smiling. "Yep."

After Will left, Enzo opened his sketchbook. He'd intended to work on the next mural he was scheduled for—something in the upper half of Maine, in an old fishing village that was trying to rebrand as a tourist destination.

But instead of whales and fish and sailing ships, he found himself drawing something else, the pencil flying over the page. Enzo told himself it meant nothing, that it was just something he needed to work out, but instead of stopping at the bare lines, he began to fill in the shading, wanting to make it as perfect as he could.

"Well, I guess you don't need to tell me after all that you think Will's hot."

Enzo looked up in surprise, glad it was only Rocco who'd caught him sketching Will's face, and not Will himself.

That would be difficult to explain.

Rocco set a cappuccino down next to Enzo's sketchpad and slumped down in the opposite chair. "Thought you might want some more coffee," he said, taking a long drink of his own iced mocha.

"You better be careful. You know Oliver keeps me *and* Luca on a three-cappuccino limit."

"For a good reason," Rocco said with a grin. "We're already intense enough."

Enzo didn't always feel like he fit in well with his family, but that much *was* accurate. He could admit that he could be a little absorbed, a little obsessive, when he wanted to be. Or when he got caught up in a project he loved.

"So, why are you drawing Will, besides the obvious?"

"Just practicing." Enzo flipped the page. Let the pencil slide over the paper, a figure emerging. A recognizable figure, albeit an exaggerated one.

Luca, shaking his finger at something off the page, his good looks and his intensity both exaggerated.

Rocco giggled. "Don't let Oliver see that," he said under his breath.

But of course Oliver chose that moment to emerge from the back of the bakery. "I give you a minute for a break and of course you come out here," Oliver complained. But he was smiling as he gazed down at Rocco. "What's this about me not seeing something?"

Rocco leaned over and covered the Luca sketch with his hand.

"Oh, we're just joking around," Rocco said, still chuckling gesturing towards Enzo. "He's drawing caricatures of the different people around town."

Oliver raised a questioning eyebrow. "And why don't I want to see? Let me guess, the best one is my husband."

Enzo shrugged awkwardly. Somehow the Luca drawing would be easier to explain than the one of Will. "If he doesn't want to be a target, he shouldn't make himself one."

Oliver didn't say that Luca wasn't, at least not these days; he only smiled. "True," he admitted. "You're not going to show me, are you?"

"Uh." Enzo hesitated, but Rocco nudged him.

"Listen, *he* married him," Rocco pointed out. "Oliver knows what he's really like. Better than either of us."

Oliver's smile deepened. "Also true." But he didn't ask again. Instead, he changed the subject. "What's this about you drinking *three* cappuccinos today?"

"Rocco gave me this last one," Enzo squawked.

"He just looked so lonely out here," Rocco pointed out, all innocence. "With his sketchbook and no coffee."

"Luca has three cappuccinos all the time," Enzo pointed out.

"And Luca shouldn't, because then he stays up way too late," Oliver said, the corner of his mouth quirking up. "You Morettis always believe you can handle your caffeine, but the truth is, you come from the womb pre-caffeinated, already."

This time both he and Rocco laughed, nodding in agreement.

"That's my way of saying you're cut off for the day," Oliver teased gently. "Now show me this picture of Luca."

Enzo hesitated again. But then Oliver plucked the sketchbook off the table before he could stop him. He flipped pages until he found what he was looking for.

For a second, he looked at the quick drawing Enzo had made of Luca, Enzo bracing for every reaction he could think of.

Then Oliver's face cracked into a wide smile, and then he was straight up cackling, head thrown back with the force of his laughter. "Oh, *oh*," he gasped, "you're *good*."

"Told you," Rocco said knowingly.

"Just don't let him see it," Oliver said, returning the sketchbook to his table.

"Yeah, it would piss him off," Enzo agreed, feeling a little pulse of shame for doing it, because he *liked* Luca. At least he did now.

"No, no," Oliver corrected gently, "he'd never let me hear the end of it. He'd *love* it that much."

"Really? He wouldn't be insulted?"

"Are you kidding?" Oliver shook his head. "You really don't know how proud he is of you, do you?"

That was not what Enzo had expected Oliver to say.

"Uh, no?"

"Are you kidding me?" Rocco chimed in. "He won't shut up about your latest mural. That galaxy one in Seattle? He talked about it non-stop, even to *customers*, for days."

"Oh. *Oh*."

Oliver shot him a gentle smile. "He's a complicated guy," he admitted. "I tell him all the time that he should tell *you*, but you know your cousin. He's so contained."

"Not as much as he used to be, before you convinced him to be a real boy," Enzo joked.

It was funny, because back when that had actually happened, he'd been so pissed off. And now it was impossible to be angry about it, because Luca and Oliver made each other better.

It was the kind of relationship Enzo measured his own by, and when every single one had come up short, he'd begun to think that maybe the kind of white-picket-fence forever love that his cousin and Oliver shared wasn't for him. He'd meant what he told Will earlier; maybe real life was full of disappointing love. And it had been easier, too, to give up on relationships because sometimes it felt like he spent every month in a different city.

"Yeah, I was really surprised when I came here," Rocco agreed. "I only knew him, a few years back, when he lived in Napa. And then I showed up a month or so back and imagine my shock when he was laughing and joking and *teasing*."

"The miracle of love," Oliver said mysteriously. He turned to Enzo. "I've got bread rising. But you're good out here, minus the cappuccinos?"

"Can I just hang out here? Do you mind?"

He realized that maybe Oliver wouldn't want him spending his morning—and maybe even his afternoon—taking one of his handful of tables.

"No, no," Oliver waved. "Feel free to stay. You're always welcome here, you know? Besides . . ." He shot him a knowing grin. "It's a small town, isn't it? Not a whole lot of choices."

Ilaria was always telling him, whenever his feelings about Indigo Bay had come up, that he needed to remember that he'd changed. *You, more than anyone else, need to remember that,* she'd added. *'Cause it's like you go back there and the minute you cross the town line, you forget, too.*

"Definitely smaller than I'm used to, now," he admitted.

"I bet, and God knows, when I first came home, it was an adjustment," Oliver said, and Enzo believed that he really understood. "Come on," he said to Rocco, "let's work on some of your pastry skills and leave your cousin to his artistic endeavors."

Chapter Six

Instead of telling her where he was going and why he was going there, Enzo told his mother he'd made plans with Rocco—it was a little white lie but the way he saw it, a necessary one, because he didn't need to encourage her to build her castle in the sky any taller than it already was.

He walked down the darkening street, noticing a number of people carrying ice cream cones and cups emblazoned with the Cherry's bright pink logo as he headed closer to his destination.

When he reached the corner the ice cream parlor sat at, with its big blank wall, he stood there for a long minute, staring at it. Imagining various different images splashed across it.

And even though he didn't really want to do it, in fact telling his mind that he didn't want to envision *the* story told by his paintbrush, he did anyway.

He could see it, clear as day, bright and undeniable, the outcropping hill rising on one side, Eliza standing on top of it, her dark hair streaming behind her in the wind as she faced the open ocean, waiting for the man she loved. There was a boat too, drifting on the waves at the far end, and the tiny figure of a man staring down the storm as he tried, desperately, to get home.

Enzo took a deep breath.

He still didn't *want* to paint this, but he couldn't deny it *was* an arresting image.

Rounding the corner, he pulled open the door to Cherry's, not surprised to see it half-full, but most of the people already sitting at tables, and only one person in line currently. He slipped in behind them, eyeing Will behind the counter, his big body moving gracefully from one task to another, scooping ice cream and mixing milkshakes and swirling dollops of bright white whipped cream on top of dishes, all topped with . . .what else but cherries?

The white T-shirt and bright pink apron he was wearing were mostly clean, a single stripe of chocolate across his pectoral muscle, and a smear of something almost as pink as the apron across its front.

He was smiling at something his employee had said, and his eyes were so blue, his teeth so white, against his tanned face, and something inside Enzo clenched.

He hadn't come back here to start anything with anyone. Certainly not the kind-eyed man with all the muscles and the ice cream shop.

He'd come home because his mother had made him such a good offer he hadn't been able to resist.

But he'd never imagined that the man would be as alluring as the blank wall he owned.

The woman in front of Enzo finished ordering and he watched as Will easily slid in front of the register instead of his employee who'd been there before.

Enzo wondered if it was because of *him*.

That thing inside him clenched harder.

"Hey," Will said, giving him an even deeper, sweeter smile. "How's it going?"

"Good. You?"

"Oh, we've been busy, but like I expected, it's been slowing down." The smile deepened even further, like nothing could have delighted Will more.

Enzo was helpless to smile back, even though there were probably half a dozen people in the shop who were going to report back to his mother—and to anyone else who would listen—that he and the newbie in town had been flirting over ice cream.

"Lucky for me," Enzo murmured. "I don't know what I want, so you'd better suggest something for me to try."

"I got you," Will said confidently, conspiratorially. "You like chocolate?"

Enzo shot him a look. "Doesn't everyone?"

"You'd be surprised. But I'm not surprised you do." Will's voice lowered and leaned in, right over the counter. "Your eyes are like the best Valrhona in my storeroom."

Enzo knew he had the Moretti good looks but it was still one of the best compliments he'd ever received. "I'd say thank you, but I didn't have much to do with them."

Will nodded, once, decisively. "I'm gonna make you my tuxedo milkshake. You good with that?"

"I trust you," Enzo said and realized, to his own surprise, that he didn't necessarily *distrust* Will.

"Go ahead and take a seat and I'll bring it out. Joy's already out there, and I've told her what I'm hoping for. She's very excited," Will said, waving towards the seating area.

Enzo wanted to warn him that he hadn't made any promises, but it was hard to burst the happy bubble that seemed to envelop him.

"Alright," Enzo said.

When Enzo turned around, sure enough there was an empty chair, right next to Joy Billings, who appeared to be halfway through her dish of ice cream.

"Hi, Joy," Enzo said, sliding into the chair after giving her a quick embrace. "It's good to see you."

"Oh, Enzo. Welcome home." There'd been a time when Joy's voice had been downright chilly, back when he'd resented Oliver for the failure of their date, but so much had changed.

He'd changed, and then he'd done everything he could—save move home to Indigo Bay—to make it right with both the mother and the son.

"I see you've discovered how delicious the ice cream is here," he said as she scooped up a bite of ice cream the exact color of coffee with cream.

"Ugh, it's so good," Joy said, making a face. "It's become my favorite new way to procrastinate when a book's giving me trouble."

"Your secret's safe with me, if you do me a favor."

She raised an eyebrow, gone mostly gray. Unlike her hair, she didn't dye those. Today her short wavy locks were a sweet shade of lavender. "Is this the same favor Will asked me for?" she asked.

Enzo nodded.

An excited gleam appeared in her hazel eyes. "Are you really going to paint the story?"

"I'm thinking about it," Enzo said. "Will wants me to. But that's not normally how I do things. I'm . . ." He cleared his throat. "I'm trying to make an exception considering how my mom didn't even *ask* him if it was okay."

Joy nodded solemnly. "I told her she should have."

"And you didn't do it yourself?" It was a fair question.

"Ah, well, she said she would." Joy shrugged. "I assumed she would."

"She probably meant to—after I'd already started it." Enzo made an irritated noise.

"Probably. I know you have every right to be frustrated, but I know she did it because she loves you, and she wants you to be happy."

"I *am* happy," Enzo grumbled.

"I know," she said sympathetically and reached out, patting his arm. "So why are you hesitating to paint the story?"

Enzo was trying to find a nicer way to tell her he thought it was a load of bullshit when she continued. "Let me guess, you think the story's silly and heavily embroidered with fiction to sell tickets to the festival."

"Maybe a little?" Enzo winced. "Though I can't blame you guys for doing it, because it's brought a lot of tourism to the town." Tourism the town *needed*. Enzo wasn't stupid enough to believe Indigo Bay would survive without it, especially during the offseason.

"It has," she agreed.

"But you're right, I . . . I'm afraid I've never really understood it. And how can I paint something I don't understand?"

"Not everyone does," Joy admitted. "Will said he hoped that I might be able to convince you, and I'm not against trying to do that. But I think it's more than that. Art is more than that. You know that, and so do I. Maybe I'm not painting with colors but with words, but you have to *care* about it, and I can't make you do that."

That was not what Enzo had expected her to say. He'd expected her to drag out every good reason, every tourist-centered, every leader-of-the-town reason. But she hadn't.

"Oh. Well."

Joy smiled mischievously. "Do you still want me to tell the story again?"

She scraped the last of her ice cream. It *was* coffee—he could smell it now, in the air. And it smelled fucking delicious. He kind of hoped that maybe Will's suggestion of chocolate might include that particular flavor.

Enzo glanced behind the counter, where Will was bent over the glass case, arm muscles bunching as he effortlessly scooped out ice cream.

He *wanted* to paint a mural on his wall, but even more than that, he wanted to make it right. And what if Will's theory was spot-on, and he'd just never been particularly receptive to the story before because he'd been too young and too pissed-off?

"I do," Enzo said.

Joy nodded. "I hoped you might. We'll wait for Will, because he loves it so much."

"I hear you're remodeling the Inn," Enzo said.

"I am. Your mom's helping me out. She's got a ton of antique dealer contacts in Charleston, from when she moved there."

Giana had only spent a year or so in Charleston, before coming back to Indigo Bay. Enzo hadn't been particularly surprised when she'd returned to the small town—he'd been fairly certain she'd only moved because *he* was moving, and she was trying to distract herself from the inevitable loneliness after he'd left.

"I'm glad she's got more friends in town," Enzo said.

"Me too. It's too bad we didn't connect earlier," Joy admitted. She shot him a little smile. "You Morettis can be a prickly lot."

It was only the truth. Hard to take offense, when he'd certainly thought it himself a dozen or a hundred or even a thousand times. "We can be," Enzo agreed.

Joy patted him on the arm again. "But you generally mean well," she added.

"Thanks," Enzo said dryly. "I'm not sure you're right, but I appreciate the sentiment."

Joy laughed. "It's good to have you home."

"I'm glad someone besides my mother thinks so."

Before Joy could answer that one, Will walked over, Enzo's attention suddenly riveted by the unbelievable creation he was setting in front of him.

It was streaked in an intoxicating swirl with deep, dark chocolate, but the milkshake itself was white, flecked with tiny little black specks. Vanilla bean, Enzo realized. And, like a crown on the top, was a swirl of whipped cream, and nestled into it was a triangle of deep, rich-looking brownie, partially dipped in white chocolate, a little bow tie drawn on with more dark chocolate, and like the jewel in the crown was a bright red cherry.

"This looks *amazing*," Enzo said, not even sure where he should start.

"It's my tuxedo milkshake," Will said proudly.

"Oh, that's a good one," Joy said. "Even though I'm very partial to the coffee bean flavor."

"Tell me," Enzo demanded as he picked up the long silver spoon, not sure where he should start. Where the bliss should begin.

"Dark chocolate swirl, vanilla bean milkshake, topped with a tuxedo brownie and whipped cream. And of course, a cherry."

"Love the little bow tie. It's adorable."

"The best part," Joy agreed. "It's all in the details, and you get that, Will."

Will flushed, making him look even more attractive. Or maybe that was the decadent ice cream masterpiece he'd just brought Enzo. "Thanks. It *is* called the tuxedo," he said.

"I don't even know where to start," Enzo said, his spoon hesitating over the top of the whipped cream swirl.

"How do you start a mural?" Will answered Enzo's question with one of his own. "I'm gonna assume you just have to *start*. Doesn't really matter where."

Enzo dug his spoon into the whipped cream and then lower, digging out some of the melty-vanilla-ice-cream goodness, and groaned a little when he put it in his mouth. For anyone who felt like vanilla was overrated, clearly they'd never had really good vanilla bean ice cream, with the little flecks of seed, the taste rich and nutty on his tongue. And then there was the deep, dark chocolate ganache ribboning the edge of the glass.

"This is fucking delicious," Enzo said, through a mouthful of ice cream. He plucked out the brownie, his teeth sinking into the perfect chewy texture, flecked with chunks of chocolate.

Will smiled, looked very pleased. "Glad you like it."

"I *love* it. Please tell me all your ice cream is this good."

Will didn't need to tell him, because Enzo already knew it had to be.

"It is," Joy said.

But Will only shrugged, flushing again in a very cute, self-deprecating way. "I do pretty well," he said.

But from the number of people streaming in and out of his shop, it was clear he did more than "pretty well."

"As for the murals . . .I usually start with an idea. In this case, *your* idea."

Did he actually *want* to paint the de facto Indigo Bay story? He'd have said before today that there was no way. And yet, doubt had begun to wiggle in. He'd stood there, in front of the wall, and he couldn't deny it had talked to him, the way blank walls tended to do before he created something really special.

Who was he to ignore the call of inspiration?

"What happens after that?" Will sounded genuinely interested, which was surprising. Most people were only interested in the beginning and the end.

"Then I do a loose sketch, make sure the layout works for the wall, and then, depending on the project, a more detailed sketch. But for this? I'll probably keep it simple." Enzo finished the brownie in two delectable bites. "Did you bake this? Or do you get these from Oliver?"

A bright wash of pink crept up Will's neck and cheeks but this time he didn't look adorable, he looked perturbed. "No, no. Of course not."

"Oh. Well, I didn't know you were a baking genius as well as an ice cream prodigy. My apologies." Enzo grinned at him, hoping that it would smooth things over.

"Oliver actually told him he wanted *his* recipe," Joy said. She was glancing between the two of them, and Enzo was afraid that when this evening was over and she reported back to Giana—because there was no question she'd demand to know about this visit—his mom would be more determined than ever to see them paired up.

"You should put make that your slogan," Enzo advised. "This town worships Oliver's baked goods."

"For good reason," Will said.

Joy nodded, agreeing. "It's a family tradition."

"Share another one with me," Enzo said, forcing himself to turn away from Will's beautiful flush, towards Joy. "Tell me the story."

"You're sure?" Joy asked.

"I'm sure," Enzo said.

A hundred Enzo Morettis sauntered through Will's brain, uninvited, but not unwanted.

Enzo smiling.

Enzo teasing.

Enzo, his dark eyes serious and intent.

Enzo, moaning with the taste of Will in his mouth.

It was . . .well, it was not surprising, exactly, because Will was at-tracted to him. Anyone with a pulse would be, because Enzo Moretti was plain fucking gorgeous. But it *was* disconcerting. Especially with how tightly his brain was hanging on to even the thought of the guy. All day, he'd been trying to get a respite, even as he'd known he'd be seeing him tonight.

Not just any vision of him either, but an Enzo Moretti eating *his* ice cream.

He was having difficulty even focusing, as Enzo slowly demolished his milkshake, bliss blooming across his handsome face.

"Well, Will, how does it begin?" Joy teased. "Since it's your favorite."

When he'd first come to Indigo Bay, scouting for the right location for his ice cream parlor, he hadn't been convinced it was the right place for him. Then one morning, over coffee and the best scones he'd ever tasted, Joy had told him the story of her ancestors, the story that made Indigo Bay so special, and he'd never wanted to leave.

"It has to begin with Eliza," Will said. "She was born in the early 1800s to one of the first families of this town."

Joy nodded, giving him a soft smile. "Right. She grew up with Nathaniel Billings. To hear it told, they were childhood playmates, always close. But when they grew up, he decided to go to sea."

"But first, he fell in love." Will sighed.

"And not with Eliza," Joy confirmed. "With a woman named Betsy. They pledged their love to each other, before he left for a long sea voyage. When he came back, they were to be married. But he didn't come back. Not for years. For so many years, Betsy married someone else."

"Betsy's the real villain in this story," Enzo inserted casually.

Will had gotten momentarily distracted by Kate and Mari having a quick discussion, and when he glanced back, he realized that Enzo had finished his milkshake and after pushing it away, he'd laid his sketchbook out in front of him. He was sketching quickly, pencil flying over the page. Like he couldn't even keep up with his own inspiration.

With scenes from the story? Will wasn't sure.

"I don't know if she's a villain," Joy said. "What other choice did she have but to move on? There'd been no sight of him, or word either, for years. She wasn't supposed to wait forever."

"Eliza did," Will reminded.

It was the thing he loved most about the story. The hope that lived in Eliza that had never died—even when it didn't make logical sense for her to hang on to it.

"It was a question I did consider at length, when I wrote their story," Joy said. "Was Betsy right to move on and marry someone else? Was Eliza right to wait so long?"

"I think it's romantic," Will said.

Enzo shot him a teasing look. "Of course you do."

"She knew he wasn't dead. She *knew* it, which was why she waited. Why she climbed up to the high point every single day. She knew he'd come back home; she knew it deep down, in her heart, that he'd come back," Joy said. "That's why she waited. Ultimately that's why I decided she waited. There's a certain kind of enchantment to it, an unshakable faith that you have to buy into."

The way she glanced over at Enzo, who didn't even notice, with his eyes glued to his sketchpad, pencil flying over the surface, made it clear what side he came down on.

But could anyone not believe and be so into illustrating each scene? From his vantage point, Will could see the quick lines he'd drawn, building up the vantage point—this was South Carolina so none of the cliffs were particularly high, but it *was* the highest point on the coast—and the figure on the top, long hair curling in the breeze.

"Ten years she waited. Even when her family began to say she was crazy. She still climbed the high point every day. Watching and waiting," Will said.

Joy nodded. "They tried to send her away. To relatives in Boston. To a sanitorium in Georgia. But she refused. Kept saying she needed to be here, for when Nathaniel returned."

"I don't know how anyone would believe, how anyone *could* believe, when all the evidence pointed to the fact he was dead," Enzo mused. But he no longer seemed as convinced as maybe he'd once been. When he looked up, Will could see the questions in his dark eyes.

"Love is funny like that. It's part hope and part magic, in the face of uncertainty," Joy added. "Then the storm blew in. It was the worst hurricane anyone could remember for a hundred years. They said it was like the hand of God, reaching out and touching the space between the land and the sea. When the weather finally cleared, the residents of the town could see a ship that had hit the rocks. And floating on a timber, in the wreckage, was a man with long dark hair and a thick beard that obscured almost all of his features."

"With blue eyes everyone recognized," Will said.

Joy nodded. "Everyone knew it was Nathaniel. Knew it had to be him. But Betsy hadn't waited for him, of course. She was married now, with three children. There was no room for him there. But Eliza took him in, despite the town's protests that it wasn't right, wasn't proper, and she nursed him back to health, physically and mentally. Winter turned to spring, and her love was so steadfast, he realized he'd fallen in love with her as well. They married a year later, and had five children."

"And one of them is your ancestor," Will said, smiling.

"Yes, indeed. I have a copy of Eliza's journal. The original is in the state history museum, but I don't need it, because every word is up here." She pointed to her head. "All her love, all her longing, all her faith. Her belief that he'd return. Then her unselfishness. She never asked him for marriage. Never expected anything would happen, because she thought he still loved Betsy."

"I could never be that unselfish. I'd have demanded his love," Enzo observed thoughtfully.

Will smiled, because he could see that. Could actually visualize Enzo in front of a man he loved, not letting him feel any differently than he himself did.

"I still think it's the most beautiful story I've heard. And you tell it so lovingly, Joy," Will said.

"Thanks, Will," she said and put her arm around him, tugging him into a quick hug. Then she stood. "It's late, but you got what you needed, Enzo?"

Enzo nodded. When she left, the tinkling bell of Cherry's indicating her departure, Will wanted to lean forward, memorize every line of

Enzo's drawings, but he figured that would be rude if he hadn't been invited to, so he forced himself to look away.

To give Enzo the time he needed.

But when the silence drew out between them, he couldn't resist looking over, just a quick glance.

"Joy was telling me earlier, before you came over, how prickly Morettis can be," Enzo said quietly, leaning back in his chair, as he tapped the pencil against the shiny surface of the table.

"I don't know if I'd call it *prickly* necessarily." *Difficult*, was more what Will would've called them. Challenging and charming and persuasive, even when you didn't want to be persuaded.

"I don't always think I'm a very good Moretti," Enzo said thoughtfully. "Maybe I'm not. But it means I'm willing to say I'm wrong, when I was wrong."

He pushed the open sketchbook towards Will, who glanced down at it.

"You were right. It's the perfect story to paint on your wall," Enzo continued.

As he stared at Enzo's drawings, he could *feel* the impact of the story in the images Enzo had created. Had an idea, already, of how beautiful it would be when it was done.

The high cliff, Eliza's figure on it, her hair swirling around her, her hand reaching out, towards the ocean, towards the big-masted ship, crashing against the shore, a figure in the water. The wild fierceness of the storm that raged around them.

"Are you sure . . .I'm a newcomer . . ." Will trailed off. He didn't want anyone assuming that he didn't deserve to have his building hold such an important piece of Indigo Bay history.

"You love it. I can see it in your eyes that you believe it. That you connect to it. That it matters to you. That's all that matters to me." Enzo paused. "All that should matter to *anyone* is your inspiration ignited my own."

Will didn't think he'd ever heard Enzo sound so earnest, so heartfelt. From what he'd seen of the guy, he liked to cultivate an easy, breezy, unbothered, snarky exterior but Will could already tell that there was more going on underneath.

What exactly? Will wasn't sure yet, but he knew he wanted to find out.

Enzo Moretti was a mystery he wanted to solve.

"Are you sure you're Enzo Moretti and not some imposter, taking his place for the next few weeks?" Will asked with a teasing tone.

Enzo made a face. "Let me guess, my reputation has preceded me. Who told you?"

"Uh." Will hesitated. Remembering everything Kate had told him about Enzo, before he'd ever showed his face in Indigo Bay.

"I'm sure they led with the disastrous date. How Oliver didn't want to date me, and I resented him for it."

"Well, yeah. They did start with that." Will squirmed uncomfortably. Recalling how he'd believed that because of that, Giana must have to recruit all his dates.

But the Enzo Moretti in front of him wouldn't need anyone's help getting a date.

"Not many queer guys in the town, back then. Different than now." Enzo looked at him pointedly. Okay, he'd probably heard—or guessed, anyway—about Will. He wasn't being exactly subtle, with the way he couldn't help but check out Enzo every time they ran into each other.

Plus, Oliver and Luca had known early on; they'd been the first people he'd told in this town, before he'd even officially moved here.

"I guess it didn't go well."

Enzo made a face. "An understatement. It was all wrong. A catastrophe. First off, we were the wrong people for each other. And I was a whiny little punk of a kid who wouldn't have known how to treat the right guy if he'd drawn out a map for me. I fucked it up by being an arrogant ass and then complained about it incessantly after."

He'd heard this story, of course. But not Enzo's version. "That's hard. For Oliver, and for you, too," Will said. He was having a hard time reconciling that guy he'd heard about with the Enzo sitting in front of him now. A nationally known and renowned mural artist. Unbelievably gorgeous and charming. The kind of guy anyone would want to go on a date with.

"I grew up," Enzo said, shrugging. "But some people haven't forgotten."

Will got the feeling it wasn't really the *town* that hadn't forgotten but Enzo himself. Because other than the fact that everyone clearly remembered, he hadn't seen anyone resenting Enzo now.

"That sucks," Will said. He understood a little about that. Sometimes he thought when his parents and his family looked at him, they still saw that little-too-eager-to-please kid. The one who'd drop anything and everything just to bring a smile to their faces.

But that kid was gone, now. Will had moved on, because he'd had to.

"Honestly, that's one of the reasons I stay away," Enzo admitted.

Will wanted to tell him he shouldn't—because he didn't think *any-one* genuinely held his bad behavior against him any longer—but he wasn't sure it was his place. Were they friends? Just no longer fighting about the mural? He didn't know.

He only knew that whenever their eyes met, something inside him lit up.

"So, what's the process here?"

"You're good with this sketch?" Enzo asked, gesturing to what he'd drawn out.

Will nodded. Probably a little more emphatically than he should've. But hey, Enzo had loved his ice cream. He was allowed to love Enzo's art, too.

"Good." Enzo folded the sketchbook closed. "Sometimes, if it's a bigger piece, I'll do a full color render, just much smaller, but for this, I don't think it's necessary. I'll finalize this sketch, make sure it's properly laid out on the wall, and then transfer the basic idea to the wall. Tomorrow. Or the day after. Depending on a few things. I've got to order some scaffolding, from Charleston, probably. We'll see how fast they can get it here. And paint, I'll need that."

"You'd think so," Will teased.

Enzo grinned at him, and there it was again. That electricity arcing through him in a dazzling wave.

This would be a lot easier if Enzo Moretti was a lot less appealing.

Or that he'd be spending *less* time outside Will's building.

Maybe Giana had been onto something, after all.

"Well," Enzo said, standing and stretching, flashing a strip of tanned bare stomach as he leaned back. "I'll let you know when I'm starting, for sure. I promise, no more unexpected paint surprises."

"It's . . .uh . . ." Will stammered. He did not want to be turned on by Enzo. Enzo was definitely *not* someone he could touch. He was way too complicated. "It's fine." He swallowed. "Give me your number," he said, pulling his phone out of his pocket. "And you can text me updates."

He told himself he was only asking for *that* reason.

"Just don't tell my mom," Enzo said with a wild grin after he'd recited his number and Will finished typing it into his phone.

Will fake shuddered. "No way," he agreed. "It's our secret."

Chapter Seven

Enzo was sweating.

And not even for a good reason.

Not even because Will had been popping his head out of his front door all morning.

Nope, it was just hot. *He* was just hot.

After months of working on the relatively mild west coast, moving up and down from Seattle to Portland and then back to Seattle again, he wasn't used to this heat or the South's oven-like humidity. And that didn't even count for the fact that he'd been schlepping and assembling the scaffolding that went up the side of Will's building.

His supplier had been able to deliver quicker than he'd expected, dropping off what he'd ordered just past noon, but he hadn't been able to spare anyone to assemble it.

Enzo, who'd watched and helped enough times, had waved him off, saying he'd take care of it himself.

What he hadn't anticipated was the temperature climbing up even higher, leaving him damp and cranky.

He picked up an iron pipe and screwed it into the main assembly he was working on, creating a platform for him to work on. At least with a smaller wall, the scaffolding could be smaller.

Wiping his forehead with the hem of his shirt, he finally gave up and tugged it off, rubbing his face dry—at least for the next ten seconds.

"Hey."

Enzo turned and there was Will standing there, an uncertain expression on his face and two bottles of water in his hands.

"Oh, hey," Enzo said and took the water Will handed him gratefully. "This is much appreciated."

Will craned his head back, staring up at the sky. "It's a hot one today. Summer on the coast's always warm, but it feels like it hits a new gear in early June."

"Yeah. And I'm not used to it," Enzo admitted, drowning half the water. He was in the middle of wiping his face yet again when he realized what he was doing.

That he was shirtless, in front of Will, who, even fully dressed, looked like he made being naked a freaking art form.

"Glad I brought you some water, then," Will said. He glanced over at the wall. So far it didn't look like much, Enzo could admit that.

"I did bring my own," Enzo admitted. "Just didn't expect to go through it so quickly."

"Yeah, it's hot today." Will flushed when he said it, looking everywhere but at Enzo.

"You don't look even the tiniest bit bothered," Enzo complained. It was true; Will looked cool and gorgeous and perfect.

Enzo felt like a sweaty, desperate mess, still embarrassingly sucking in his stomach, even though after how much his mother had freaking intervened, there was very little chance Will was ever going to be interested.

Will shrugged. "I've lived in the South my whole life. It's hot here, sure, but Florida's worse."

"And I've been in the Pacific Northwest for six months," Enzo admitted.

"There is that." The corner of Will's mouth quirked up. "You want another bottle of water?"

"Uh, no, I should probably grab something to eat. This is taking me a bit longer to do than I thought it might. Guess it's easier to watch someone else do it than do it yourself." He was just trying to decide if he should ask if Will wanted anything when he walked down to deli, when he heard a sound that he'd probably be hearing in his nightmares.

"Enzo!" his mother called out. "Oh, and *Will*. Just who I was hoping to catch! What a coincidence!"

"Coincidence my ass," Enzo muttered under his breath. "Quick," he said, eyeing his mom as she walked around the corner, "you may want to run. Or else she's gonna find a way to shove us together."

Will gave half a shrug. Like he wouldn't mind it. "It's all good," he said. Then turned to his mother, giving her the exact same smile he'd bestowed on Enzo. "Hey, Giana."

Enzo tried not to be jealous. Mostly failed. Even as he reminded himself that he didn't *want* Will to be charmed by him, especially.

It was bad enough Giana was here, looking between them like she'd just won the lottery. It was bad enough they'd been flirting last night in front of Joy.

If she got enough encouragement, Enzo had a feeling she wouldn't be willing to drop the idea of him and Will together. She *was* a Moretti after all, and once they were convinced something *might* be true, they didn't ever want to let go of it. It was one of their best traits, and also one of their worst.

"It's like you were practically reading my mind. I'd hoped you'd be together and here you are," she said, positively glowing—and not from the heat, either—as she gestured to the basket on her arm. "I made some extra food, when I was putting together a little picnic for Enzo here. You could always share it with him." She shot him her most winning smile. Much tougher men had fallen victim to that particular smile.

Enzo, himself, for one.

"Uh." Will hesitated.

"You two can go off to the park. It's nice and cool on the grass, under the shade."

"Mom," Enzo said, forcing himself not to roll his eyes. "Will's too busy to go off and share a romantic picnic with me."

She did not look deterred. "Who said it was romantic, Enzo? *You* said it was romantic." She shot Will a conspiratorial look. "Will, I hate to break it to you, but I think my Enzo might have a little bit of a crush."

Enzo stifled a groan. "I'll take this," he said, pulling the basket off her arm. "If it'll make you stop."

"Stop what?" Butter wouldn't melt in her mouth but she looked so secretly thrilled Enzo was afraid that maybe he had been giving out too many vibes that he'd been actually open to dating Will. He *was* attracted to the guy—he wasn't dead, thank you, Rocco—but that didn't mean he was looking for his very own happily ever after.

"All of this," Enzo said, gesturing between him and Will.

"Enzo," she said, ignoring his entreaty and giving him a little friendly whack on the forearm, "do make sure you put your shirt back on. We don't want Will thinking you're not a perfect gentleman."

"Of course not," Enzo grumbled.

Will shot him a sympathetic smile. "Thanks for the food, Giana. We'll be happy to share it. Maybe not in the park. I've got work to do. And it's so hot. Enzo could use a break. Maybe Cherry's back room would be romantic enough?"

Enzo lost the war with himself and finally rolled his eyes. "If it's air-conditioned, that's all I care about," he bit off.

"Wonderful," Giana said. "I'll leave you two to it." She turned and left with only one additionally exaggerated wink.

"You don't have to do that. Uh, invite me into your back room," Enzo said after she'd cleared the corner. But he still kept his voice quiet. God only knew she might actually spy on them around the wall, thinking she was being subtle.

Except she was about as a subtle as a sledgehammer.

But Will waved his concern away. "You're hot. You *could* use a break. And I just bet that Giana made me her famous artichoke spread, because she knows I love it. Who am I to turn that down?"

"You think she planned this then?" Enzo was pretty damn sure, but he thought it might be worth asking. He grabbed his T-shirt and the empty water bottle, trailing Will as he led them to Cherry's entrance. The seating area was empty, probably because it was dinner time and the Indigo Bay residents had yet to become so obsessed with Will's ice cream that they started indulging in it instead of regular meals.

Will laughed as he skirted around the corner of the counter, Enzo following him past the swinging double doors to the back. "You know she did," he said. But he didn't seem as perturbed by it as Enzo was. Probably because he wasn't the guy who looked so desperate for a date his mother had decided to find him one.

A woman with red-streaked dark hair was standing in the large back room, sucking down an iced coffee like it was going to save her life. She looked familiar. Then, spotting him, she raised an eyebrow.

Enzo realized two things at the same time. One, he had yet to put his shirt back on, and two, this was Kate Stewart, who'd been a few years behind him in school.

"I think you picked up a gigolo, boss," she teased.

Enzo pulled his T-shirt back on, flushing with embarrassment and hoping that Will didn't notice.

"You know Enzo, I presume?" Will asked.

"Oh yeah, though not as well as you're probably going to get to know him. I didn't know Giana's schemes were working out so well."

"They're not," Enzo said flatly. "But it's hot outside and she brought food."

Will nodded. "Enzo needed a break and I thought we could get her off our backs at the same time."

"Is that going to work?" Kate questioned.

Enzo wished he knew the answer.

"Come on back. I've got a little office. We can chat," Will said. Clearly he wasn't sure either, considering the way he ignored the question.

Will had not been lying about the *little* part. His office was only big enough for one chair and a small desk, a laptop and a charger sitting on it.

"Take the chair," Will said, gesturing towards it. "You need the rest."

"God, do I look that bad?" Enzo joked, while secretly worrying that maybe it was actually true.

Of course it didn't actually *matter* if he did or not.

But he did set the basket on the desk. "I gotta wash my hands," he said. *And make sure I'm not embarrassing myself even more.*

Will popped his head out of the office and gestured down towards where Enzo could see shiny kitchen equipment. "There's a staff restroom down that way."

Enzo found it and took his time, grimacing in the mirror at the smear of dirt on his cheekbone, the way his hair had flattened out with sweat. He washed up carefully and fluffed out his curls out as best he could, deciding that at least he'd return to Will's office *clean*.

When he did, Will had opened the basket and set out the food.

Giana had not lied; she'd made enough for two of them, easily. Which begged the question of just how she'd intended to get the two of them to share it, if Will hadn't happened to come outside at just the right time.

When Enzo said this, more theorizing than wanting an actual answer, Will smiled. "You don't think she has video equipment set up everywhere?" he wondered. "Maybe she's got a spy relay system, up and down Main Street?"

"Oh, she might," Enzo said, flopping down onto the chair, then looking over the different takeout containers that he was opening.

There was a nice selection of antipasti, along with fresh bread from Oliver's. "She *did* make her artichoke spread. She really must like you."

"Or," Will joked, "she really hopes I'll like *you*."

God, that was probably true.

"She doesn't make it for just anyone," Enzo said, ignoring *that*.

"I know she won't give me the recipe. I tried replicating it, but I'm no cook."

"I don't know, those brownies from last night would beg to differ." Enzo picked up a slice of bread and spread tapenade on it, added a few slices of prosciutto and a nice wedge of what smelled like smoked mozzarella. Chewed and swallowed, making happy humming noises in the back of his throat as he did so. Now that he'd finally cooled off some, he realized he'd been even hungrier than he'd imagined.

Will leaned over the desk and grabbed them two more bottles of water from the mini fridge underneath.

"Thanks," Enzo said.

"That's just simple baking," Will argued.

"Oliver would probably disagree with that assessment."

"True." Will dipped a crostini in the artichoke spread and made his own set of happy noises as it disappeared into his mouth. "Maybe if I date you, Giana would be willing to give me this recipe."

"Wanted only for my mom's artichoke spread," Enzo said mournfully.

Will laughed. Nudged him with an elbow. "Might actually be a solution," he said.

"What do you mean?" Enzo ignored the way his voice went high and surprised. Hoped that Will would, too.

"She's gonna be doing this all summer, isn't she? As long as you're here, working on the mural?"

Enzo wanted to tell Will that no, she wouldn't, because he'd be taking care of it, he'd be *convincing* her to stop it, but he knew what his mother was like when she got her teeth into an idea. And frankly, Enzo had a feeling he and Will didn't look all that averse to each other. Which was not going to help the situation.

"Probably, yeah. I can talk to her but well . . ." Enzo winced. Picked up a chunk of salami, sandwiching it between two pieces of provolone.

"That was what I thought," Will confided. His blond hair shone under the lights, and he looked so clean and new and shiny, so *gorgeous*, Enzo ached with it.

Like this guy would ever need help getting a date.

"Yeah, well, I can still talk to her," Enzo said, pushing down his humiliation.

"That's what I'm trying to say. We don't try to convince her to stop. Instead, we tell her we're dating. And then maybe she'll leave us alone. It's what she wants. So we'll just give it to her."

"Uh," Enzo stammered.

Will nudged him again. "Not like for real," he joked. "Unless there's something you want to tell me."

Um, yeah. You're gorgeous and if things weren't so weird with my mother and *the fact I've got no intention of staying here, I'd totally date you. For real.*

But their situation *was* weird and complicated, and he had every intention of seeing Indigo Bay in his rearview five or six weeks from now.

"It's a thought," he said. "Would it really make her leave us alone?"

Will shrugged. "She's *your* mother. What do you think?"

"I think it would take more than just a declaration. We'd uh . . .have to prove it to her. Go on a few dates."

"And?" Will grinned. "You're not so bad, Enzo Moretti. Especially once you've cleaned off your face."

"Ugh," Enzo complained. Of course Will had noticed the dirt.

"I mean, it's just a few evenings. We're both going to be busy. You with the mural. Me with Cherry's. Easy enough to pawn her off with that excuse, too."

"True." Enzo couldn't believe he was considering this. But then, his mother *was* abominably persistent. "I can't believe you suggested this."

"I've spent the last two months trying to convince her I don't want your phone number." Will took a bite of focaccia and chewed, swallowing. "And that hasn't worked, obviously."

"Obviously," Enzo echoed.

"So I thought, well, we could try something else," Will said. "But if you're not interested . . ."

Oh, I'm interested.

"I just think I'd like to try to convince her first, before we uh . . .do anything drastic."

"Going on a fake date with me is drastic? You Morettis *are* overdramatic." Will's grin was so broad Enzo discovered he had dimples too. Honest to fucking God *dimples*.

"I want to believe she isn't completely unreasonable." It was hard to admit this. "That she can see the truth when I ask her to." *That she can see I'm not sticking around.*

"I get it," Will said sympathetically.

"Somehow, I actually think you do." Maybe Will had a story too. After all, why was he here in Indigo Bay.

But instead of Will confiding about any of his own troubles, he said in a lighter tone, "Well, I'm not just here for the artichoke spread."

"It's damn good though," Enzo agreed, dipping a crostini into the container and popping it into his mouth.

"I don't suppose she's ever given *you* the recipe?" Will asked hopefully.

"She probably has, but I'm not sure I ever bothered to keep it. I'm really not a cook. I'm a good eater. That's all."

Enzo told himself that Will's shocked expression was *fine*. He was used to it, by now.

"But you're—"

"A Moretti? I know," Enzo said wryly. The cheese was curdling in his stomach, but he didn't want Will to know so he took a long sip of water and then wrapped some prosciutto around another chunk of provolone.

"You know, you're not required to be good at everything." Will shot him a sweet look. "You're already a nationally renowned mural artist, so famous you're in constant demand. Would you really want to trade that to be able to cook like your mom and Luca?"

"No." Though he'd asked himself that question enough back before he'd left Indigo Bay. He forced himself to smile. Reminded himself that before this moment, he'd actually been having a pretty good time—and that his Moretti deficiencies were not Will's fault. "So, that's what you'd get out of fake dating me? My mom's artichoke spread recipe?"

"Enzo Moretti, did I damage your ego?" Will teased.

"That was actually my own mother. Over and over again," Enzo grumbled.

Will laughed, and that somehow did more to soothe his bruised ego than anything else. "The answer is no, that isn't all I'd get out of it. You're a cool guy. Could be a friend, even. I wouldn't mind spending more time with you. Of course if I did, your mom would probably be lurking around every corner, waiting for one of us to drop to one knee."

Enzo didn't have to hold back his shudder. "She probably would, wouldn't she?"

Will nodded as he finished off the rest of the artichoke spread, Enzo deciding as he scraped the rest of the spread out of the container that this probably made him a good boyfriend, already.

"Just let me talk to her first," Enzo said. "Maybe I can make her see the facts of the situation. That I'm not sticking around."

"No matter how much you like me?" Will's voice was teasing again, but Enzo couldn't deny the little thrill that wound its way through him at the idea of it.

But they didn't like each other *that* much. They'd just managed to make it past *I think you might be vandalizing my building* and *you're accusing my painting of being illegal graffiti.*

"Right," Enzo agreed. He snagged the last piece of salami. Popped it into his mouth. "Thanks for the water and the break. I'd better get back out there and finish up my scaffolding before it gets dark. And I assume in a little bit that you're gonna get busy."

"Hope so," Will said, smiling, helping Enzo fill the basket with the empty containers. He gestured towards the basket as Enzo closed it up. "You want me to keep this in here, 'cause you know she'll be back for it?"

"No. I'll take it. And talk to her," Enzo said firmly.

He was already dreading it, but he knew he needed to try.

He was desperate enough that he'd even considered enlisting Luca and Oliver, but he didn't want to. He wanted to prove he was an adult; that he could take care of difficult situations himself. Luca might've saved his future by insisting he attend art school, in spite of his mother's protests, but Enzo wasn't about to rely on him for Giana interventions forever.

"Sure," Will said. "But the offer's open."

Chapter Eight

Enzo expected his mom to return to the scene of the crime sooner rather than later, but to his surprise, she didn't.

When he finally finished up the scaffolding, it was nearly full dark—and she'd still not stopped by.

Gathering his phone and the basket, he rounded the corner and discovered a whole crush of people inside Cherry's. He'd been planning to stop in and maybe re-configure the plan, but Will looked run off his feet, and *happy*, and so Enzo left him alone, trudging the few blocks back to his mom's house.

Unlike Cherry's, her house was dark. Unexpectedly. Where was she? Enzo paused in front of her door, considering texting and asking, but a shower and his bed were calling, and he was honestly too tired to deal with this tonight.

He'd find her in the morning, and this time, he had a feeling she wouldn't be so intent on avoiding him. After all, she'd want to know all the details of their romantic rendezvous in Cherry's back room.

He took a long, cold shower, and when he was finally clean, slumped down on the futon that doubled as his couch. Discovered he was too tired to even flip on the TV. But not too tired to glance over at his phone, especially when he realized Will had texted *him* while he'd been thoroughly scrubbing himself down.

How did it go?

Didn't see her actually. She's not home, either. He omitted that it was weird for him not to find his mother absent at nearly eight PM on a weeknight. **Don't tell me you're that eager to fake date me? The artichoke spread is good but not that good.**

My tastebuds beg to differ.

Enzo laughed, head slumping back against the edge of the futon. He should really drag his exhausted ass to bed.

You guys looked busy tonight.

Busier every night, Will texted back. **I'm gonna need to hire some more help.**

You thought about asking Rocco? I know he works at Rudy's but only during the weeknights. I think his weekends are free.

Great minds. I've already called him up. But I think I'm gonna need another more permanent employee. I know Rocco's not planning on sticking around.

He wasn't. Eventually he'd find a business he wanted to buy in another small town, and leave.

I wish I knew someone to suggest, Enzo replied.

It's alright. Part of being a business owner.

Let me guess. One of the worst parts.

Right up there with being the person everyone calls when something goes wrong.

Luca likes to say everyone who starts their own business secretly has a savior complex, Enzo texted back.

He's not wrong.

Is that why you're trying to bail me out with my mom?

Enzo regretted the text the moment he sent it. It sounded needy and desperate like, *tell me instead that you liked me too much to resist.*

But they both knew that wasn't true.

Maybe I'm trying to bail us both out.

Enzo relaxed against the futon cushions again. How did Will always know the right thing to say?

You're annoyingly perfect.

If you were my fake boyfriend, you wouldn't find my perfection annoying :)

True. I'm gonna talk to her tomorrow.

Good luck. And good night.

When Enzo fell asleep ten minutes later, still on the futon, it was Will's face, bright smile, and those irresistible dimples swimming in front of his eyelids.

At least before he'd fallen asleep at nine, like a freaking old man, Enzo had remembered to set an alarm so he was up bright and early. A little sore, but a lot rested.

He threw some of his work clothes—a worn-out pair of loose shorts, and a paint-stained tank that had once been white—and ducked into his mom's house, the back door open, before he headed out to Will's building.

And sure enough, there was his mother, enjoying her coffee at her little nook table.

"Oh, Enzo, I didn't expect to see you this morning," she exclaimed as she looked up.

Enzo knew his way around his mom's kitchen as well as anyone's and grabbed coffee and popped a bagel in the toaster.

"Why not?" he questioned innocently.

"Well, you and Will had that *very* romantic date yesterday. Thought maybe he might've crashed here last night. Or maybe you spent the night at his room in the Inn?"

"Mom," Enzo said, leaning against the counter and crossing his arms over his chest, "you need to stop."

"Stop what?" She sounded so baffled, so innocent, he almost believed it.

"Stop trying to push Will and me together."

"Why?" Her eyes were wide and surprised. "You two are so cute together, just like I knew you'd be."

"Mom," Enzo chided. Took a long sip of coffee. "Even if I liked him like that—"

"Enzo," she interrupted, "I wasn't born yesterday. I heard about you two flirting the other night at Cherry's. And then earlier, at Oliver's. You two aren't being very subtle. I'm just trying to help your relationship along. There's no law against that."

Enzo opened his mouth and snapped it shut again. There was no reasoning with her, especially not when she'd already decided they were *in* a relationship. Maybe Will was right, and the only way to convince her to stop was to convince her all this was unnecessary.

Enzo took a deep breath. Ignored his bagel that just popped up in the toaster. "Mom, it doesn't need help. It's . . .uh . . .already going just fine."

He wasn't stupid, despite popular belief. He knew what he was saying and what he wasn't saying and also how his mother would undeniably take it.

"Oh, *oh*," Giana exclaimed, looking happy enough that she might burst.

"If you keep interfering, you might screw it up," Enzo cautioned, shoving that hot burst of guilt down hard. He shouldn't be feeling it, but he was anyway. He wasn't lying to her, but apparently that didn't matter to his conscience.

"I definitely do not want that. Neither of us do," she agreed. "I knew the moment I met him he'd be perfect for you. And right here in Indigo Bay!"

"What a coincidence," Enzo said dryly, turning to get his bagel because he wasn't sure he could keep a straight face much longer.

"The very best kind." Giana clapped her hands. "Are you going out again, soon? And *not* to his back room, with you sweaty and disheveled, Enzo, darling. He needs to see you at your best. You are *very* handsome. I'm sure he agrees."

"So handsome you have to work hard to get me a date?" Enzo decided it was a positive development that he could at least joke about this now. Maybe Will had been right, and this had been the way to do this to begin with. After all, he genuinely liked the guy. How hard would it be to spend some extra time with him while he was here?

Not that hard.

Or really fucking hard.

"You know it was for you," Giana reminded him after he'd buttered his bagel and sat across from her. "I just want you to be happy."

"I know I keep saying this, but I *am*," he said.

"Well, you are *now*," Giana agreed, smiling.

Ugh. Enzo had never felt a kinship more viscerally than he did right now. Was this what women felt like, when they were constantly reduced to and defined by their relationship status?

"What are your plans today?" she asked. Enzo already knew she was forcibly returning the subject to the question he hadn't answered yet. *When is your next date with Will? When will you get married? How about that picket fence? And babies? Those big blond babies I want so badly?*

Maybe it was unfair since she hadn't specifically mentioned marriage and children—that had been Luca as, Enzo hoped, a *joke*—but he had a feeling it was only a matter of time.

"I'm working, Mom," he said.

She made a frustrated noise as he sipped his coffee and ate his bagel. "I mean, your plans with *Will*."

"I know I'm working, and he's working." He flashed her a conciliatory grin. "But good news, we'll almost certainly see each other, as we'll be basically in the same place."

She relaxed then. "Oh, right. Yes, of course. Well, I trust that you know how to treat a man right."

Enzo made a face and told himself she was not referring to his disaster of a date with Oliver, *years* before this.

"I do," he countered and decided he was done with this assumption once and for all. He didn't know when Will's next free evening was, but he intended to take him out, *very publicly*, and make sure the whole town was aware of what a goddamn brilliant date-r he was now. That he was a catch. That men actually *liked* him.

Will likes you.

Well, he'd better, because Enzo intended to romance the hell out of him, in front of everyone.

"Of course you do," Giana said. She gave him a small proud smile, and he couldn't deny the delight in her eyes as she gazed at him. It made it hard for him to be too angry or frustrated with her. "You're a fine man, Enzo. I don't know how you managed it, because I'm afraid I was not the mother you needed, for far too long, but you did it. All by yourself."

"Oh, I think you had something to do with it," Enzo said softly. It *was* the truth, and he was handsomely rewarded for it with another of her beaming smiles.

"Thank you," she said. "For being understanding even when you didn't want to be."

"It was always just us, against the world," Enzo reminded her.

It had always been hard to be angry with her when she'd been loved and then abandoned, almost certainly in death, by Enzo's father. They'd never found his body and Enzo had a feeling they never would, if his mom's stories about his profession and associates were true.

It hadn't been fair that the world had been cruel and left her saddled with a child and no way of making a living. He knew it had been harder on her than she'd ever let on.

"Always," she agreed, and this time he didn't see the shadow of bitterness, the fleeting sadness he usually saw cross her face whenever the past came up.

Maybe she'd finally made her peace with it. Enzo hoped so.

He pulled out his sketches from his back pocket as he finished his bagel and his coffee.

"Oh," his mother said, inhaling sharply as she leaned over the table, "is that the mural?"

Enzo nodded.

"It's . . ." She glanced up, meeting his eyes. "It's stunning, darling. You're so talented."

"Thanks, Mom. Don't you think you might be a bit biased?" He shaded in a corner. He'd been toying with the idea of adding a frame around the main image, almost like he was bringing Joy's story to life.

"I'm not," she said, rising and grabbing his empty plate and cup. "All those people who clamor for your work prove that I'm not. And doesn't Will love it, too?" she asked archly.

"He likes it fine," Enzo said.

She raised an eyebrow. "I think his feelings are a bit stronger than *fine*."

"Maybe," Enzo said. He wasn't usually this modest, but there was something special—something private—about the way Will had looked when he'd first seen Enzo's drawings. Something that eclipsed the faux dating arrangement he'd suggested.

Something *real*.

"I'm sure he's wild about it." His mother patted him on the arm. "Just like he's wild about you."

Will shaded his eyes and looked up at the wall of his building, wishing he'd brought his sunglasses outside because it was nearly noon and unbelievably bright, the sun bearing down on them with ferocity.

Enzo was a dozen feet up, brush moving with casual flicks—while the lines developing underneath it were the opposite of haphazard.

He could see the beginnings of a cliff and a woman's figure, blooming onto the wall in stark white lines.

"Hey," he called up to Enzo.

Enzo glanced down. "Just a second," he said. He drew a handful of additional lines and then he was climbing down.

"Is that safe?" Will asked.

Enzo raised an eyebrow, pulling his silver aviator sunglasses off and tucking them into the worn neckline of his paint-splattered tank top. He'd pulled his hair back today, a sweat-soaked bandana holding it in place.

"If it was taller, I'd wear a safety harness," Enzo explained. "This is too low for me to bother." He flashed Will one of those Moretti grins. "You worried about me?"

Yes. "I don't want my insurance to skyrocket because you broke your legs outside my building," Will said instead.

"Pragmatic. I like it."

"It's coming along." Will shaded his eyes again, glancing up at the wall.

"This is just the first sketch. To get an idea of how the design fills the space. It'll all get covered, eventually."

"Makes sense," Will said, nodding as his eyes traced every line Enzo had painted today.

Will didn't want to be fascinated by Enzo's artistic process, but he was. Undeniably. All morning he'd been almost unbearably tempted to step outside, to check on Enzo's progress, to see *exactly* what he was doing, but he'd forced himself to stay inside and to work his way down his to-do list.

As a reward for finishing the last of his prep work for the day, he'd finally let himself come outside and check on Enzo's progress.

Kate had given him a hard time as he'd walked out, because okay, yes, first he'd checked his hair and his face in the employee bathroom before he'd ducked outside, but he'd been working all morning on ice cream mixes, and had even baked a few batches of brownies and cookies, so he'd wanted to make sure he wasn't covered in chocolate—or worse.

"I had a client freak out once because she thought I was going to paint the whole thing in white," Enzo said, wiping his face with his forearm. "We had a good laugh over that one."

"I wouldn't expect you could freestyle paint this whole thing, or even *want* to," Will said.

"Oh, I *could*," Enzo boasted, but his eyes were glimmering with amusement. They were almost mocha colored in the bright light, not the deep, dark chocolate brown he often fantasized about. That he'd imagined just this morning, as he'd mixed the rich chocolate batter for his brownies.

Will chuckled. "Maybe don't try it on *my* wall, though."

"Don't worry. I'm gonna paint you something beautiful."

Will had never doubted it. Okay, *yes*, he had. But only when he'd been convinced Enzo was a vandal who only wanted to cover his building with graffiti.

"I know," he said.

"I talked to my mom this morning," Enzo said. "When's your next evening off?"

For a moment, Will didn't quite grasp why he was asking. Or what his day off had to do with Enzo talking to his mom.

And then he realized.

"The conversation didn't go well, then?"

Enzo shook his head. "She's basically already convinced. You're right, the path of least resistance is to just go along with it. So, when are we gonna have our big date?"

Will's eyebrows raised. "Who says I even *want* a big date?"

"If we're doing this, we're doing it right. No questions. No half-measures."

That didn't really surprise Will much. Enzo *was* a Moretti, after all. They were kinda notorious for going all-in.

Look at Luca, moving to Indigo Bay and changing his whole life when he'd fallen in love with Oliver.

"Alright. In two days. You gonna be ready for it that quickly?"

Enzo laughed. "Oh, baby, I'm ready right now."

"Baby, huh? Fake date me for five minutes and I'm already *baby*."

Enzo looked intrigued. "You want me to call you something else? Some other kind of cute pet name?"

"Honey? Cutie? Darling?" Will grinned. "How about Daddy?"

Enzo rolled his eyes, but he was smiling.

"Then you'd have to explain to my mother what that means," Enzo said. "We'll put a pin in this. Maybe that can be one of our discussions on our date. What charming nickname I'm going to murmur in your ear."

Will had been the one to suggest this plan, but he could admit now that he hadn't thought it through as much as he should've.

Because Enzo would want to commit to this—he'd *said* he did, just now, in case there was any question—and that was going to mean playing it up in public. There would absolutely be cute pet names and Enzo dipping his head low, murmuring into his ear in that deliciously melodic voice. Then he'd flutter those lethally gorgeous eyes in Will's direction and expect Will to melt like his highest quality chocolate.

Well. That wasn't going to be a problem. Melting would be the least of his worries.

"Works for me," Will said. "Explain to me again how you screwed things up with Oliver."

"By being totally the wrong guy for him. And also being an arrogant asshole," Enzo joked, the self-deprecating light in his eyes proving that if that *had* been true at any point, it wasn't any longer.

Enzo Moretti had grown up.

Very, *very* well, if Will had any say.

"I'm kinda thinking," Enzo continued, before Will could come up with something to say that wasn't, *I don't believe it, it's impossible to believe something so ludicrous,* "that maybe dating you is gonna redeem me in the eyes of the town."

"Oh?" It was the most—the *best*—Will could get out and that was saying something. Fake Boyfriend Enzo flustered him even more than Regular Enzo. He didn't know whether to be delighted or horrified by this.

"All anyone believes I'm capable of is one terrible date with Oliver, eight years ago, and then sulking about it afterwards. I'd like to prove I'm better than that."

"Fair," Will said. Still wanted to tell Enzo that he thought it was preposterous that anyone looked at the Enzo of today and still thought about that sullen kid.

Preposterous for anyone to think he couldn't get anyone he wanted, if he set his mind to it.

Including me.

Will pushed the thought away. This was just to get Giana off their backs. It wasn't serious. It *couldn't* be serious, because in five or six weeks, Enzo would leave Indigo Bay and he wouldn't be back anytime soon. Considering that Will had just opened a business here, there wasn't a future there.

"So something in this for both of us," Enzo said.

Will nodded. "So Wednesday night?"

"Yep. Be prepared to be knocked off your feet by all the pretend romance."

Maybe the way to go about it was to make it so over-the-top there was no way for Will to want it for real. No way for Will to mistake it for something real.

"I'll be ready," Will told him. Took a step closer, then another. Pretended his heart didn't beat a little faster at the nearness of him.

The sharp sweat tang of him. He was hot *and* gorgeous. And in the eyes of everyone else, *his*.

"Good," Enzo said. But he didn't step back.

"This is where I'm gonna make sure you don't stand me up," Will said, lowering his voice and his head, tilting it down so he could graze his lips just over Enzo's damp temple. Reaching out, he steadied him, digging his fingertips into the taut muscle of his waist.

"Not a single chance of that," Enzo murmured.

"No," Will agreed. He knew he should move back, move away, but he didn't want to. Enzo fit against him even better than he'd imagined, in those hazy, muggy dreams he kept pretending he wasn't having. No way Enzo slid through them, teasingly delectable, everything Will wanted to take a bite out of.

It was Enzo who moved back, clearing his throat.

"Well, I was thinking we'd go to Rudy's. Get a nice public steak. Canoodle a bit."

Will was gonna have to brace himself for that second part.

"Works for me," Will said.

"I can't believe I'm asking this," Enzo said, rubbing his neck, shooting him a sheepish glare, "but where are you staying? Are you renting?"

Will winced. "Worse than that. Well, don't tell Joy that, because her hospitality is spectacular, but I'm renting a room in the Sweetheart Inn. I keep telling myself I'm gonna find a place and move my stuff out here, but we keep getting busier."

"Oh, but you know what that means?" Enzo sounded delighted.

"No?"

"It means I can pick you up *very publicly*." Enzo rubbed his hands together, clearly excited about this development.

This had been Will's idea—his apparently very stupid idea—but he asked anyway, "Are you sure?"

"Oh yeah," Enzo said. "I know I said it before, but *get ready*. Nobody romances like an Italian, and no Italian romances like a Moretti."

"I'm looking forward to it," Will said weakly. Not entirely sure that he was.

"Good." Enzo nodded.

"I . . .uh . . .have to get back to work," Will said, and Enzo nodded absently, his attention either on romancing or on the mural, his gaze sweeping over the wall already.

"See you later," Enzo said.

When Will walked back into Cherry's, his face was flushed and his heart beating a million miles a minute. Not only because it was hot as Hades outside, either.

"You look dazed," Kate said.

"I'm . . ." *I'm thinking I might have underestimated how this was going to be.*

"Enzo Moretti's pretty potent, I guess," Kate teased.

"He's something," Will said. He didn't really want to lie to Kate, but this was his *real* reaction to the man, so it was hardly like he was pretending otherwise.

"Giana must be over the moon," Kate said.

Will leaned against the cold ice cream case and waited for it to cool him down. It didn't really work, which said everything. "We're going on a date Wednesday night," he said.

Kate looked shocked, which was surprising, considering what she'd *just* said—and probably how enthralled Will had looked when he'd walked back in just now.

"Seriously?"

"You said it yourself. He's pretty potent."

"And famously not an actual inhabitant of this town," Kate said.

Will had not anticipated this very logical argument.

"Neither was Luca, before he moved here," he suggested.

Kate shot him a look. "That was different. He'd never lived here before. He didn't have a chance to hate the nosy gossips, the way you can never escape every stupid shit move you've ever pulled, and the stifling narrowness of the expectations."

It was Will's turn to be surprised. "I didn't know you disliked it here that much." All of the above was true of any small town, including Indigo Bay, and he'd known that when he moved here. Small towns were a Johnson's specialty, and he'd grown up in them. He'd learned there were downsides, like anywhere, but he didn't want to live in some big, impersonal city. He wanted to know the little kids who came in for ice cream cones, and their parents, too.

Kate waved a hand. "Oh, I *don't*. I'm a realist, though. And all of that? Is all stuff I've heard Enzo say, about a thousand times. He couldn't wait to get out of here. As soon as Giana reluctantly let him go, he was *gone*."

"I know that," Will said.

"Then what are you doing with him?" Kate's tone turned concerned. "He's gonna break your heart."

"Maybe it's not about the heart. Maybe it's just…he's a really, *really* hot guy, and it's been a while for me," Will said. Honestly, that was probably more of a convincing argument than the Luca one.

He should've started with: *I'd just like to get this guy underneath me. And over me. And in me. ASAP.*

Kate would get that.

She laughed, all her concern melting away. "Okay, fair. You deserve it, boss."

"I do," Will agreed, grabbing a water bottle from the fridge under the counter and taking a long drink. He needed to cool down, not keep thinking about Enzo in bed.

"Giana's gonna hold out hope that you've got a magic cock, you know?"

Will choked on the water.

"What?" he said, coughing.

Kate gave him a hearty slap on the back and a very knowing grin. "She's totally gonna hold out hope that your magic cock makes Enzo decide he likes Indigo Bay well enough, as long as you're in it."

"I guess," Will said.

This fake dating thing had been going on officially for twenty-three minutes so far, and already Will had regretted agreeing too many times to count.

How would he feel on Wednesday night?

But as a harried mom with four children walked in to Cherry's, the tinkling doorbell singing and Kate moving to the counter to help them, Will knew he'd agree to do it again, no matter how hard it was.

Chapter Nine

Will took advantage of his day off to catch up on paperwork and go to the gym.

And, knowing what he was about to endure, he got off twice. First, in the early morning, hand slicked over his cock, coming all over his stomach, and again, during the shower he took after his punishing workout.

It was all pointless, though, because the moment he walked onto the long porch that ringed the whole first floor of the Sweetheart Inn and saw Enzo leaning against one of the intricately carved support poles, he became hard, instantly.

Enzo, in his paint-smeared clothes, dirty and sweaty and flushed, was hot enough.

Dressed in a pair of dark jeans and a short-sleeved black button-up that clung to his chest and his biceps, his hair curling over his forehead, gaze intent on Will, he was so gorgeous Will wanted to cry with it.

"Hey." Even his voice was deeper and rougher, the sound sliding over Will like velvet over his skin.

"You . . . uh . . . clean up good," Will said. He'd almost decided against saying it, but then he reminded himself that he was *supposed* to be bowled over by him. That was the whole point of this.

That he looked as awestruck as he felt.

Enzo's grin was crooked and charming. "Well, *yeah*. I was hardly going to show up in my painting clothes." He paused, maybe just noticing that Will was still hovering in the vicinity of the door, unsure how close they were supposed to get. He knew Joy had been downstairs, and there was almost no way she wasn't watching them now. But he also didn't know how close Enzo *wanted* him to get. "You gonna come over here?" he murmured, gesturing with one of his hands.

Will didn't typically notice hands. To him, they'd always been *tools*. But Enzo's were long and slender, beautifully formed, like the works of art he created with them.

"Uh, yeah. Wasn't sure you wanted—"

"Come over here," Enzo said firmly, and a moment later his arms were folding around him, tugging him close. It was just like the other day, except that instead of the sharp-sweet tang of Enzo's sweat, he smelled delicious. Practically freaking edible.

Will slid his hands over his back, felt Enzo's muscles tense and relax and told himself that this ludicrous idea still made perfect sense.

"A day off looks good on you," Enzo said. His fingertips brushed Will's chin.

Will's breath stuttered. Wildly trying to convince himself this was all pretend.

But the look in Enzo's eyes looked so real.

"Uh, thanks?"

"And . . ." Enzo smoothed a hand down his chest. Probably feeling the way Will's heart was rabbiting like crazy. "You look good, too. Real good. Good enough to take a bite out of."

Please do.

But instead of leaning in closer and encouraging him, Will look a step back. It would be so easy to lose himself, to fall into the magnetism of this man, but he needed to resist.

Kate's warning slash reminder was still echoing in his head. *He's not sticking around.*

"Where are we going?" Will asked. "I'm hungry."

"Me too," Enzo said and waggled his eyebrows.

Will laughed, the sound surprised right out of him. "You're ridiculous." But the over-the-top comment had been a much-needed bucketful of cold water to his desire.

They were play-acting, that was all. Putting on a good show. Enzo had already told him he was going to make it good. So of course it needed to be convincing.

"Oh, but sweetheart, you love it." He paused. "Let's go. We've got reservations at Rudy's."

Rudy's was the most popular restaurant in town, and as a result, would be full of Indigo Bay residents, even on a Wednesday night.

No doubt the rumors were already circulating because Enzo had made the reservation for two—though Will supposed they could assume Enzo's plus one was Giana.

Will told himself he was not surprised as Enzo reached out and took his hand, squeezing it gently as they walked down the stairs towards the sidewalk.

It was only a five minute walk from the Inn to the other side of the tiny Indigo Bay downtown, where Eliza sat, on the other side of the park.

"How's the mural coming along?" Will asked, shortening his longer strides to match Enzo's.

At least once he'd been tempted to swing by Cherry's, ostensibly to check on things there, but really to see the mural—or maybe even to see Enzo—but he'd resisted, promising himself he'd get plenty of Enzo tonight.

"More progress," Enzo said. "I've got the outline mostly done. Though I might do some more fine detail."

Will could hear the deep satisfaction of a job going well in Enzo's voice. An undeniable excitement.

"Good. I can't wait to see it tomorrow morning."

"It's not much to look at, yet," Enzo cautioned.

"Says you. Says me, the person without a single artistic bone in their body? It's pretty freaking incredible."

"Aw, my mom was right. You *are* a fan," Enzo teased as they turned the corner. The park, flanking Indigo Bay's main square, was still green.

"Hard not to be," Will said, shrugging awkwardly. He didn't think he'd be *this* bad on a regular date. Maybe that was how he should approach this. His palm was damp, and he was afraid he'd gross Enzo out, but he showed no hesitation in gripping it tighter.

They walked around the statue of Eliza, Enzo's gaze skimming over it.

Will thought he was going to make some comment on the artist or his creation, but instead, Enzo turned to him and said, "You're wrong, you know."

"I'm wrong?"

"You have *plenty* of artistic bones in your body."

"I do?" Will braced himself for Enzo to make some joke about a *certain* bone, but instead, Enzo's expression turned serious and intent.

"What you've created with Cherry's? That's a form of art. Every time you invent a new, insanely delicious ice cream flavor? Or a new sundae? Or devise a milkshake that makes me want to weep it's so goddamn good? That's art."

"Oh. *Oh.*" Will couldn't pretend he was anything other than pleased.

"You're very talented," Enzo said.

Will grinned at him. "I guess we've both got a thing for competency porn."

Enzo shot him a hot look as Will let go of his hand to open the front door at Rudy's, ushering him inside.

Maybe this wasn't a real date—maybe they were pretending to be crazy about each other—but Will *liked* treating Enzo like he was special.

Because he *was* special.

Enzo sauntered through the door and approached the hostess station. "Good evening," he said. "Reservations for two. Moretti."

The young lady had an appropriate reaction to Enzo's appearance.

Enzo believed everyone in town remembered him as only that young, messed up kid. But *this* girl wouldn't. Not now. Her jaw dropped and well, it made Will feel a little better that at least he wasn't alone in being blown away by how stunning Enzo Moretti was.

"You must be one of Luca's brothers," she said in an awed voice.

"Cousin," Enzo said in clipped tones.

Will didn't think. He just slid up next to him and put his arm around Enzo's waist, tugging him closer in what no doubt looked to everyone else like a firm declaration of possession.

Enzo leaned into him, glancing up at him from under those curling black lashes. Did he even flutter them a little?

Jesus, he was potent.

No wonder the hostess was stammering, searching through her tablet.

"I requested a booth," Enzo said. He glanced up at Will, longer this time, his gaze going positively gooey. *It's fake, it's fake, it's all goddamn fake.* "So I can cuddle with this handsome hunk of a man."

"He is . . .uh . . .yes," the girl said. "I've got your reservation right here, Mr. Moretti. If you'll follow me."

Will had grown up in small towns. He knew exactly how they were and so did Enzo, obviously, because as they followed the hostess to their table, he was undeniably aware of every gaze in the place following them and the whispers in their wake.

Will kept his arm firmly around Enzo's waist, even though the aisle between the two rows of booths wasn't that big, because he was supposed to be persuading the town they were dating, and if he was really dating Enzo, he wouldn't let go of him for a second.

"Here we are," the hostess announced, stopping in front of a cozy-looking booth.

"Oh, perfect. Thank you," Enzo said, shooting her the most potent smile in his arsenal.

At least Will had believed it was, until Enzo turned to him as he slid into the booth. "You gonna share with me?" he asked, raising an eyebrow.

Will's fingers gripped the seat cushions. "Like I'd want to let go of you for a moment," he said.

Enzo beamed, taking his seat next to Will like it had always been his. "Good," he said. "You want some wine? Did you know since Luca moved to Indigo Bay, he's been an unofficial wine consultant for Rudy's?"

"I did hear that rumor," Will said. "But I'm not much of a wine drinker." He shrugged at Enzo's semi-outraged expression. "I grew up in *Florida*. You think we have decent wineries there?"

"I grew up here and we definitely didn't, but then I moved to San Francisco and lived with Luca's sisters. I wasn't used to real wine, or *dry* wine, and at first, I didn't like it either. But it grew on me. Now I love it. Especially when we're talking the *good* stuff, and Luca makes sure they stock the good stuff here."

"For him and Oliver?" Will questioned as Enzo picked up the wine list and began to peruse it.

Enzo nodded. "Do you want to get something else? I was going to get a bottle of this pinot noir, but if you're not going to have any . . ."

"Oh, maybe I'll try some," Will said. After all, what would it hurt? "If you think it's a good starter wine."

Enzo flashed him a smile. "I think you'll like it. Luca mentioned it was nice and fruit forward. Suggested I try it when I said we were coming here tonight."

Will tensed. Realizing for the first time that pretending they were dating for Enzo's mom meant they were pretending to date for *everyone else,* too, including friends like Oliver and Luca. Friends he didn't particularly want to lie to.

"What did you say to him?" Will asked, hoping his question sounded casual enough.

"You mean, did I tell him the truth?" Enzo's voice dropped lower, and he slid in closer, practically murmuring into Will's ear. If anyone saw them together, they'd believe, no question about it, that they were incredibly intent on each other. That they didn't even see anybody else.

"Yeah," Will said.

"I told him I was taking you out on a date, and he told me I had good taste," Enzo said, grinning. "Don't worry, I didn't lie. Just slightly stretched the truth."

"Alright." Will relaxed. "It's . . .it's awkward, isn't it?"

"Yeah, a little. But we're gonna be just fine." Enzo leaned in even closer. "The real question isn't who we're gonna tell the truth—or who we're *not* gonna tell—but what I'm gonna call you."

"Yeah?"

"We gotta come up with the *best,* most convincing pet names," Enzo said.

"Pet names?"

Will looked up and Rocco was standing in front of the booth, a black apron wrapped around his waist, and wearing a polo shirt with Rudy's logo embroidered on the upper right-hand corner.

"I forgot you were working here, too, now," Enzo asked, sounding surprised.

"Rocco's everywhere," Will said. "You still good to stop by on Thursday morning for some quick training?"

Rocco nodded. "Yep. What can I get you to drink? Wine? You know Luca is curating the list these days."

"I was thinking of this Sonoma County pinot noir? What do you think?"

"Oh, that's a good one. Really nice drinkable wine. One of Oliver's favorites. You guys gonna share it?"

"Yep, two glasses. And some of those parmesan cheese straws, alright?" He glanced over at Will. "You good with that?"

"Sounds great. Those are the best."

Rocco leaned in. "You do know they buy those from Oliver's bakery, right?"

Enzo chuckled, and Will felt the sound resonating through Enzo's body, echoing into his own. "I didn't, but I guess I'm not surprised."

Rocco nudged Will. "You're the only one in town who isn't secretly—or not so secretly—buying baked goods from Oliver."

"That's because Will's *amazing*," Enzo answered. He draped an arm around Will's shoulders. It couldn't have been that comfortable because Enzo was shorter and smaller, but he didn't hesitate. "Such an incredible baker. Even more incredible than Oliver."

Rocco looked skeptical, and Will couldn't blame him, because he was *not* a better baker than Oliver. "Sure," Rocco said. "I'll go grab your wine."

When Rocco left, Enzo dropped his arm, but didn't let go of Will completely. Instead one of those beautiful artist's hands wrapped right around his bicep and squeezed. "Now, what about these nicknames?" Enzo said persuasively.

"We can't just call each other Enzo and Will?"

"Oh, we *can*. But not in public! We need to convince everyone we're falling madly in love."

Will raised an eyebrow. "And if you were falling madly in love with me you wouldn't call me Will?"

"Oh, I would. But my mom doesn't know that. The sappier I am, the more convinced she'll be."

"Okay then. What about baby?"

Enzo shot him an incredulous look. "Really? That's the best you can come up with?"

"Pookie?" Will suggested, scraping the bottom of his brain. "Dumpling? Sweetums?"

Enzo laughed. "Cutie Patootie? Peanut? Boo-Boo?"

And now Will couldn't help but join in. "Where did you even come up with these?"

"My endless imagination," Enzo said, waggling his eyebrows.

Well, Will could at least equal him. "How about Pumpkin?" he suggested.

"Do I look orange to you?" Enzo asked.

Will looked him up and down, waggling his eyebrows suggestively. "I don't know. I haven't seen all of you, yet. Maybe there's a big lumpy orange part."

"Oh, Stud Muffin, I promise you, all of me looks this good." The exaggerated leer Enzo gave him made it clear he wasn't serious, but Will had a feeling that while he was kidding, what he said was actually the truth.

Enzo would look so good without a stitch on. *Not just good. Fantastic. Amazing. Tasty enough you wouldn't be able to resist taking a little bite.*

"What about Honey Butt?" Will suggested.

Enzo shifted, and something flashed across his face—so quick Will almost missed it, but he was looking for it—that reminded Will of his own conflict. The outwardly pretend ridiculousness compared to his own interior longing.

"I *do* have a very good ass," Enzo agreed.

It was why Will had suggested it. A ring of truth in the middle of all this ludicrous posturing.

"You do . . ." Will trailed off, realizing he was going to have to say so, in front of the whole of Indigo Bay, including Enzo's mother. "What about Honey Bunny?"

"Oh, that's cute," Enzo said, smiling. Not the over-the-top exaggerated grin of earlier, but something real. "And I'm gonna call you Stud Muffin. If the shoe fits . . ."

"I'm flattered," Will said, but Enzo just rolled his eyes.

"You have mirrors. You know what you look like," Enzo teased. "You're one hundred and ten percent hunk."

"Is that Honey Bunny saying that or Enzo?" Will wondered in a low voice. Hoping Enzo would understand the difference.

"Both," Enzo said.

Rocco arrived with the wine then, opening the bottle with a flourish and presenting Enzo with the taste to verify its quality.

"Okay, this is delicious," Enzo agreed as he swirled the cherry red liquid in his glass. "Really fruity but deep, too."

"I'll tell Luca you approve," Rocco said dryly. His gaze shifted to Will. "Would you like me to pour you a glass?"

"Sure," Will said.

Rocco did so with an adept flick of his wrist, settling the bottle on their table and promising that the cheese straws would be out shortly. "Would you like to order?"

"Oh, *Honey Bunny*," Will said, forcing himself to keep an even tone of voice even as Rocco's eyebrows edged up towards his hairline, "what were you thinking? The flank steak with the baked potato and the brussels sprouts?" They hadn't discussed the menu, but he knew what was good here, and he had a feeling Enzo did too.

Enzo nodded. "Medium rare on the steak. What about you, Stud Muffin?"

"Yep, you got it, Honey Bunny."

Rocco burst out laughing. "Are you two okay? Are you drunk *already*? I just poured the wine."

Leaning forward, Enzo nodded, shooting Will a rapt look. "We're drunk on love," he said.

"Alrighty then," Rocco said. "Well . . .you enjoy that, and I'll put your food order in."

"I'm not sure he was convinced," Will said once he'd disappeared.

"How could he not be? We were so full of love we were practically vibrating with it."

"Well…uh…" He knew they were probably overselling their story, but he didn't want to say so, because what if Enzo stopped? Enzo was *so* pleased with himself, and this was the most fun Will had had in months. Maybe years.

If he was honest, maybe the fun would stop.

And he really, really didn't want it to stop.

He wanted Enzo to keep himself plastered up against him, one hand on his arm, another creeping up his thigh. Wanted to keep gazing into those amused dark chocolate eyes.

"It's okay, we're still getting good at this," Enzo said, squeezing his bicep reassuringly. "We'll get better."

"You're so patient you're practically a saint," Will told him wryly.

"Oh, Stud Muffin, not a saint when it matters."

Will didn't think he'd ever get tired of Enzo laying it on thick. Especially with these outrageous comments were accompanied by an intense fluttering of his eyelashes.

"I'm looking forward to discovering just what a devil you can be," Will murmured, his tone unexpectedly serious. Unexpectedly *real*. He couldn't help wishing, not for the first time, that his desire might actually come true.

Enzo leaned in. He was only a breath away from Will's face; it would be so easy to kiss him. For *real*.

Will wanted to. Wanted to kiss all that sweet bullshit right off his lips.

But he didn't. Because he'd already told himself this was the line *he* was drawing. He couldn't kiss Enzo in public and then keep his distance in private. His heart wouldn't take that kind of misdirection.

"Now this is *actually* convincing."

Will glanced up and Rocco was standing in front of their booth again, a basket of cheese straws in his hands.

"I hardly believed you before," Rocco continued, "but this *now*, looks damn good. Like you're about to start making out, damn the gossips."

"I . . .uh . . ." Will stammered as Rocco set the cheese straws onto the table. Afraid that Rocco was a little more right than he wanted to admit.

"It's okay. It's hot. I love it." Rocco winked at them. "Enjoy these. I'll be out in a few with your food."

Ironically, after Rocco was actually convinced was when Enzo shot back half an inch. He took a long sip of wine, and Will decided that might not be a bad idea for him, too. And was pleasantly surprised by the rich taste coating his tongue.

"This *is* really good," Will said, gesturing with his glass.

"Luca's a genius with wine. Could've probably been a sommelier but where'd he find the time?" Enzo shrugged. "That's what he should've done instead of playacting at starting a gelateria."

"What?" Will couldn't believe what Enzo had just offhandedly claimed. Will was in the ice cream business so he understood exactly what Enzo had revealed. In the United States, they had ice cream parlors. In Italy, they had gelato and gelaterias.

"You didn't know?" Enzo took a closer look at his face. "Oh man, you didn't know."

"How serious were they?" Will didn't want to apologize for opening Cherry's, but he respected and admired Luca and Oliver enough that the last thing he'd have wanted was to step on their toes.

"It wasn't that serious. They talked about it a lot." Enzo waved a hand. "But honestly, they're *much* happier that you opened Cherry's, instead. At least Oliver is. He'd never see his husband if Luca did everything he wanted to."

"Oh. Well." Will squirmed uncomfortably on the bench seat until Enzo's hand clamped down on his thigh. And that was both distracting and arousing enough he stopped wiggling.

"I promise you, it's fine. Everyone's happier that you did it, instead."

"If you say so," Will said. Wanting to believe Enzo was right. Worried he was not. He'd need to talk to Luca himself. Make sure they were indeed as good as he'd believed they were.

"Trust me," Enzo said, "if they weren't happy about Cherry's, you'd have heard about it. Luca wouldn't have made friends with you, even if Oliver broke ranks and did it anyway. And you know my mother *never* would've stopped squawking about it."

That was true about Giana. She was hardly subtle and absolutely incapable of keeping a secret.

"Eat a cheese straw and stop angsting about it," Enzo encouraged. "I want to see you put it in your mouth *real* slow. Torment me a little. Make me wish we weren't in the middle of this busy restaurant."

Will laughed, because what else was he supposed to do? It was impossible to be faced with such an incorrigible request and not be amused by it.

"Worried about my gag reflex?" Will joked.

"Not in the least," Enzo said with relish. "Especially not after you stick that whole pastry into your mouth."

Chapter Ten

IT WAS THE STRANGEST date of Enzo's life, and, also, surprisingly, the most fun he'd ever had on one.

There were no expectations, no danger zones, no concerns about saying or doing the wrong thing, no awkwardness. It all dissolved in the headiness of doing and saying the most outrageous thing Enzo could come up with. Daring Will to do the same.

By the time they'd come to the end of the meal, his stomach hurt from laughing so hard and his cock was aching in his jeans. If he'd thought Will was gorgeous and wonderful before tonight, he was viscerally aware of it now.

Undeniably convinced that if he'd actually been sticking around Indigo Bay, he'd take this man to the Inn, press him back against one of those columns lining the porch, and give him a goodnight kiss either of them would forget anytime soon.

But he wasn't staying and this wasn't real.

The thought was a bucketful of cold water metaphorically dumped all over his desire—but it didn't douse it entirely.

Maybe that was the shy, almost ashamed way Will's gaze flicked to his. The real truth lingering there, that he couldn't hide entirely, no matter how outrageous their nicknames were.

Enzo had made a big deal of paying for their dinner. Of saying loudly they were going to go take a romantic walk through the park, under the stars. Rocco had rolled his eyes a bit, but the way Will tucked his hand trustingly into Enzo's *and* the faint flush across his cheekbones from the wine—and maybe everything else—made it all feel a little too real.

They were meandering through the park now, Enzo keeping half his brain on the statue of Eliza and half his brain on Will's warm hand tucked into his own.

"So, how are we going to do this?"

"Do what?" Enzo asked.

"You know I'm living at the Inn. After . . . uh . . . that kind of evening, do you really think you'd leave me without . . ." Will trailed off, and Enzo saw his gaze dart to his lips.

And okay. *Fair.*

"I get the feeling you're only willing to take this so far," Enzo theorized.

He was only willing to take this so far.

If he kissed Will, he was going to want to do it for real. He was going to want it to *be* real.

Will nodded. "I don't want to cross too many lines."

"Me too," Enzo agreed. "Not that doing it would be unpleasant, the opposite actually, I just think it would be—"

"Confusing. Complicated," Will finished for him. "Too confusing. Too complicated."

"Yes." Enzo was relieved they were on the same page.

Just another page in the growing book of evidence that his mother hadn't been completely wrong and they were more than a little right for each other.

Their permanent location notwithstanding.

Obviously Will lived here. And Enzo had made a very serious promise to himself that he'd never live here again. He was frankly happier living out of a suitcase, not having any kind of home at all, than coming back to Indigo Bay forever.

"Alright, so how are we going to do this?" Will repeated. "Nobody would ever believe you'd leave me un-kissed if we were . . .what did you call it? *Falling wildly in love?*"

"True." It was a conundrum. Will had a very good point. Joy would undoubtedly be at the Inn. Probably situated in a way that would make it impossible to avoid the inevitable while maintaining their fiction.

"We could just part ways here."

"And I let you go home alone? I don't even drop you off at the Inn?" Enzo shook his head emphatically. "I'm trying to prove I'm a better date than I was with Oliver. How would that prove anything?"

Will looked torn. For a second, Enzo was almost tempted to say, *fuck it, we both want to do it, for real, and so let's just do it. How bad could it be?*

Bad, because Will would want him to stay. Bad, because *he* might want to stay.

They were playing with fire here.

"I have an early morning. So do you. We could just use the excuse of our work."

"How about this? We'll use that excuse and when you see Joy, make sure to tell her I gave you a *very* romantic, very private kiss out here, in the park, under the stars. Luca kissed Oliver for the first time right by this statue. Peak romance at work there. She'll buy it. Then repeat it to my mother, for sure."

"What if I'm not convincing?" Will actually looked worried about this.

"How about this: we'll do everything but, and that'll give you a template for the story you need to tell," Enzo said and tugged him in closer. They stopped near the statue. Enzo's body tucked into Will's bigger one. Maybe if he'd realized just how well they fit together, he wouldn't have been quite so willing to agree to this. Or to the boundaries. But those ships had sailed.

"What do you mean?" Will asked in a hushed whisper. "What are we doing?"

"This," Enzo said and tucked his head in close, arms encircling Will's taut waist. Will's hand hesitated over his back—Enzo could feel the warmth of it—before he gave up and he swept it up and down Enzo's back in mesmerizing strokes.

He was hard as a rock and only by angling his hips just enough could he hope to keep it secret. But then Enzo had a feeling Will was doing the exact same thing.

We're pathetic. Smart but also very, very stupid.

"Okay?" Enzo asked, tilting his chin up, and nobody would look at them right now, Will's gaze intensely fond, Enzo probably as awestruck as he felt, and think any of this was fake.

"It's good." Will licked his lips, and his gaze flicked to Enzo's. But they'd agreed they weren't doing it. They weren't closing this distance between them.

"Could be better," Enzo said wryly.

Will nodded and tucked his head in, dipping it low, lips barely brushing over Enzo's neck. Enzo felt himself inhale sharply. But he didn't move. Didn't think he *could* move.

"As good as we're getting," Will finally said, right before he released him.

Enzo didn't want to leave the warm circle of his arms, but if he didn't, he *wouldn't*.

"Did that . . .uh . . .give you enough inspiration?"

"Yeah." Will's voice was deep and a little rough, scraping over Enzo's nerves. "Plenty. I know just what I'll say."

Enzo was not tempted at all to follow him to the Inn and listen to Will telling his side of the encounter. Nope. Because if he did, that would totally defeat the whole point of what they were trying to do. Because if he did, there was no way they'd avoid kissing for real.

And you really want to.

"Text me after and let me know how it goes," Enzo said.

Will shot him a knowing grin. "You wanna know what I'm gonna say."

"Well, *yeah*." He was trying to be good, trying to do the right thing, not *dead*.

"Between the two of us, you're the one famous for his imagination," Will teased. "I think you'll be able to fill in the blanks."

Enzo made a face but he nodded. "Fine. Yes." He did not add that he'd be filling in those blanks while he touched his cock and imagined that his hand was bigger and calloused with work. That it was attached to a big mountain of a man with kind blue eyes.

"Goodnight, Enzo," Will said. "Thanks for dinner. For uh . . .the laughter. And everything."

"Honestly, it was my genuine pleasure, Stud Muffin," Enzo said and meant it.

Will smiled and turned away, heading towards the Inn.

Enzo knew he should turn and go, too—the *other* way—but instead, he stood there for a long time, watching as Will's figure disappeared into the darkness.

Finally, when he couldn't see it any longer, he turned and headed towards his mom's house.

And, to his surprise, it was dark *again*.

Where was his mother and what was she doing during these long evenings?

It was almost ten at night. She should be *home*. He'd fully expected that she would be, and she'd be incredibly eager to hear how it had gone. That he'd be giving his own recital of the date.

Enzo stared at the empty dark house and then finally went up the stairs to his old apartment over the garage. Regretting that it was *also* dark. And lonely.

There was no mountain of a man waiting for him, and no blue eyes full of laughter as Enzo called him the most ridiculous nicknames he could come up with.

Being alone had never bothered Enzo before. He remembered when he moved out of Chiara and Ilaria's loft to his own tiny studio, and how he'd gloried in the silence. How he'd never once come home and thought, *isn't it just a little too quiet?* like he was doing now.

"Stop it," he told himself, out loud. "Just fucking stop it."

His brain didn't need to supply any more reasons to want Will Johnson. Or any more reasons it was a terrible idea. Including that he was apparently now *missing* him even though he'd just walked away.

Will swore he could feel Enzo's gaze on him long after he turned and headed back to the Inn. Even though he told himself it wasn't real, that Enzo wasn't watching him, wasn't following him, he felt the weight of that stare on him all the way back to Joy's house.

Just like he'd expected, there was Joy sitting on one of the long, shallow porch swings, but to his surprise, she wasn't alone.

Nope. Even Giana was lying in wait for them.

Her eyes brightened when she saw Will and then dimmed when she realized he was alone.

Great.

It was going to be awkward enough to relate the story of his date with Enzo to Joy, but to do it in front of his mother?

Well.

Buck up, Buttercup, he could hear Enzo teasing in his head. *Steady on, Stud Muffin.*

"Good evening, ladies," Will said, stopping in front of the pair of them.

"I hope *your* evening was good," Giana said, a twinkle in her eye. "Especially since you're here alone. I was expecting to see Enzo with you."

I just bet you were.

"Ah, well, it was late, and we've both got an early start in the morning," Will said, waving his hand. "You know how it goes."

"Was it not delightful? Was Enzo not a gentleman?" Giana asked.

"G," Joy said under her breath, nudging her, "leave him alone."

"He was a perfect gentleman." *Kind of perfect in general.*

"Oh, of course he was," Giana trilled, clapping her hands together. "But no kiss goodnight?"

It would've been far easier to perform this just for Joy, but Will steeled himself. Winked at Giana. "Oh, I wouldn't want to kiss and tell," he said lightly. "But I appreciated how Enzo made sure it was very private, very personal. *Very* romantic."

It had been unbearably romantic. The stars shining overhead, the rustling of the leaves the only sound breaking the silence around them. Enzo's dark eyes intent on his. The way his body had fit so perfectly against Will's.

Will was pretty sure he'd wanted the kiss nearly as badly as Enzo had.

But he'd restrained himself, because they'd drawn the line, the *right* line, and Will had to admit he admired and respected Enzo even more as a result.

"Oh, I knew it," Giana said, turning to Joy. "Didn't I tell you a hundred times they'd be perfect for each other?"

"A thousand," Joy retorted dryly, but she was smiling too. "Enzo's a good boy. A good Indigo Bay boy. He knows the right place to kiss a man he's into, and it's not my front porch, Giana."

"Was it in the park?" Giana asked excitedly. "By the statue?"

Will had worried this would be hard, but it was actually way easier than he'd imagined. He nodded, and Giana shrieked in delight.

"This is the best news," she said.

Will gave them both another smile, agreeing without words that, *yes*, it most definitely was. Then he bid them goodnight, heading into the house. As he walked up the stairs to his room, he pulled his phone out of his pocket.

They both ate it up, he sent to Enzo.

Enzo's reply came in almost instantly. **Both? You mean my mom's there? With Joy?**

Did you not expect that?

No. I didn't know they were that close.

They were sitting out here on the front porch. Just chatting, I'd imagine.

Huh. So they both enjoyed it? Did you spin your tale well, Stud Muffin?

Will unlocked his door and settled against it as it closed. Squeezed his eyes shut. Wished, even as he tried to pretend the thought wasn't spinning through his head over and over again, that Enzo wasn't on the other end of a text conversation, but they were talking about it. Laughing about it. That he was right here, right now, and that in a minute, they'd settle into the bed together and their amusement would morph into white-hot lust.

Well as I could, Will said. **A little hard to go into some of the finer details in front of your mother.**

Aw, and she's worried if I'm a gentleman.

You are. In case you were wondering.

A guy who wasn't would have said screw the consequences and thrown caution to the wind, but Enzo hadn't, even though he had to know that any desire he felt was easily reciprocated by Will.

Turns out you haven't been brainwashed by the town! Or maybe you've actually been un-brainwashed?

As Will pulled his shirt off and unzipped his jeans, settling on the edge of the bed in just his boxer briefs, sadly *alone*, he thought of what he'd known of Enzo before he'd come back.

What Giana had promised him Enzo was like, every time she'd come in, singing his praises. The casual references Luca and Oliver had made to their cousin. The stories Kate had told him when he'd asked.

The only thing I thought about you before you showed up was that you must need help getting a date, or else why else was your mom so insistent I talk to you?

Ouch.

Good news, you definitely don't need the help.

An understatement.

Thanks for making me feel better.

It's unfair the whole town judges you by how you were when you were twenty-one. We're all idiots at that age.

Even you?

Even me.

Will thought of himself, when he'd been twenty-one.

He hadn't been wild by any stretch of the imagination, but he'd stayed out too late, partying on the beach, hooking up with anyone he felt like, rolling into one of his parents' stores with only a few hours of sleep, hungover and jittery with the caffeine he'd drunk to combat his exhaustion.

Nobody had ever judged him for that. Okay, well, they *had*, but only a little. He'd still worked hard, but had he cared as much about the work? Back then, no.

It wasn't like a whole town had condemned him, not like they had Enzo.

Of course, Will hadn't known *that* Enzo. He only knew this Enzo. But he understood, a little, why Enzo didn't want to come back here, and why he'd refused the idea of moving back permanently. Why he'd carved out a life for himself elsewhere.

Huh, Enzo texted back. **I think I'd liked to have met you, back then. Think of all the trouble we could've gotten into.**

Will wanted to tell him, *imagine what we could get up to now.*

But he didn't need to say it because he had a feeling they were both thinking it.

I think we're having a pretty good time now.

Definitely the most fun that Will had ever had on a first date. Even a faux first date.

Could be even better.

Will stared at his phone's screen. He *knew* Enzo felt the same. He'd felt it the whole date, and especially at the park, when they'd playacted their first kiss.

God, pretend I didn't say that. It only makes it harder, Enzo texted before Will could figure out how to reply.

Easier, too? To know it's not just me.

You're working tomorrow? Enzo sent, and Will was actually glad that he'd changed the subject. He wasn't sure how much more teasing he could take before he decided they might as well just give in.

Yeah, I'll be in. Maybe we can grab lunch again, together. Plan our next big date.

Maybe they didn't technically *need* to do another one, but Will already wanted to.

Sounds good.

Enzo decided to avoid his mom's kitchen the next morning, because he wasn't particularly interested in the interrogation she'd give him. So instead, he lit out early, to try to avoid the heat of the day, and stopped by Sweetie Pie's to get a coffee and a hand pie before he started work on Will's building.

But Rocco wasn't the one staffing the front counter when Enzo walked in—and neither was Marjorie, Oliver's long-time employee.

It was Oliver himself.

"Morning," Oliver said, grinning, as Enzo approached the counter. "Have a good night?"

Enzo pointedly ignored him, pretending he wasn't glad that the news had already made the rounds. If it hadn't, he'd have been disappointed. After all, he and Will had practically designed the date to be the hottest gossip in town. "You heard about the date, huh?"

"I think everyone did. Rocco said you two were practically glued at the hip." Oliver leaned over the counter. "I'd say he was exaggerating, but he was so flabbergasted by it, and these nicknames he claimed you kept using, that it must be true. Rocco's smart, but he doesn't have your imagination."

"It's . . .uh . . .it's new but it's . . ." Enzo had thought it would be easier to talk about this. After all, he'd basically done it with Luca, before the date.

Oliver raised an eyebrow. "Luca said you were going out with the guy, not that you were going to fall in love with him on the spot."

Okay, admittedly, convincing his mother was easier, because it was exactly what she wanted to see, but Oliver? Luca? Even Rocco? They were going to be tougher nuts to crack.

But that didn't mean he wasn't up for the task.

"What did you tell me about Luca, when you first met him?"

"That he was an annoying, overbearing jerk?" The soft smile that bloomed over Oliver's face told the whole story, though.

"A *hot* annoying, overbearing jerk, though," Enzo teased.

"True," Oliver admitted with a grumble. "But Will's not annoying or overbearing."

"Exactly." Enzo grinned. "He's nice like you, the perfect foil to my Moretti-ness, just the way you are with Luca, *and* he's hot."

"Should I be penciling in a wedding date?" Oliver joked.

"No. But you can get me a large iced vanilla latte and one of those sausage and egg and cheese hand pies." Enzo glanced over at the case, brimming as always with Oliver's delicious baked goods, each one looking better than the last. "And a cherry streusel muffin. I've got cherries on my mind."

Oliver chuckled under his breath as he opened the sliding door to the back of the case and pulled out the hand pie and the muffin, setting the former on a piece of parchment paper so he could heat it up in the toaster oven on the back counter. "I just bet you do," he said.

"Rocco's not here today?"

"Oh he's in the back. Working on the bread order." Oliver waved back there. "I'm sure if he hears you're here, he'll come out. He's *really* confused."

"He was the one who kept telling me how hot Will was. How could he be?"

Oliver laughed. "Yeah, I don't think Rocco was expecting that you'd go that route, if you went any route at all. I think he was thinking more of the few weeks of torrid hookup variety, not a sappy love affair." He paused. "Are you really calling him *Stud Muffin*?"

"I love cherries and I love muffins and he reminds me of both," Enzo said with a sly grin, grabbing his muffin and popping a piece of streusel in his mouth. He watched as Oliver went over to Taylor, his bright red Italian espresso machine, and began to make his latte.

"I bet Giana is literally over the moon." Oliver's comment was casual, but Enzo knew him well enough to hear everything he wasn't saying.

When was the last time you gave your mother exactly what she wanted? Wrapped up in a present with a gigantic bow on top?

The answer was never.

He'd never done it.

Maybe this would be tougher than he'd imagined.

"I haven't seen her, so I don't know how she is," Enzo said. It wasn't exactly a lie. He *hadn't* seen her. "And what's this about her spending all her time over at the Inn with Joy?"

Oliver waved his hand absently. "Oh, you know, they're friends. After Giana tried living in Charleston for a bit, she came back here and they hit it off. Giana . . .I don't know . . .chilled out some. Or my mom finally had the time? I'm not sure. But they're practically inseparable these days."

None of this made sense. Giana was not magically *more* chill. If she was, then Enzo wouldn't be calling Will *Stud Muffin*.

"It's good for my mom to have a friend," Oliver continued as he poured a shot of espresso into the cup half full of ice. "Keeps her from working too hard. Either at the Inn or her books. Besides, I think Giana told me she was helping Joy source some antiques for the Inn expansion."

Enzo didn't point out that Joy working *less* seemed incongruous if they were adding onto the Inn. He just took his coffee, his hand pie, and muffin nothing but a wrapper full of crumbs he tossed in the garbage on the way out, nodded to Oliver, and left.

Chapter Eleven

"YOU'RE SMILING AN AWFUL lot today," Kate pointed out as he leaned against the long back counter during a break in the afternoon. "Must've been some date with Enzo Moretti last night."

For a half a second, Will was *almost* tempted to tell Kate the truth. Because if he did, then he could confide her in that he'd woken up this morning—but it really hadn't felt like he'd woken at all.

It still felt like he was dreaming.

"It was," Will said, his smile deepening. He told himself he was just trying to be convincing, but it felt a lot closer to the truth than felt comfortable with. "He's . . .well, he's something else."

Kate rolled her eyes, but the look in her gray eyes was warm and affectionate. "Yeah, he sure is. Caught you good, didn't he?"

Will flushed. "Right. Uh, well, yeah. And he's painting the mural, of course."

"That all you want him to do?" she teased. "Paint your blank wall?"

"Yes. No. I don't know." Will hesitated. It was difficult to walk this fine line, but if he was really doing this, he'd say more. Kate was a new employee and a newer friend but she was *still* a friend, and it wasn't like he had a lot of those to choose from right now. "He's not sticking around. He doesn't like it here, and the worst part is that I understand. It's why I didn't want to stay in Florida. My family—"

"And you know, all the anti-LGBT policies," Kate added with a serious, knowing nod.

"Right. Just . . .on one hand, part of me is like, what's the point of starting something? And on the other . . .why can't we just enjoy each other for as long as he's around? Maybe he'd come back more often if he had reason to. Maybe if we went *all-in* he'd change his mind? Love does that, doesn't it?"

"Maybe." Kate didn't sound convinced—but Will wasn't hardly convinced either. *Try harder.*

"All I know is that he's not like anyone I've ever met," Will said, punctuating that statement with the sappiest lovestruck sigh he could conjure. He wasn't an actor; he was just doing his best.

He fully expected Kate's expression to grow more skeptical still, but instead, she smiled. Soft and understanding. Maybe his acting was better than he'd imagined.

Or it's not really acting.

"You're down bad," she said.

And well, maybe he was a little, but that was only because all these over-the-top declarations held a worrisome kernel of truth.

"Yeah," Will agreed.

"When are you going out with him again?"

"Uh, I think we're gonna share dinner again today. He's still working on the mural—"

Kate laughed. "Like a sweaty, messed up Enzo, do you?"

He could lie—or he could tell one hundred percent of the truth.

"Yeah," Will said, flushing. Still unsure which one he'd chosen.

His phone buzzed in his pocket and he pulled it out, glancing at the screen.

"I gotta take this," he told Kate and ducked to the back, to his little office. He basically never shut the door, but he did this time.

"Hey, Mom," he said. Felt himself already internally bracing for what was to come, because it wasn't like his mother to call him just because she wanted to. Only because she needed something.

They'd gotten into this ugly pattern years ago, and he didn't know how to break it. The only thing he'd been able to do was escape.

"Oh, good, I got you," Carla said with relief. "I'm so stuck, Will. I'm hoping you can help me out."

Of course she was hoping that. He didn't even roll his eyes at this point because it was so expected.

"Whatcha need?" he asked. Trying not to be hurt that she hadn't talked to him in at least two months and she hadn't even bothered to ask how Cherry's was going. The last time they'd talked, he'd brought up that business still hadn't picked up in a way he'd been hoping it would—though of course, with the Sweethearts Festival, plus the warmer weather arriving and the town discovering him, that *had* changed.

"Oh, you know how we're opening that big new store out on Tybee?" she asked.

He didn't, actually, but he wasn't surprised. Tybee Island was a big tourist draw, and it was exactly the kind of thing that Johnson's would take advantage of. Honestly it was only a surprise that Johnson's hadn't set up shop there before.

"Seems like a good choice," Will said.

"*Well*," Carla said in a huff, "the manager we hired to take care of the opening, he flaked right out on us. And he came *so* highly recommended too. So many wonderful references."

"That's too bad." Will thought he deserved a pat on the back or maybe even a gold star for keeping his voice so even, despite the fact that he knew exactly what was coming.

"It is," Carla said, her tone exasperated.

He waited, hoping that she'd ask, *and how are you doing?* But she didn't. He shouldn't be surprised at this point—or even disappointed—but it turned out that even moving away and opening his own business hadn't made him immune from the desire for his parents to be proud and interested in him.

"So," she continued, "we're searching for a replacement. The renovations are almost complete, the store just needs final touches, to be stocked, employees hired and trained, and the opening handled. We'll be there for that weekend, of course. Us and Brewer. But we *need* someone to manage the opening."

"Of course." Will considered suggesting that Brewer, his older brother and not only the apple of his parents' eye but their heir apparent, might bother himself to cover the gap, but if Brewer was willing or capable, then his mom wouldn't be calling.

"But other than that, it wouldn't be a huge time commitment. And you seemed like the obvious choice because your store's been open for *months* now, surely it's running itself by now."

She hadn't even *asked*, she'd just assumed.

Will sighed. "Cherry's isn't like Johnson's." He'd told her that a number of times. Enough times that it should've stuck, but it never had.

"I know that, but surely you can make a few weeks of time for family? We are *really* in a bind, Will."

Before his move to Indigo Bay, he'd have said yes. He'd have given in and gone to Tybee and done exactly what his family needed from him—for probably very little acknowledgment or thanks, unless you counted the large bonus his father likely would've routed into his bank account—but now, not only did he not want to, but he *couldn't*.

He'd planned and built and opened Cherry's for so many reasons, but one of them undoubtedly was that when his family inevitably came calling, he had a very good reason to say no.

"I can't," Will said. "You know I can't."

"You have a manager, Will. I know you do. Why did you hire her if she wouldn't be able to handle things while you were gone?" There was less judgment than disappointment in his mom's voice. Curiosity too.

There was no question that Kate would grow into a good manager. But Cherry's did a lot more than just sell bulk candy and fudge and simple ice cream cones and sundaes. Johnson's didn't make its own ice cream—but Cherry's did. He'd known that making every single thing he served from scratch would be a ton more work. But he'd also known it would mean he couldn't be at his family's beck and call.

But more than that, it meant he could hold his head high and know that he was responsible for every smile, every sticky face, every kid cajoling his parents to go back.

Cherry's had meant he could draw a line in the sand and not wiggle over it, even if he wanted to—and he didn't, not really—because there was something more important than just his personal feelings now.

If his mother understood anything, she *would* understand that business trumped those, every single time.

"I can't. You knew when I moved away, when I decided to open Cherry's, I wouldn't be able to help out as much. I told you that."

She sighed. "You did, but you said *not as much*. Not when we really needed you, Will. And we *really* need you."

Guilt swamped him. Maybe he should move heaven and earth to go to Tybee. To help them out, when they needed it.

"Can't Dad go?"

"Well, he *could*, of course . . ." The way she trailed off made it clear that of course he could, but he didn't want to. Will couldn't deny Patrick Johnson had already put his years and years of time in, traveling from one Johnson's location to another, overseeing their expansion, managing the day-to-day operations, and now he didn't want to anymore. Will couldn't blame him. It was a lot of work.

But that doesn't mean you need to do it, either.

"Or Brewer?"

"He's so busy, Will. He's managing the whole chain. He can't take the time out to open a store."

Will wasn't really surprised at that argument either. Brewer had never wanted to get his hands dirty with the actual running of the business. He preferred his suits to stay pristine, lording over everything from behind a desk.

"I'm sure you'll find someone," Will said. Ignoring, as best he could, the strong surge of responsibility he felt. "If I can think of anyone that could do it, I'll let you know."

"If that's all you can do," Carla said.

"It is," Will said firmly. For her. For himself, too.

"Right." She paused. "Is it going better, now that you've been open for a few months?"

"Yeah," he said. "A lot better. We're busy."

"Good." She sounded pleased at that, at least.

It wasn't like Will didn't think she'd ask at all. Or care. She was too business-minded to ignore the fact that he'd come here, to Indigo Bay, and not just started another outcropping of Johnson's, but something that was entirely his own concept. Still, it hurt to know that played second fiddle to their own business concerns.

Not surprising. There was a reason he'd ended up making the break when he had. He'd begun to realize, two winters ago, that every year he became more and more entrenched in the Johnson's business, and eventually, he wouldn't be anything more than a slave to it. And he hadn't wanted that. Hadn't wanted any of it.

He'd told Kate the bare rudimentary background and then a little more about his family's never-ending expectations, as they'd grown to be not just employer and employee but friends.

Still, when he finally stood and walked back to the front counter, he hadn't realized his face would be reflecting all of this. But Kate took one look at him and shook her head. "Again?" she asked under her breath as he checked the stock of the various ice creams sitting in the big glass-topped freezer.

But Will didn't want to talk about it; honestly, he didn't want to *think* about it.

Vanilla was running low, so he headed to the back. Grabbed a fresh five-gallon bucket and lugged it up towards the freezer. Pulled the nearly empty one and began to scoop out the remains, using his big metal scoop to pile it on top. He'd done this so many times, probably numbering in the thousands over the years. When he'd first started working in the family business, his mom had always reminded him to not make the new ice cream "look like garbage; pile it up nice, make it look appealing."

"My mom wanted someone to go to Tybee, to open their new store," Will said.

Kate's expression morphed from curiosity to sympathy.

"Their manager ditched. Hoped I might have some 'free time' on my hands to help them out."

Kate laughed, humorlessly. "Does she not know you're working sixty-hour weeks?"

"To know that, she'd have to *ask* about that."

"Ah." Kate's single syllable contained multitudes.

What else was there to say? Everyone had issues with their parents. At least Will's parents loved him, and they didn't try to stifle him or change him, the way Giana tried to do with Enzo. It wasn't their fault, necessarily, that they got distracted by just how *useful* he could be.

It had never bothered Brewer. They'd read him and slotted him into the place he was most suited. Then they'd tried to do the same with Will.

But he was never going to be the owner. He was only going to be the lackey, at everyone's beck and call.

"I'm gonna get some of these replaced and then . . ." Will trailed off, glancing around. His two employees besides Kate were working—one at the register, the other competently scooping ice cream and making sundaes and milkshakes.

"And then you're gonna take off for the rest of the evening?" she asked archly. "Why don't you go find Enzo?"

"I—"

"No," she said firmly. "We have this. I promise. Take the night off. You deserve it, and I can tell it bothered you."

"We'll see how busy it is when I finish up swapping out this ice cream," Will said. Sure that it *would* get busy and the three of them wouldn't be able to handle themselves.

But when he finished lugging the last of the new buckets in and piling the older ice cream on top, he realized when he looked up that it *had* gotten busier, but his employees were handling it alright. Not to the point where he'd feel okay leaving for weeks and going to Tybee, but enough that he could take this bad mood out of here.

"See?" Kate asked under her breath, as he surveyed the line, moving fairly quickly, and the happy families and couples, gathering around various tables.

"But I had *yesterday* off," Will said.

Kate threw her arms up. "Oh my God, *two* evenings off in a row! What will happen!"

It was impossible not to laugh at Kate's dramatics. "I guess I'll see you in the morning," he finally said, because one of the things he *had* learned from his family was the technique of letting go.

"We'll call you if we need you, but don't expect a call. Enjoy Enzo," Kate said, shooting him a knowing grin.

Will laughed. "Noted."

But he had no intention of finding Enzo and poisoning him with his bad mood.

Instead, Will stopped by his room at the Inn, and for the first time since he'd taken it, began to think that maybe it was time to look around for a more permanent kind of home. If he was really building a life here, why was he continuing to live in Joy's bed and breakfast?

Maybe he couldn't really blame his parents for thinking he wasn't staying permanently in Indigo Bay once Cherry's was established, if he was literally still living in a hotel?

He grabbed a few things and then headed out, to the place he always visited when he felt like he needed to just *get out* and have a few minutes to himself.

The walk was short, and he knew it like the back of his hand now, even in the dusk with all its lengthening shadows.

He climbed the dunes, between the reeds, and took his first deep breath of sea air.

This time Enzo decided it would be *his* responsibility to make sure Will took a break and had dinner.

He popped down to the deli, ordered two sandwiches of his favorite cold cuts, full of cool, crisp shredded iceberg, juicy ripe tomatoes, and sharp thin slices of red onion, all doused in the Morettis' famous homemade dressing. But when he pushed open the door of Cherry's, he was surprised to not see Will behind the counter.

Kate looked over at him, a startled expression on her face. "Enzo! I thought Will was with you."

"Uh . . .no?" Enzo's fingers itched to reach for his phone and check it, because maybe Will had sent him a text to meet him somewhere else for dinner? But he knew his inbox was empty because he'd been staring at it while he'd been down at the deli, waiting for them to put the sandwiches together. "I thought we were eating together."

Kate's smile was sad. "Ah, well, that makes sense. He was in a rotten mood so I sent him away. To be with you, I assumed, but he probably didn't want to talk about it."

"Did something happen?"

Kate shrugged. "His parents are difficult." She shot him a frank look. "You wouldn't know anything about that."

"Not a thing," Enzo said. "Where did he go, do you think?"

"You're going after him," she said with an approving nod.

He didn't tell her that it wasn't because, like the whole town assumed, he was falling wildly in love, but the truth was, with what they'd already shared, he'd have done it anyway.

He understood enough to know it was worse to be alone, even when you thought it was what you needed.

"Yeah, of course I am," Enzo said.

"You're not what I remember."

"You're not what I remember either. You were a punk and a brat in high school. Lots of dyed black hair and thick eye makeup," Enzo said with a grin.

Kate laughed. "You know the big dune?" Then she paused, still chuckling. "Of course you do. You grew up here. He'll be over that way."

Ten minutes later, he'd grabbed a sweatshirt from his loft on the way to the beach spot Kate had described, and, with his sandwiches in hand, he took the path through the tall grasses. Just as she'd predicted, there Will was, sitting on top of the tallest dune, staring out at the sea.

He looked so peaceful, knees tucked up under his chin, watching the waves as they rolled in and out Enzo almost didn't want to bother him.

Okay. That wasn't true. He still *wanted* to. But he wasn't sure he should, no matter what Kate said.

What they had wasn't real.

But Enzo liked to think because of all this fake dating, at least they were friendly. Maybe not friends yet. But *something*.

Still, he knew that what he should do was turn around, head back to his place, and then send him a text, suggesting they meet up in the morning.

But before he could, Will glanced down, and their eyes caught.

He was unbearably handsome like this, the sunset glow shading his face, the remnants of the sun glinting off his hair.

Then there was his smile, friendly and welcoming, and okay, he actually seemed pleased to see Enzo.

It wasn't particularly easy to scramble up a dune, and Enzo hadn't done it in long enough that he was sure he looked even more awkward than normal. But Will didn't say anything as he finally made it to the top, brushing sand off his calves as he plopped down next to where Will was sitting.

"Kate said you'd be here," Enzo said. Hoping that it didn't look like he was tracking Will's movements around town.

"Sorry," Will said. "I know we were supposed to have dinner. I guess I missed it."

"It's alright." Enzo pulled the two paper-wrapped sandwiches out of the front pocket of his sweatshirt and handed one to Will, who took it with a grateful look. "Dinner was happy to come to you."

"You didn't have to," Will claimed.

Another guy might've been frustrated with Will. After all, he seemed determined to be a bit of a martyr. But in this case, Enzo actually understood the instinct because he'd done it enough to himself.

"It's all good. I'd have missed this sunset, and it's spectacular," Enzo said casually. He nudged him. "Eat your dinner."

And for a while, that was all they did, munch away at their sandwiches.

When all was left was paper and a few stray pieces of lettuce, Will spoke up.

"I had a weird afternoon," was all he said.

"You want to talk about it?"

Will chuckled under his breath. "Not particularly."

"But you're gonna tell me anyway."

"Seems to me," Will said, "like you've got parental issues of you own, so maybe you'd understand."

Enzo took a risk and put his hand on Will's bare knee. Felt the shiver that went through him and through his own body, too. "From personal experience," he pointed out dryly, "keeping it to yourself doesn't help you deal with it any better."

Will was quiet for a minute. "It's kinda funny, because you wanted to leave here, to avoid the way your family makes you feel. But I came here because Indigo Bay saves me from *my* family."

"Why?"

"Did your mom tell you how they own a whole chain of stores? Like Cherry's but—" Will paused. "Nothing like them, too. Johnson's serves ice cream and bulk candy and fudge and there's fifteen stores stretched across the Southern coast. My great-grandfather started the first one, but my grandfather and father expanded. And then expanded again."

"And what, you're supposed to be the new head of the business?"

"Um, well, no, not even that." Will winced. "That's my older brother, Brewer. But they like to . . .well, I *did* work for them for a long time. Most of my life. It's how I learned so much about business and also about ice cream. But they always knew I'd do anything for them. That I'd always be there to step in. To bail them out. To go wherever they needed. I realized that I was getting lost. What *I* wanted. What mattered to me, what made me *me*, was getting lost. They weren't happy about me taking time off, but I did, and then I realized what I really needed to do was quit. So I did. I came here, I built Cherry's, and in a way, I designed it so I *couldn't* be at their beck and call anymore.

Only my own. 'Cause I knew I'd want to do it, anyway." Will hesitated. "My mom called today. Wanted me to come help out at the new store on Tybee Island. I had to tell her no. Didn't feel great."

Enzo thought he understood what Will was really saying. He'd wanted, he'd *hoped*, for some kind of happy medium. A place where he could be what his family needed and also be his own man. It was the same thing Enzo had fought and fought against, for so long, before he'd finally just had to leave.

Only after leaving Indigo Bay had he learned how to truly be Enzo Moretti.

"It's definitely an irony that Indigo Bay is where you came to find yourself," Enzo said wryly. "But I'm glad you did. Don't get me wrong—there's nothing wrong with this place. Actually as small towns go, it's pretty neat. More accepting than I ever expected it would be."

"But?" Will asked.

"Sometimes I think the problem isn't this town, it's me," Enzo said quietly.

"There's nothing wrong with you." Will declared it firmly, with a confidence he shouldn't possess. After all, they didn't know each other all that well. Not yet, anyway.

"You don't know that."

"I know enough. I know someone who maybe doesn't *get* Eliza's story, but still senses the way it makes the rest of us feel, who understands the way love and hope intertwine together, isn't a bad guy." Will's gaze was warm.

"It was your idea," Enzo joked. It was easier to tease than it was to sit here and just *feel* Will's earnestness. Not because he didn't enjoy it; but because he wasn't sure he deserved it.

Will raised an eyebrow.

"I'm not painting the story *only* because you asked me to," Enzo corrected. "If the cutest guy you've seen in ages tells you what you to paint, you don't say no." He shot Will the most charming smile he possessed. "At least not right away, you don't."

Will flushed. "I'm not cute," he stuttered.

"You totally are. And if you don't believe me, go look in a mirror." Enzo barely managed to tear his eyes away from his tanned handsome face. Which really, said it all, considering the glorious sunset in front of them. "See, you feel better already, don't you?"

"Yeah, actually," Will said. "Being near the water helps, always. But it helped to tell you, too."

"Good." Enzo nodded. "The ocean always helped me, too. Something about how it's so consistent, no matter what, no matter what changes, it's always there."

Will nodded.

"Don't get to it as much as I'd like, these days," Enzo said. "But back when I was a teenager, me and a few others would raise hell on this beach. Throw bonfires. Drink too much shitty booze. Tear our clothes off and go skinny dipping in the dark."

"That'd be a sight to see," Will said.

"Not so much, back then," Enzo admitted. "I was a skinny little brat. Very full of himself, despite that."

He could feel Will's gaze skim over his body now. And yes, he *had* grown into himself, finally. Physically too.

Maybe he'd never have broad shoulders like Luca, or a face that made grown men weep, like his cousin Ren, or the spectacular golden brown eyes of Gabe, another cousin. But *he* could look in a mirror now and not feel like he'd ended up the runt of the Morettis. A *non* Moretti.

"Somehow, I doubt that," Will said, tone full of amusement.

Enzo was tugging off his T-shirt before he could decide this was insane and they most definitely should not be doing it. The line between the two was already blurred enough. *So,* he thought, *what's adding a little water to it?*

"Well," he said, "you game?"

Will looked shocked. He hoped it was more because he'd taken his shirt off unexpectedly and not because of what he'd seen underneath. "You mean . . .go skinny dipping? In the ocean?"

"Come on, don't tell me a coast boy like you doesn't know how to swim?" Enzo teased, standing. It was still warm, with the last of the sun's rays continuing to heat the air, and the ocean was definitely warm enough to swim in, considering it was June and these beaches were packed with people during the day, doing exactly that.

Though it wasn't like that had stopped Enzo when he'd been that young, punk kid. They'd gone in all kinds of weather, stupid and reckless.

This was reckless too, in an entirely different way.

"I know how to swim," Will said slowly.

"There you go," Enzo said. He tucked his T-shirt and sweatshirt together.

Still, Will looked uncertain. Way too uncertain. Enzo decided it was time to put his money where his mouth was and reached down, flicking open the button on his jeans.

Will's jaw dropped even farther.

"But we don't have towels or . . ." Will trailed off as Enzo lowered his zipper. Leaving his jeans hanging on his hipbones, barely.

He'd had a hookup once mention he looked insanely sexy half-dressed like this, and even though nothing between them was supposed to be real, this *felt* real. Real enough that Enzo was kind of counting on that being true and not just something the guy had said to boost his ego.

"You need a towel?"

"We're gonna be *wet*. The ocean is wet, Enzo," Will said, still sounding way too reasonable. Way too logical.

"A+ reasoning. We'll figure that part out after. Come on, stop thinking so hard." Enzo reached out and grasped his shoulder. Squeezed. "Have a little bit of fun. We both know you work too hard. And isn't that what you're trying to do here? Find *you*?"

Will nodded. Licked his lips. "Alright," he said. He pulled off his own T-shirt and Enzo nearly swallowed his tongue. A man who sold ice cream for a living should not have abs like that.

"I like to work out," Will said, having the nerve to sound self-conscious as Enzo stared at his bare chest.

"An understatement," Enzo mumbled under his breath. He'd been so ready to get naked, only a few seconds earlier, but now he was suddenly self-conscious himself. He'd had a feeling Will's clothes were hiding a wet dream of a body, but he'd underestimated just how hot the guy actually was.

"Hey," Will said kindly and reached out for Enzo, squeezing his bicep reassuringly. "You've got *nothing* to worry about, I promise. Now, where's that smug little kid? I bet he's in there somewhere."

Oh, he was. Enzo had never been able to destroy him completely. His chin lifted, he toed off his shoes, and then he shed his jeans the rest of the way.

Will nodded in approval, dropping his shorts, leaving both of them clad in nearly identical boxer briefs, Will's dark navy blue, and Enzo's gray.

"You ready?" Enzo asked. Not sure he was quite ready himself.

"I thought we were gonna go skinny dipping," Will said, taking an unfortunate step back, away from Enzo. But then he tucked his fingertips under the waistband of his boxer briefs and just tugged them right down.

Enzo was devastated. All his half-formed plans shattered around him.

Jesus.

No. he's not here right now. And he's not gonna be here, not with Will looking like a fucking snack.

Enzo tried to drag his mouth closed. Didn't quite succeed.

"What is this? I thought you were so eager to go skinny dipping?" Will asked. "What about having some fun?"

"I can think of some fun we could have," Enzo said, before he could snatch the words back.

Will laughed. "Skinny dipping, then," he said and, without a shred of embarrassment, started down the dune, leaving Enzo behind with a picture fucking perfect view of his pale, gorgeously muscled ass.

"Fuck," Enzo muttered. Then before he could think—or *over-think*—he shed his own boxer briefs and followed, skidding down the dune awkwardly, glad that he was actually behind Will. And not only because he got another really great view of that ass.

He watched as Will strode right into the water, no hesitation at all, proving that he *was* an ocean kid, just the same as Enzo.

The water hit Enzo's ankles, lapping around his legs as he followed Will into the waves.

It was still warm from the hot day—and the many hot days that had preceded this one—but cool enough to tamp down a fraction of the arousal he'd felt ever since Will had tugged down his boxer briefs.

Spray dotted Will's tanned broad shoulders, and he glowed reddish orange as the final dregs of the sun set.

He'd stopped, waiting for Enzo to catch up and they stood together, watching it, the waves covering them from the waist down.

But even then, the guy was gorgeous, and Enzo had trouble not looking at him.

"I . . .uh. . .hope that was okay," Will said, breaking the silence.

Enzo glanced at him with surprise. "What was okay? You stripping down and giving me a show I won't forget anytime soon?"

The flush creeping up his cheekbones was a delightful giveaway to what Enzo kept hoping were Will's real feelings. Even as he told himself he *knew* this couldn't go anywhere.

Maybe Will was the opposite of Enzo. Knew how to keep his mouth shut when he should.

But Enzo didn't ever know when to quit.

"Isn't this better than camping out in your cramped little office?" Enzo wondered.

"Yeah. Pretty good view." But Will's eyes were glued to him, not to the last gasp of the sunset.

"Mine isn't too bad either." A freaking understatement.

They swam there for a minute, treading water, regarding each other.

It felt like they were edging way too close to something that wasn't fake at all.

But then how could it be? They weren't doing this for anybody but themselves.

Maybe what they needed was another one of those over-the-top fake dates to remind him exactly why they were doing this. Why they kept circling each other. And why it couldn't be anything more than the deep down yearning that kept tugging him towards Will, even as he knew better.

"We need to go out again."

Will raised an eyebrow. "Yeah?"

"Oh yeah. Lots of cutesy nicknames, all the cuddles, the whole shebang," Enzo said. "*Stud Muffin.*"

Will laughed and flicked water at him. Enzo shook it off, pushing his hair back, ignoring the way Will's gaze traced his face. Ignoring the way he kept returning that particular look.

Waited a second, until Will was good and lulled into complacency before splashing him back, harder this time.

Unsurprisingly, that kicked off a water fight. Will was as good of a swimmer as Enzo and they circled each other, playing earnestly, but never getting too close.

Enzo knew *he* was far too aware of how Will was totally naked under the water—and he had a feeling Will was equally as attuned to that particular fact. It meant they kept their distance, but even that didn't diminish their fun.

When they finally came to a stop, Enzo's hair dripping as much as Will's face, he turned to Enzo, suddenly serious.

"If you think we need to." *Oh. The fake date.* "But I won't be able to get an evening off until next week."

"What about brunch?"

"Brunch?" Will scrunched up his nose.

"Don't tell me you don't like brunch."

"I *do*. But weekend mornings are for ice cream prep. I can't take it off. What about Monday night? We're closed."

"Alright. Well, this weekend I can work on the mural and when I'm not, I can swan around Cherry's, staring longingly in your direction."

"Is that just an excuse for me to feed you ice cream?"

It hadn't been, actually, but if Will wanted to pretend his ice cream was the only reason Enzo wanted to be around him, then Enzo wasn't going to enlighten him.

"Sure," Enzo said. He gestured towards the beach. "Come on, we'd better get out. It's going to be full dark soon, and even though I stayed out way too late when I was young and stupid, we'd better not."

There could be sneak riptides, and also critters hiding in the dunes.

Plus it was always better to walk back to town when you could at least see your hand in front of your face.

"You gonna get out first?" Will had the nerve to blush again. Like he hadn't been the first one to strip down completely.

"I can't believe you're embarrassed now. Trust me, you've got nothing to be embarrassed about." *Nothing,* Enzo nearly repeated a second time, but he'd already made Will's myriad attractions clear. He didn't need to pump the guy's ego up any further.

"Maybe I'm just jealous that you got a good look at *my* ass on the way out here, but I didn't get even a peak at yours," Will teased. "Fair play and all that."

"Fine, fine. But don't expect too much," Enzo grumbled. He had a skinny ass. He knew it.

But when he walked out of the ocean, the sand crunching beneath his feet, he could feel Will's gaze on him, and then came the inevitable wolf whistle.

Will caught up to him a moment later and Enzo smartly kept his eyes forward, on their way back to the dune.

"Trust me, I'm not disappointed," Will said earnestly.

"Thanks," Enzo retorted, but he *was* pleased. Undeniably.

"See," Will said a second later, as they were clamoring up the dune and Enzo was actually very glad for the near-dark, "a *towel* would've come in real handy about now."

And okay, yes, it was awkward. Enzo could admit that. But it had been fun too. So much fun. He wanted to say he couldn't remember the last time he'd had this much fun, but it had been the other night, when they'd gone to Rudy's and pretended they were wild about each other.

"Next time you're in charge of towels," Enzo said as he pulled out his briefs from the pile he'd shoved them into.

"It's a deal," Will said, pulling on his shorts.

Chapter Twelve

Their date at Rudy's had been good enough, Enzo mused, but he needed something bigger, better, even more elaborate than a steak, a good bottle of wine and a faux goodnight kiss in front of Eliza's statue for this next one.

So he went to his cousin.

Five years ago, he'd never have considered Luca an expert on romance. In fact, he didn't think *Luca* would've considered himself an expert on romance. An expert on lots of other things, sure, but not romance. Not until he'd met Oliver.

When he took a break for lunch, Enzo texted Luca, and when he found out he was at the deli, he headed in that direction.

Found Luca in a T-shirt and an apron, gloves on, sleeves metaphorically rolled up, mixing up meatballs in a gigantic metal bowl in the back kitchen.

"Hey," Luca said. "You're lucky you caught me before I got my hands in this. What's up?"

"What are you making?" Enzo leaned in, sniffed. The mixture was raw, sure, but it looked and smelled delicious.

"A variation of Nonna's meatballs with ground chicken, roasted garlic, and blanched broccoli rabe," Luca said. "Gabe said he'd done

one, as a special, at the food trucks in Los Angeles, and it was popular, so I thought I'd try it here."

"Sounds good." Enzo's stomach grumbled. "How long til they're ready? I'm starving."

"Been working all morning, huh? Give me twenty minutes and I can get them on a sandwich for you. You can be my first taste tester."

"Perfect," Enzo said. "And yeah. Just finishing up the outlines. I think tomorrow I'll be able to start on the actual paint. I'm running out to Charleston tonight, to get paint. You need anything?"

Luca shook his head. "It's coming along. I walked by it yesterday and I swear I can already feel the waves and the wind," he said, giving Enzo an approving smile. He finished mixing with one last flourish, and turned to the sink, meticulously scrubbing his hands. "So, you gonna tell me why you really came by? If you just wanted food, you'd have called the main deli line and ordered."

Enzo leaned against the long stainless steel counter and forced himself to relax. He'd told Luca about Will already. Talking about him more wasn't a big deal. After all, *everyone* was supposed to be buying into the show, not just his mother.

"I'm taking Will out on Monday," Enzo said.

To his surprise, Luca frowned. "Again?"

"Of course *again*. To hear the rest of the town talk about it, our first date was the greatest in the history of Indigo Bay."

But Luca was still frowning. "No, that's your mother who keeps saying that to anyone who will listen. I was convinced, after Rocco talked to me, that you were just doing it to get her off your ass. Not because you really liked him."

"I . . .uh . . .that's not true."

But his stuttering surprise at Luca's painfully pinpoint accuracy had probably ruined his denial.

Luca glanced over at him as he grabbed a metal ice cream scoop and began portioning out the meatballs onto a tray. "So you like him and all this is for real? You know he's—"

"I know he's staying, yeah. He has a business here. It would be hard *not* to know that," Enzo interrupted. "You did it with Oliver. Started something even though you didn't think it was going to be forever."

"I was lying to myself," Luca said steadily. "I don't think you're lying to yourself. You don't love it here."

It was true. He didn't. He never had.

He *could* admit that this visit was leaps and bounds better than every other one he'd had. It helped, of course, to have a purpose and a job to do—and one he was very good at, that he loved. But he had a feeling it was more than that, too.

It was Will.

But it wasn't just him. It was that Enzo had grown up, finally, and he could see this place more accurately, now that he'd been in so many other places.

His travels had given him perspective.

Maybe not *that* much perspective, but he could admit that he didn't think he'd ever returned to Indigo Bay, spent at least a week, or even a few days, and hadn't already wanted to leave again.

But he hadn't felt that way this time around. Not once.

"No, I don't want to stay, but . . ." Enzo hesitated. "I don't hate it the way I used to."

Luca rolled his eyes. "Don't tell me the power of love has changed your mind."

"Why not? Didn't it change yours?"

"It wasn't that I didn't want to stay. I didn't think I *could* stay," Luca said. "Will's a good guy. A solid guy. A friend. And I wouldn't be proud to call him that unless I warned you not to fuck with him."

"Trust me, I'm not."

But aren't you? Aren't you fucking with yourself?

"It kind of feels like you're doing *something*," Luca said. "Rocco said you guys were calling each other ridiculous nicknames. *Stud Muffin*." He frowned. "I know you, Enzo, and this isn't you."

"Maybe it's me, now," Enzo claimed. But he knew how weak his argument was.

Luca shook his head. "No, it's not. If this is some kind of elaborate scheme to get Giana off your back, I applaud it, but she's going to be pissed when the truth comes out."

"Maybe."

"Disappointed *and* pissed."

Enzo swallowed hard. "Okay, that's probably accurate." But he couldn't quit the charade now. Not when he enjoyed it so much. Not when the thought of stopping made him desolate in a way he didn't want to examine too closely.

"You know it is," Luca said pointedly.

"Okay, fine. The truth? Maybe I went out with him because I was curious, and to get Mom off my back. I'll admit that. But now . . ." Enzo took a deep breath. "I really like him. I *do*. There's nothing fake about that."

"And you want to keep this up?"

If Will didn't think they were faking it for the town's gossip mill, Enzo wasn't sure he'd want to keep hanging out. If he'd let Enzo continue to call him his *Stud Muffin*. And letting him touch him.

"We're in this, now," Enzo said.

"You know." Luca turned to him and put a hand on his shoulder, gaze sympathetic. Or maybe even empathetic. Because yes, while his situation with Oliver had been slightly different, there *were* similarities. "You *can* like him. You're allowed. But you know if you do, if you really let yourself go there, leaving is going to be wretched. For both of you."

Enzo swallowed hard. "Yeah. Probably."

He didn't want to say, *But he's the guy. How could he not be, when I've never wanted to spend so much time with someone just pretending to like them?*

Maybe he didn't need to, though, because the look on Luca's face made it clear he understood anyway.

"You want to have what you can, while you can have it." Luca nodded absently, his eyes distant, like he was remembering a time when he'd felt the same. "I get that. So you want to take him out on Monday. You want me to get you into the restaurant."

"You and Oliver run the nicest place on the coast. But it's booked up months in advance." Enzo made a face. "You guys need more tables."

"Then we'd be busier than we are, already, and that'd be no good, because I actually *like* seeing my husband," Luca said with amusement.

"Come on, Luca. Fit me in."

"You'll never be able to go back from this," Luca warned.

Enzo understood that he meant in multiple kinds of ways. If Giana heard that Enzo had begged Luca to fit him and Will in for a romantic date, she'd believe *this was it.*

And maybe if he took Will on a romantic date, he'd end up believing the exact same goddamn thing.

It wasn't like he wasn't already in deep. It had been two days since their skinny dip in the ocean, and it felt like Will was constantly in his thoughts.

He sketched something and wondered, *what will Will think of it?*

He painted on Will's wall and thought about him looking at it every single day as he walked by it.

He ate something and wanted to know what Will's face would look like if he tried it too.

He turned on a ridiculous, over-the-top romantic movie on TV and wondered if he could convince Will to re-enact any of the scenes with him.

He was haunting Cherry's, spending too much time in there, just surreptitiously watching the man.

It was becoming a real problem.

"I know," Enzo said, agreeing with Luca's assessment. Agreeing and wanting to move forward anyway.

"Alright," Luca said with a nod. "I'm proud of you, you know?"

Enzo cracked a smile. "I thought this was supposed to be the baseball bat talk."

Luca laughed. "Don't you think I'd be giving *him* that? You're *my* cousin."

But the cousin you didn't really like and didn't want, forever.

"I . . . uh . . ."

Luca did a double take. "You *did* think that I would." He paused and set down the ice cream scoop. Turned to Enzo, put both hands on his shoulders, and gave his most earnest, most soulful Moretti look. Luca didn't often use it. Of course he didn't usually *need* to. His hard-ass Moretti look worked better.

But not right now.

"You're a great guy, Enzo. You've grown up into a great man. If you didn't know I'm proud of you, I'm sorry. I'm not very good at showing it. Oliver tells me I need to be better. We didn't start out on a very auspicious foot, I'll admit, but you saw you needed to change, and you *changed.* You fought for every single change I see in you now. How could I not be proud of that?"

Enzo was speechless.

He didn't have a father. He didn't have brothers. He'd never had any family besides his mother, really, especially because the rest of the Morettis were all on the west coast. Even though he'd been brought into their fold during his time in San Francisco, he still hadn't been one-hundred-percent convinced that Luca even *liked* him, even though they'd mended their differences ages ago.

But this was more than like. Luca *loved* him, like he loved his father and his brothers and his cousins.

Like Enzo was one of the people Luca worried for and watched out for. And even when Enzo hated it, he could still appreciate that Luca did it out of loyalty and responsibility and *yes*, pure, unadulterated affection.

"Oh. *Oh.*"

"Yes," Luca said firmly. "You're a Moretti, but I care about you not only because of that. Because you're Enzo."

It was maybe the nicest thing anyone had ever said to him. And it meant even more because it was coming from Luca, who was notoriously close-lipped when it came to his emotions.

"Thanks, uh . . .I didn't expect that."

"And I'm sorry for that," Luca said firmly. "Now, if you want that reservation, then I'll make sure you get it."

"Really?"

Luca returned to his meatballs, and the moment between them technically ended, but Enzo had a feeling the warmth of it would fire him for a long time to come. "Really."

<hr>

"I can't believe you actually got us into Luca and Oliver's place," Will said, shyly glancing over at Enzo as they walked past the park. He looked really pleased, his hand squeezing around Enzo's.

Enzo had never felt any particular desire to hold hands with anyone. But doing it with Will was *nice*. So nice he might want to do it even if they weren't parading by where half the town could see them.

It was a cool-ish evening, and Enzo thought they'd passed all the biggest gossips in Indigo Bay—except his mother, of course.

"Luca and Oliver love you. You provide them with ice cream for some of their desserts. You don't think they'd have gotten you in, if you'd asked?"

"Yeah, but the Lowcountry Bistro is . . ." Will waved his free hand around. "You know. Romantic. Meant for two. And uh . . .before you, I didn't have *two*. I only had me."

"You could've taken Kate," Enzo suggested with a sly grin.

"Then it *definitely* wouldn't have been romantic."

"Guess you were just waiting for me, then." Enzo paused, grinning. "*Stud Muffin*."

Will laughed.

"Guess I was. The food though, it was so good. Different than what I expected, but delicious."

"Luca would never tolerate less. Oliver, either." It had been amazing, but that was exactly what Enzo had expected of his cousin and his husband. And they'd given them a nice private table. When Luca had shown them to it, the gleam in his eyes had told Enzo that this was entirely on purpose.

He'd given Enzo exactly what he wanted, deep down—privacy—but not what he'd claimed to need—a public display of their date.

"True. I'm still impressed." Will shot him another one of those fond, affectionate looks that Enzo was beginning to realize weren't fake in the least. "And you made it happen."

"All I had to do was ask," Enzo said modestly.

They turned the corner and they were already at the Inn. How had that passed so quickly? Enzo had deliberately been walking slowly. Knowing how he wanted the date to end. Also knowing how it *should* end. Will had drawn the line, and Enzo wasn't going to cross it, unless he invited him to.

"But you *asked*," Will said, squeezing his hand again. "How are we going to play this?" he asked, gesturing towards the screen porch. There were Giana and Joy again, sitting on one of the swings, chatting.

But as soon as they saw them, they clammed up, staring at Enzo and Will as they approached the porch stairs.

Great.

"I . . .I'm not sure," Enzo said. He wanted to kiss Will, but he did not want to kiss Will if he wasn't as into it as he was, and he did not want to kiss him just to convince his mother and Joy that they were wild about each other.

"I have an idea." Will turned to him, voice and expression equally earnest. "Come upstairs with me."

"What?" Enzo asked flatly, even as his whole body thrilled at the thought of it.

"It's our second date. You look . . ." Will sounded flustered now. "You look like that. And you got us a table at the Bistro. I would *not* let you go home alone."

Enzo understood what he was saying. *He'd* not have wanted to go home alone, either. If this was real, he'd have been trying hard to win an invitation to Will's bed.

"I . . .uh . . .same," Enzo agreed.

"Then, come upstairs," Will said with a devastating smile that left him weak in the knees. "They'll know exactly what's going on. And if they don't? Well, we'll make *sure*."

"You want to fake having sex?" Enzo asked.

Could he be excited and disappointed at the exact same time?

Will nodded, looking more the former than the later. And how could Enzo puncture all that with the hard reality of their situation?

"Oh yeah," Will said. "Don't you?"

Actually, I'd rather have it for real, but if this is what I can get, I'll take it.

"Sure," Enzo said. He slowed, pausing right out of what he hoped was his mother's hearing distance. "How far are you wanting to take this?"

Will grinned. "How far are *you* willing to take this, *Honey Bunny*?"

The thing was, Enzo didn't back down from a challenge. Even when it was a challenge he didn't particularly want to win. "Oh, it's on," he said, and he tucked his head in between Will's neck and his shoulder, murmuring with intent into his ear. "I think it's time we took this upstairs," he said.

Will's skin was slightly damp with the heat, but he smelled so good Enzo wanted to bury his face into it and *lick*.

His arm tightened around Enzo as they walked up the stairs, fingertips digging into his waist, like Will was just as eager as Enzo to be alone.

He glanced over at his mother as they crossed to the front door.

"Hello and goodbye," he called out. "See you later."

Will was laughing under his breath when they walked into the Inn and headed towards the stairs. "You're incorrigible."

"But you love it," Enzo said.

The stairs weren't quite so wide across so Will was forced to let go of his hand.

"I kinda do," Will said. "It's fun. When I suggested this, I didn't think it would be nearly as fun as it has been. I kinda thought it would be a chore."

"Aw. You thought hanging out with me was gonna be terrible?" Enzo teased.

"The first time we met? Yeah, I might've. Of course by the time I suggested we fake it, I'd already figured out that your head wasn't *nearly* that big." Will shot him a smile as he unlocked his door.

"Maybe not the *only* part of me that's big," Enzo said with a nudge.

Will looked delighted. Sadly, it wasn't because he wanted Enzo to drop his pants anytime soon and prove it.

"See, this is exactly the vibe we need," Will said with absolute sincerity. "We need to make sure everyone in this Inn knows exactly what we're doing."

Enzo didn't normally spend much of his time on regret, but he could fully admit now that he regretted convincing Will that all this over-the-top behavior was necessary. He'd sort of imagined them coming up here. Hanging out for an hour. And then he'd leave, pasting on his most satisfied smile as he paraded past his mother and Joy.

"How are we gonna do that?" Enzo asked, afraid he already knew the answer.

Will's blue eyes twinkled with mischief. "If we were dating for real, and we came back to this room, how would it go? I'd pin you to this door." Punctuating his statement, he smacked his hand against it, and Enzo nearly jumped. Not really from surprise—though he was surprised enough—but from the way all his nerves drew tight and anticipatory.

Yep, he totally wanted Will to pin him to the door *for real*.

Instead, he nodded and pushed his body against the door too, landing against it with a dull thud, loud enough that he expected at least *someone* heard it.

"We'd be kissing then," Will continued, "and moaning a little."

"Loudly?" Enzo asked, trying to remember the last good makeout session he'd had, and if he'd been that loud.

"Not yet," Will said, glancing over at him, heat in his eyes. "But soon." He smacked the door a few more times, a little quieter than his initial impact, but enough that it wouldn't go unnoticed.

Enzo's skin felt too tight. This was fun yes, but it was also driving him more than a little nuts. He nearly opened his mouth and said, "fuck the charade, let's do this for real." What stopped him was what Enzo imagined Will's inevitable question would be. *Are you staying here in Indigo Bay then?*

He didn't fucking know. He didn't *want* to. And he'd sworn he never would. Especially not for a guy.

But Will wasn't just any guy, was he? He was *Will*. He had blue eyes and the brightest smile and abs that Enzo was desperate to lick his way down.

It wasn't just the way he looked, either. It was how he smiled when he handed a little kid an ice cream cone as big as his head. And laughed. His kindness. His willingness to give to others. His patience with Giana, when she hadn't really deserved it.

Ugh.

"I think now," Will said. "Full confession. I'm a pretty good kisser, so you'd definitely be moaning now."

Enzo wanted to moan now, for real.

"Who's got the big head now?" he said instead.

Will looked slightly sheepish, but not even close to ashamed. "Just telling it like it is."

"So I gotta moan now?" Enzo didn't think he'd ever moaned, *sexually*, on cue before. Usually when he did it, he wasn't thinking about it. Wasn't thinking about anything.

"Don't tell me you've got performance anxiety," Will joked.

Enzo rolled his eyes, but maybe he did, a little. He let out a little moan, probably not nearly loud enough, but didn't you have to work up to that? That was a good excuse. If Will called him on it, he'd just say it was a work in progress.

"Oh, yeah, that's good, let me hear you, Honey Bunny," Will said, his voice inching upwards. He sounded as hot and bothered as Enzo felt.

There was part of him that hoped, fervently, that Will was feeling this as much as Enzo was. That was also going out of his mind with how much he wanted—no, he *needed*—this to be real.

But he couldn't ask and open that can of worms. Instead, they were going to have to plow through this.

Metaphorically.

He moaned a little louder then. And then again. Will did, too, and Enzo tried to pretend he wasn't going to be hearing that noise an hour from now when he was finally alone and could wrap his hand around his cock and give in to the pleasure teasing him.

"Oh, yeah, that's so good," Enzo called out. Will gave him an approving nod, and okay, maybe he was actually decent at this. "Give me more, Stud Muffin."

"Oh, baby, I got it all for you," Will said with a nice heavy moan as additional ammunition. He smacked the door again and then again.

Enzo risked a glance at him. And yeah, it was not full dark in the room—there was a light on in the corner—and Will was definitely hard in his slacks. Then there was the flush on his face, the brightness in his eyes . . . well, it helped but it didn't help, also, that Will was just as affected by this as Enzo was.

"I think," Enzo said in a low voice, "it's too been long since I've actually done this for real."

Will smiled, understanding in his eyes. "Uh, yeah. Me too. Though . . ." He stopped. Hesitating.

"What is it?"

"It's never been like this before," Will said. "And we're not even doing it for real."

Enzo wanted to squeeze his eyes shut and run away.

But he didn't. Because he was a goddamn grown-up, and it was partially his fault they were in this mess.

"Yeah," he agreed.

"Do you think we should . . ." Will gestured towards the bed.

Do this for real? Pin me to the nearest horizontal surface and kiss me like you mean it? Absolutely.

"Uh, yeah, sure. Yes." Enzo nodded and kept nodding, feeling unhinged as they pushed off from the door and approached the bed.

"More moaning," Will directed.

"You know, if you ever have to leave the ice cream business," Enzo said, adding a few loud noises for good measure, "you have a real future as a porn director."

Will laughed. "I think I'll stick to the ice cream business." He landed with a resounding thump on the bed.

Enzo laughed, too, because if he didn't, he was going to cry. Because then Will went up on all fours and made a fun growling noise.

"You're kinda killing me," Enzo said.

"I know." Will flushed. "I'm killing myself. But the sooner we get through this . . ."

Enzo nodded. When had this gone from a fun time to pure fucking torture?

Right around, *I'm a pretty good kisser.*

Or maybe when he'd stupidly convinced Will to get naked last week.

Or even before that, when Will's eyes had fluttered, the first time Enzo had called him *Stud Muffin.*

Enzo moaned again, slapped the wall hard, in conjunction with a few of Will's thrusts.

Yep. Cause now Will was thrusting and the bed was squeaking and it was all too much. Enzo started to laugh and couldn't stop.

"Don't stop now," Will cajoled, but he was laughing, too, under his breath. "Big finish!"

Enzo slapped the wall hard, three times, and let out the loudest moan yet, practically a scream, and Will joined him, the two of them sounding like yowling cats in heat.

And okay, it had been sort of torturous, but also pretty fun, in the end.

All until, their breath returning back to normal, there was a knock on the door.

"Oh shit," Will hissed under his breath.

The knock sounded again, louder this time and far more insistent.

"Shit, shit, shit," Will repeated. He looked around, eyes wild.

"Will?" Yep, that was definitely Joy's voice.

Will tore his shirt off, then his pants went next. Shoes. Socks. Enzo averted his eyes at the last moment, though it wasn't like he hadn't seen it all before, when they'd gone skinny dipping.

Grabbing a sheet, Will pulled it off the bed with a sharp movement and then wrapped it around his waist. "Get down," he mouthed to Enzo, who crouched low, on the other side of the bed, and then he opened the door.

❦❦❦❦❦❦ ❦❦❦❦❦❦

Will told himself he was embarrassed. Humiliated. Flushed so bright a red that Joy would never believe that he and Enzo had actually been having sex in their room.

"Yes?" he asked.

She looked equally as uncomfortable, so that was something, at least. "Will, honey, there's been a few . . .uh . . .complaints from some of the other guests that you're being . . .um . . .loud. Too loud. Do you think you could keep it down?"

Will apologized to her silently. And to his own pride. "I'm sorry. We got uh . . .a bit carried away."

Joy's eyes twinkled with amusement. "I'm sure you did," she said. "Next time just try to get carried away quieter, okay?"

"Okay, will do," Will said and then shut the door.

"Phew," Enzo said from the other side of the room. "That was . . ." He trailed off.

"Yeah."

Will didn't know what else to say, twisting the corner of the sheet even tighter in his fist. Joy was right. He'd gotten carried away, one hundred percent. And then convinced Enzo to get carried away alongside him. Part of him had hoped, maybe, that if he pushed it, Enzo would break down and say *fuck it*. And kiss him for real.

But Enzo wouldn't, Will was beginning to realize. Because he'd said on their first date he didn't want to cross that line, and Enzo was clearly going to respect it, no matter how much it sucked.

Right now, Will's blood was pumping so hot and insistent under his skin he nearly turned to Enzo and said, "Let's do this for real." But he didn't. Because the second he thought it, he also thought of how much *more* he'd like Enzo if they did. If they kept doing it, and kept hanging out, and then in a few weeks, Enzo left.

Would it break his heart? Maybe not entirely, but enough that it was worth being smart about this.

No matter how much Will wanted to throw *thinking* out the window.

"So, what now?" Enzo asked, voice quiet.

Will was acutely aware of his still-subsiding erection. The desire still raging through him. And his unclothed state.

"I . . .uh . . .should get dressed," Will said.

This time it was Enzo's turn to flush, and he whipped around so fast he looked unsteady. "Oh yeah, of course," Enzo said.

"I was thinking . . ." Will let the sheet drop and picked up his boxer briefs and shirt, putting them on, but when he got to his jeans, he set them on a chair next to the dresser. He trailed off, because now that he'd started to say it, wouldn't this just be more torture? And didn't he want it—didn't he *need* it—to end?

And don't you want to finally be alone and wrap your hand around your cock? Get yourself off?

Oh, he did.

No. What he *wanted* was for Enzo to do it. His own hand could only provide a very temporary respite.

"Yeah?" Enzo's voice cracked. Like maybe he was thinking about Will getting dressed.

"Would you really go back to your place tonight? If we were . . ." Will swallowed hard. When they'd started this, when *he'd* suggested it, he'd never imagined it would feel like this. One breath away from the lie falling apart into tatters. "Falling for each other, would you really leave?"

Enzo turned around. His fists were clenched tightly. "I wouldn't let you out of my sight," he said seriously.

"Exactly." Will swallowed hard. *What are you doing?* "You should stay here. You wouldn't ever leave me. Not after . . .uh . . ."

Enzo's face creased into a fleeting grin. "Our bedroom gymnastics?"

"Yeah. And uh, after just one round," Will added.

Enzo's grin returned, much wider this time. "Oh yeah. That's what I'm talking about."

"If you don't want to . . ." Will trailed off.

"We said we'd do this, and we're doing it," Enzo said with determination.

Well, shit.

He'd wanted Enzo to leave, but he'd wanted him to stay, even more. Even if it meant lying next to him, without touching him the way he craved, deep down.

"Alright. I'm . . .uh . . .gonna get ready for bed." It was only just past nine, but they both got up early for work. Will, because there was always too much to do, and Enzo because he wanted to get as much work in before the heat of the day.

"Sure. I'll just be out here, doing the same." Enzo waved around him. Then his face split into a knowing smile. "Take your time."

Will was bright red by the time he made it into the bathroom, because of course Enzo had figured out what he was going to do. He was probably going to do the same.

That was all it took to make him hard as a rock again.

He shed his boxer briefs again, wrapped his hand around his dick, and thought of how Enzo moaned. His face as he'd fallen against the door. The tension in his face and body as he'd vibrated with desire. But what really pushed him over the edge was that knowing smile as Will had shut the door.

And what he was almost certainly doing on the other side of it.

Will heard a rustle and gasped under his breath. Imagining what Enzo would look like if he opened the door now. If he let Will look his fill. Because Will had a feeling he would.

A moment later, he was coming hard, in his hand, pulse after pulse, and even after it was over, he wished it hadn't happened like that.

That he'd stayed.

That things were different.

He took another few minutes. Washed his hand and the rest of him. Brushed his teeth.

Stared in the mirror and waited for the inevitable glow on his cheeks to fade, but that took even longer than the pleasure to dissipate entirely.

Finally, he didn't have any other choice but to open the door and walk back out into the bedroom.

Enzo was lounging on the bed. He'd taken off his pants and his shirt, and was only in his boxer briefs and a white tank. Will swallowed hard. He looked so gorgeous like this, all relaxed, bedroom eyes soft and blurred with the pleasure he'd just given himself.

Will imagined he might look like this after *he'd* just pleasured him.

"Come on, get in," Enzo said, patting the bed next to him. "You'll sleep better, now."

"Yeah." Will was tired but keyed up at the same time. Still, what else could he do but slide in next to Enzo?

You idiot, this was your stupid idea.

"See, that wasn't so bad?" Enzo teased in a low voice.

"Could've been better." Will cleared his throat.

"Eh. We said it would complicate everything. Or you said it. And I didn't exactly disagree because you weren't wrong."

And what's wrong with a little complication?

Will knew he was in trouble when his own brain had decided to play devil's advocate.

"Yeah," Will said. He leaned over, clicked the light off, and then rolled back over, staring up at the shadowed ceiling. It was easier than looking back over at Enzo, who no doubt resembled some kind of Renaissance masterpiece, with the dark carving out the hollows of his face.

"Well." Enzo let out a breath. "I think we did at least really convince everyone."

At what cost?

That question was still echoing through Will's mind as he fell asleep a few minutes later.

Chapter Thirteen

WILL WOKE UP WITH a mouthful of hair.

He was tucked around a slim, firm body and didn't ever want to open his eyes.

Mostly, because there was only one man who could be in his bed, and it was too good of a dream to shake off.

Then a moment later, before he could really sink into the warm lassitude of this feeling, his phone alarm blared, ruining everything.

Enzo wiggled out of his arms, and Will rolled over. Not sure what he should say. Should he apologize for spooning the hell out of him?

Well, it had probably been inevitable.

If they ended up in the same bed together, they were going to end up touching.

Will finally leaned over and turned off his alarm.

"Good morning," Enzo said in what sounded like a deliberately cheery voice. "Sleep well?"

"Really good, actually," Will said. "You?"

"Great," Enzo said, but Will wasn't quite sure he believed him.

"I was thinking, I've got to get home. Shower. Change for painting work. So I thought I'd do a big walk of shame," Enzo said.

Will risked a glance at him. His hair was mussed. From sleep. Maybe from Will's hands. Nobody would ever be able to say for sure.

"Okay," Will said.

"But I'll see you later?" Enzo said, and there was a hopeful light in his eyes as he looked at Will that looked completely genuine.

"Yeah, I'm sure," Will said.

He was always a little slow to wake up in the mornings, and waking up with his arms wrapped around Enzo meant he was even slower today.

"Alright," Enzo said cheerily, and a minute later he was gone.

Leaving Will staring at the door.

Thinking that there was no way Enzo hadn't just made his walk of shame but his escape.

You can't blame him for that. Not after what kind of torture you put both of you through.

Still, despite that, despite all the frustration coursing through him, he had things he *had* to do.

It helped, to go through his regular routine. Stretch. Ab work. Shower. He considered grabbing breakfast from Joy, but instead he skirted past the dining room and headed out, thinking he'd grab coffee and a pastry at Oliver's. He couldn't face the innkeeper, not yet, not after last night was still so fresh in his mind.

God, he'd gone to the door in just a sheet, because he and Enzo had been having fake sex way too loudly.

But when he opened the door to Sweetie Pie's, he was both surprised and not surprised to see Enzo there, in a paint-splattered tank that had once been white, and a pair of navy athletic shorts that hugged his ass and thighs in the best possible way.

"Oh, it's you," Enzo said, turning when Rocco gestured behind him.

"Hey," Will said awkwardly.

And then, making it worse, there was Giana too, beaming at the pair of them like they'd just invented sex.

"Good morning," he mumbled.

"Must be a *very* good morning," Rocco teased.

Will flushed, unable to keep it from rising up his cheeks.

"It was," Enzo said, wrapping his arm around Will's waist, beaming up at him. Because of course they couldn't stop playing now. And really how was this any worse than him going to the door with only a sheet wrapped around his waist?

Will inwardly groaned but leaned into Enzo's touch anyway.

He *wanted* to.

"Did you two have a nice date last night?" Giana asked.

"Very," Will said, as Enzo nodded, adding, "Oliver and Luca set an excellent table."

"Well," Giana said brightly, "you can tell them yourself."

And sure enough there was Oliver coming out of the back, Luca trailing behind him, chatting in low voices about a supplier.

"Oh, hey, you two are here. I didn't realize," Luca said, giving the pair of them one of his nicer smiles.

"If you'd believe it, they didn't even come in together," Rocco said dryly.

"I'd believe it," Giana said loyally.

"Well, I gotta take off actually," Luca said. "I'm at the deli this morning."

Oliver gave his husband a soft smile as he leaned in, brushing a quick kiss across his mouth. "See you later, honey," he said.

Next to Will, Giana made a sweet cooing noise.

After Luca had left, the door shutting behind him, Rocco turned to Will. "What can I get for you?"

Will ordered his coffee and a muffin as Enzo stood next to him, talking to his mom and sipping his own coffee.

When Rocco handed him his own, there was no reason to stick around. And in fact, he couldn't, not really.

"Hey, I got to take off, too. I've got a long list of prep to do today," he told Enzo.

"Oh, okay," Enzo said. "I'm gonna stick around a bit longer. Talk to Oliver about something. But I'm sure I'll see you later."

Will nodded and turned to leave, but before he could, Giana made an affronted squawk.

"That's all?" she said. "Luca *kissed* his partner."

"Maybe Will's not into PDA," Enzo said, frowning.

"That sure didn't seem to be the case last night," Giana said knowingly.

Great. Will went bright red again. Naturally, Joy had told Giana about all that.

"I . . .uh . . ." Will stammered, and then he chanced a look at Enzo.

He might be dressed in his oldest work clothes, hair frizzing in the humidity already, a speck of milk foam on his upper lip, but he'd never looked more kissable than he did right now.

So Will just did it. Leaned in. Brushed a kiss across Enzo's mouth, and before he could overthink or freak out or even worse, *see* Enzo's expression, turned and walked out.

He could hear Giana behind him, sounding excited and probably counting down the days before one of them was going to get down on one knee, but he didn't have to be *there* for it.

Five minutes later, he unlocked the front door of Cherry's, but didn't bother to re-lock it behind him. Kate would be along soon, and they'd be open in a few hours anyway. Besides, if anyone came by wanting ice cream at nine in the morning, Will wasn't going to turn them away.

But even as he got out ingredients for brownies and cookies, he was thinking about the kiss.

Wishing he'd stuck around. Not only to see Enzo's face, but to kiss him a lot more. Because he'd probably never get the chance again, and that particular fact sucked.

Even a single brush of his lips against Enzo's had lit him up inside in a way he couldn't remember a kiss ever doing before.

We could have something special. If he lived here. If he didn't feel the opposite way I do about this town.

He was midway through mixing up his brownie batter when he heard footsteps. Assuming it was Kate, he called out, "Back here, in the prep kitchen!"

"You kissed me."

Will looked up in surprise.

It was definitely not Kate standing there, breathing hard, like Enzo had actually *jogged* over from Sweetie Pie's in the morning heat.

"I did." There was nothing else Will could do but own it.

"You said you didn't want to. Not for . . .not for something fake." Enzo gestured around. "Not for my *mother*'s benefit."

"I didn't. I just . . ." Why had he done it? It had been easier, probably, but they could have brushed Giana off.

He'd done it because he was tired of *not* doing it.

Last night, and then this morning, had pushed him past the edge.

"I didn't want it to be like that," Enzo said, prowling closer, expression dead serious, his eyes intent on Will's face.

His hand, gripping its spatula, deep in the brownie batter, froze. "You didn't?"

"I wanted it to be real. Like this."

That was all the warning Will got before Enzo was cupping his cheeks with his palms and he was kissing him.

Really kissing him. Lips strong and fierce on his own, tongue sneaking in his mouth, a pleasurable assault that Will had never welcomed so much in his whole goddamned life.

He groaned in the back of his throat and let the spatula fall right into the batter. He could clean it off later. He couldn't kiss Enzo later. Not like this anyway. He wrapped one arm around Enzo's waist and dragged him closer, until every inch of that delicious body was pressed against his own.

"God," Enzo gasped as he came up for air, "you smell like *chocolate*."

"Surprised it's not you, with those eyes," Will murmured, and that was all it took for them to be kissing again, over and over, mouths sliding wetly, perfectly against each other. He lost himself in the fog of

Enzo's passion, eating every bit of it up, one kiss sliding into another and another until he didn't care about anything else.

This was how he'd always imagined it would be between them.

From the first moment, when he'd walked around the side of his building and seen this way-too-hot guy painting on it. When Enzo had turned around and given him that searing, approving look.

And a hundred times after that.

A thousand.

A throat cleared behind them.

But Will didn't want to let Enzo go. He only lifted his mouth off his for a second. Keeping it a breath away.

"Hi, boss," Kate said, sounding amused. "And hi, boss's hot hookup."

"Maybe we should've been doing that all along, if we wanted to prove it was real," Enzo murmured.

"Come on," Will said and took him by the hand and tugged him towards his office. It was just big enough for him to shut the door behind them. Enzo hopped up on the desk and dragged Will in between his legs, covering his mouth with his own again.

It would be so easy to get lost in his mouth. Lost in the heat between them.

Will wanted to. But actually, he hadn't brought them in here to do this.

They *needed* to talk about this. As much as he didn't want to.

As much as he was afraid this wouldn't change anything—and everything at the same time.

"We should talk about this." Enzo was surprisingly the one to say this, after he pulled back a fraction.

His lips were red and wet from Will's mouth and he was mesmerized by watching them move . . .but that was *not* the point of taking Enzo in here. It was to *actually* talk.

"I get it," Enzo continued, a self-deprecating chuckle escaping him. "I've got about a hundred moments where I *wanted* to kiss you and I didn't to make up for."

"Really?" Will had known it wasn't just him yearning, but he hadn't realized Enzo was perhaps in just as deep as Will himself.

"Oh, yeah," Enzo said. He leaned in and his lips brushed Will's again. "That's what I wanted to do this morning. Why do you think I ran away so fast? I wanted it so goddamn bad I thought I'd give in for sure."

"I wanted you to," Will confessed. "But then I thought . . ."

Enzo nodded solemnly. "Yeah, I know. This isn't . . .it's not a hot hookup, not like Kate said. I mean, I hope it's *also* that. If I have to think about you jerking off in the bathroom alone one more time, I'm going to go insane."

"It's been less than twenty-four hours since I did that," Will pointed out.

"Still," Enzo said, grinning. "But it's not that for me. Not *just* that. I know I don't live here, and I don't know if I'll *ever* want to live here. But if you're here, I know I'm going to be spending a lot more time here."

Will was floored. "Are you serious?"

Enzo nodded. "I realized, I've never come home and spent so much time here and *not* wanted to ditch this town already. That's because of you."

"But I don't want you to . . .*stay* here because of me."

Enzo reached up and cupped his cheek. Much as he'd done right before he'd laid that hot-as-hell kiss on him earlier. "I'm definitely not staying *staying*. I still work. I'm still gonna do that. I wish I could tell how it's gonna work but I do know this. I'll never regret spending more time here in Indigo Bay if it means spending more time with *you*."

It wasn't a perfect speech. It wasn't out of a movie, or designed to pull at every one of Will's heartstrings and convince him that the white picket fence was in their joint future—but it *was* real. And that was the most important thing.

What else was Will supposed to do after a speech like that, with Enzo staring earnestly up at him, but kiss him again?

"I wish we'd done this last night instead," Will murmured as he dipped his head low, capturing Enzo's mouth. They kissed for a moment, for probably a whole minute, before he reluctantly stepped back. "I wish we didn't have to work today."

Enzo tried to reel him back in with a foot tucked around his thigh.

"Well, *I* can play hooky," Enzo teased. "I'm actually ahead of where I'm supposed to be. I don't think I've ever been so dedicated. I was kinda obsessed with hanging around here. Can't imagine why . . ."

Will laughed. "Nope. No clue."

"What are you doing after work?" Enzo asked, hope lighting up his face.

Will's pulse accelerated as he leaned in. Enzo didn't have to do anything to cause it other than merely *exist*. "I don't know," he said, intoxicated by the look of pure desire in Enzo's dark eyes. "I was kinda hoping I'd be doing *you*."

"Oh, I like you," Enzo breathed out, and there was fire in his gaze now. Searing Will all over.

"Yeah? You wanna show me later just how much?"

Enzo nodded. "It's a date."

"Without a date?"

"I think we've been on enough dates without any of the benefits," Enzo pointed out wryly.

"Exactly," Will said. He took a step away and another. Before the thought of those benefits tempted him into kissing Enzo again. "Sadly, I actually *do* have to work."

"And I should too." Enzo sounded as reluctant as Will felt.

Will tried to look anywhere but at Enzo, flush high on his cheekbones, erection still visible in those worn shorts riding high on his muscular thighs.

Because if he didn't, he wasn't going to be able to walk away. He definitely wasn't going to be able to walk away without his own matching erection.

"You good?" Enzo asked, his voice teasing. He slid off the desk. The only problem was even though he was on solid ground now, Will was always going to picture him like that, an irresistible vision.

"I'm not *good*, but I'll manage," Will said honestly.

Enzo laughed again, and he was rapidly returning to that nearly irresistible temptation as he straightened his clothes and fixed his hair.

Hair Will knew he'd been the one to mess up.

Turning towards the door, Will pictured a whole lot of unsexy things, and he was nearly there, when Enzo said, "One sec."

Will should've protested, but how could he, when Enzo's mouth was already on his, a brief but hot kiss, Will's lips still tingling even as he pulled away.

"One more for the road," Enzo said seriously, and Will groaned a little.

"I'll meet you at the Inn, at what . . .ten?" Enzo questioned as Will reached out and latched onto the door handle like if it was solid and real under his fingers, then maybe he wouldn't reach for Enzo, instead.

Will nodded and opened the door. They were safe now. Mostly. "Ten sounds good."

"See you then," Enzo said with an extra spicy smile as he sauntered past Will.

When Will finally returned to the kitchen and to Kate, his spatula was nearly entirely drowned in brownie batter.

She gave him a speculative look. "Christen your office?" she asked.

Will shook his head. "Of course not," he said firmly. "We just . . .needed to . . .uh . . .*talk*. Privately."

Kate chuckled under her breath. "Yeah, I'm sure that's what you were doing. *Talking*."

"Hey," Will said, both embarrassed and smarting from the fact that his employee, his *manager*, thought he'd just fucked off to screw in his office. He wasn't that kind of boss. He wasn't that kind of business owner.

"Yeah?"

"I wouldn't. I won't. I *don't*," Will told her firmly. "Cherry's means a lot to me. This thing with Enzo is . . ." *Intoxicating.* "New and exciting, but Cherry's is still my priority. Always."

Kate looked over at him, respect in her expression. "I didn't mean to . . .you know what I meant." She sighed. "Sorry. I really didn't think you'd be unprofessional. But the way you were wrapped around each other when I came in . . .it was like nothing else existed."

Nothing else did *exist.*

"I . . .well, uh . . .like I said. It's pretty new." Will bashfully rubbed his neck. Couldn't tell Kate just how new it was. They were already supposed to have been doing this for nearly two weeks.

"Right," she said knowingly.

He dug his spatula out of the batter and ignored how Kate laughed when he tried to scrape it off before taking it over to the sink to rinse.

Gave himself a little pep talk while he was at it.

You can think about the way Enzo felt like and tasted like and looked like, but you gotta get some work done too. It can't happen again, if you don't.

What he *couldn't* think about was how Enzo was just outside. Only a few steps away.

He lasted all the way through prep. He got the baking done by the skin of his teeth. Helped Kate open. Make more ice cream. He ate lunch, mechanically shoving crackers into the container of chicken salad he kept in the walk-in for days he didn't want to go out.

The difference today was that he *desperately* wanted to go out. To see what Enzo was doing. To just plain *see* Enzo. But he resisted.

All the way past lunch, to the lull of the afternoon.

Kate didn't tell him to take a break. But after reviewing a handful of resumes for his new part-time employee and updating Cherry's website with the new flavors of the week, he finally gave in.

Ducked outside, ignoring Kate's knowing glance.

It was unsurprisingly hot, sun shining in his eyes as he rounded the corner.

Enzo was there, halfway up the wall, lounging on the scaffolding like the height didn't bother him one bit, sucking down a water bottle with force.

He'd shoved a hat on his curls and taken off his shirt, his back a long tanned line, smooth and perfect.

Will swallowed hard.

Wanted to lick the sweat up his spine.

His cock was a hard, aching weight in his jeans as he stared, like a total creeper.

He nearly said something, but then, as he watched, Enzo plucked a paintbrush out of the back pocket of his jeans and dipped it into the can at his feet and then began to paint.

He was creating the outcropping, the high point Eliza stood on, Enzo realized, as he dabbed and brushed, something blooming out of nothing—out of just his imagination.

Will didn't know how long he stood there, mesmerized, as Enzo unleashed his unbelievable skill and vision onto his wall.

He was beginning to understand why Enzo had been so pissed off when Will had thought, even for a minute, that he was vandalizing his building with graffiti that was rough, uncreative, without purpose. Nothing like what Enzo was really capable of.

He'd known that Enzo was going to keep doing mural painting. It was his calling and his *job*, so of course he would. He'd go on traveling around, to different cities, gracing them with his talent. But now he really understood. Enzo was special. His creations were special. It would've been an utter shame for him to be trapped here in Indigo Bay.

Will wanted him, but he wanted him like *this*. Being the best version of himself.

How was that going to work?

He lived here and Enzo didn't?

That didn't sound so great, but then the alternative, Will reminded himself, was worse: no Enzo at all.

Enzo had said he didn't know how it was going to work, and Will would just have to trust him.

He was so lost to the work he didn't even notice Will watching him, and finally, when the bright heat of the sun got to him, Will turned and walked back inside.

It's going to work out; it has to. It can't feel like this and not work out.

But Will knew that life didn't, sometimes.

By the time Enzo got home, showered the sweat of the day off, and then took off for the Inn again, he was buzzing with anticipation and exhilaration.

Only by pouring himself into the work today, pushing himself hard into a focused zone, had he been able to resist the urge to beg Will to play hooky with him. To return to the bed they'd just left.

He didn't know where his mother was—and didn't really want to be thinking about her right now—but she wasn't on the front porch like she'd been last night, so he headed straight into the Inn and up the staircase.

The point this time wasn't necessarily to be seen, though Enzo wasn't *against* being seen.

He was just too focused to want to be bothered with anybody else right now.

There was just Will. *Only* Will.

Breathless from his jog up the stairs, he paused in front of Will's door and knocked.

Like he'd been waiting, Will opened it on the first knock and immediately took Enzo's arm, tugging him in.

He was in a white T-shirt and blue shorts, hugging all those rippling muscles Enzo wanted to explore more closely. His mouth watered.

Enzo had dressed relatively simply too. T-shirt. Shorts. Easy to remove, though he wasn't exactly proud that the thought had crossed his mind more than once as he'd been getting dressed.

For a second, Will stared at him, eyes flicking to his mouth, and they didn't say anything.

Enzo swallowed hard. "Hey," he said. Suddenly feeling awkward and a little stupid. Should he have not been so goddamned eager?

Then Will bent towards him, his mouth reaching for his, and it was all over.

They both went up like dry kindling, stumbling to the edge of the bed, lips fused together, hands everywhere. Then Will's fingers found the hem of his shirt and tugged it up, over his head.

Enzo did the same, groaning as he finally got to touch Will's bare chest, follow every smooth line of muscle he'd been dreaming about seeing up close and personal.

"God, you're so hot," Enzo murmured against his lips.

"That's you, Honey Bunny," Will said, his voice rough and desperate as he flipped them. He pressed Enzo to the edge and then stepped between his legs again. The bed was lower than the desk had been earlier today and so the angle wasn't quite as extraordinary, but it was still damn good. It was still way too easy for Enzo to drag him in with his legs, flicking off his shoes as he wound himself around his man.

Will's hands found their way into his hair, tangling through the curls, soothing and gripping all at the same time, pinging Enzo with pleasure and pain until he was dizzy with it.

"That good?" Will asked, one hand dropping to Enzo's shoulder and then farther down to his waist, tracing up and down his back.

Enzo kissed him back harder, answering without words just how much he liked it.

Telling him just how much more he wanted.

Will's shoulders were big and broad, easy for Enzo to grip. Surprisingly soft too, despite how gorgeously ripped he was. It seemed impossible this was a man who made ice cream for a living, but then he lifted Enzo right up, like he weighed *nothing* and put him farther back on the bed, crawling over him like a predator who'd just discovered a particularly tasty bit of prey he wanted to snack on.

"Want you," Enzo groaned, as Will's mouth slid from his, down lower, to his neck, and then lower still. Coasting down his chest, licking over a nipple, and then finding the trail of dark hair that led to his shorts.

"Yeah?" Will's fingertips grazed his cock, hard and aching, and Enzo arched up underneath him.

"God, more, *more*," Enzo begged. He already felt mindless with pleasure, desperate for Will's big, competent hands to take him and then drive him wild with it.

Will tugged down his shorts, Enzo exhaling short and sharp as he leaned down, warm breath ghosting over where he wanted his mouth the most.

There was no room—no place whatsoever—for insecurity, because Enzo was so aroused from the thought that this was *finally* about to happen. Then there was the hot look Will shot him from his baby blues as he glanced up at Enzo, taking in all of him now that he was naked.

"Been thinking about this. Ever since we got naked on the beach, and I thought, if I ever see you like this again, I'd get to touch." Will did now, stroking a fingertip up and down Enzo's thigh, making him shiver with it.

"Thought about touching you too." Enzo paused. "A lot. A *lot*."

Will laughed.

There *wasn't* any room for awkwardness or hesitation, because they'd felt the same. Even back then.

Before then, *way* before then, if Enzo was being totally honest.

"You wanna touch me, too?" Will asked, licking his lips.

God, Enzo wanted those lips on his cock. Wrapped *around* his cock.

But yeah, he was all about reciprocation. Definitely. You didn't get a guy that looked like Will in your bed and not spend a *lot* of time fantasizing about it.

Will looked at him, the corner of his mouth quirking up. "You thinking what I'm thinking?" he asked.

And Enzo was hardly going to argue.

"Oh yeah, Stud Muffin. Let's do it."

Will slid off him, eyes never leaving Enzo's body as he shed his own clothes, revealing the rest of his gorgeous tan, turning the pale color of vanilla as he pulled down his boxer briefs.

His cock was big and hard, and he reached down, groaning as he stroked himself.

"That's mine," Enzo said, leaning over and smacking his hand away. He wiggled closer and wrapped his hand around. Will gasped but then Enzo removed his hand.

He scooted back on the bed, motioning to Will to come closer. "Come on, baby," he crooned. "Come over here and make me feel good. While I make *you* feel good."

"Don't have to tell me twice," Will said and climbed back on the bed. A moment later, he was caging Enzo again, but this time, it wasn't Will's mouth that Enzo lifted his mouth to.

His cock tasted even better than it looked. Enzo loved how it twitched against his tongue, loved the noises Will was making as he lowered his own head.

And then they were just as muffled as Enzo's own moans as Will put his gorgeous mouth to good use.

Blowjobs were usually pretty goddamned amazing, but like this, pleasure circling pleasure, giving and taking, they were even better. Enzo nipped his balls and then stroked them with his fingertips.

Opened his legs wider when Will went deeper, sucking him hard, and slid a finger down, grazing his hole.

Enzo made a garbled noise as he sank just the tip in, and Will lifted his head. "Like that, do you?"

Pleasure was fizzy in his veins, the intoxicating brew making him giddy as he pushed Will, sucking him harder, playing insistently with his balls, angling his head at just the right angle so Will could sink practically to his throat.

"Jesus God," Will cried out as he licked the tip of Enzo's cock, a whole finger deep in his ass now.

Then he found the spot that lit Enzo up, and it only took a few strokes before he was nearly choking around Will's cock, coming like a freight train as Will strung it out, finger massaging his prostate with every pulse of his orgasm.

Will was still hard against his tongue as he came down.

He made a disappointed sound as Will lifted himself off, tongue flicking out to clean his lips from Enzo's come.

Enzo heard how rough his voice was already when he asked, "You wanna fuck my face, baby?"

Will groaned in approval, and Enzo sank to his knees next to the bed, hungrily guiding Will's cock back into his mouth. It was easier like this, less of a difficult angle, and he could really work all the spots that seemed to make Will loud and appreciative.

And then somehow it became a game. Just like before, except this was real.

How loud could he make Will?

Could he make him scream?

Then Will gripped his hair, with that intoxicating grip—soft but hard; gentle but insistent—and took over, Enzo slicking his tongue along the underside as Will thrust.

"God, baby, I'm so close," Will babbled loudly.

Enzo wanted him louder.

Wanted to wake up the whole goddamn Inn again.

Slipped his thumb up, right behind his balls, and the moment he touched Will's hole, his hips stuttered, and Enzo knew he had him.

Half a dozen unsteady thrusts later, Enzo was wiggling a second finger along his thumb, and Will shouted, coming with long, hot pulses down his throat.

"My God," Will said, sounding shattered as he collapsed onto the bed, knees shaky.

"Good?" Enzo sounded like he'd been sucking cock. But probably the whole Inn had a decent idea what they'd been up to at least tonight—if not last night—so it was hardly time for him to get embarrassed about it.

"The best. Oh my God," Will repeated, a glazed look of contentment on his handsome face.

Enzo lifted himself up and tucked himself in, right under Will's arm.

They were allowed to cuddle now. In fact, it was practically encouraged.

For a long minute and then another, they lay there in happy satisfaction. Quiet. Nothing, Enzo thought, needed to be said.

But then there was a knock on the door.

Will groaned. He glanced over at Enzo. "I think next time we've got to go to your place."

Laughing, Enzo rolled over and tucked himself under the sheet as Will grabbed his boxer briefs and shoved them on, walking on still-unsteady legs to the door.

And sure enough, Enzo could see Joy, her mouth in a thin, unhappy line, on the other side.

"Will, *really*," she said.

"I'd apologize, but I'm not really sorry," Will said, and Enzo could tell from his voice that he was smiling.

Joy shook her head, rolling her eyes. "Of course you're not. Get familiar with Enzo's place, alright? I know he has one. And it's thankfully far from any neighbors who could complain."

"Got it," Will said and closed the door.

A second later he returned to the bed, tugging Enzo over so he was lying half on his chest. "You totally did that on purpose," he said a minute later, not sounding particularly upset.

"Make you loud? I don't know, I could absolutely suck your cock less brilliantly next time, if you want to be quieter," Enzo teased.

Will laughed again, and a part of his heart that he thought had always been cold, always been untouched, throbbed.

It wasn't enough that the sex had been *just* as good as it had promised to be.

It had been fun too. They could laugh about it. He'd never had so much fun with another guy before. Never been quite so unworried about it all.

"Don't you dare," Will said drowsily. "You spending the night again?"

"I don't want to be anywhere else," Enzo said, and it was the truth.

Chapter Fourteen

"You're not too worried about the walk of shame?" Will asked as Enzo returned from the bathroom a few minutes later and stretched out next to him.

"I did it this morning, didn't I?" Enzo shot him a smoldering look from under thick dark lashes. "Besides, walk of shame implies *shame*, and I don't have an ounce of shame. I'd do that again."

"Right now? Already?" Will squawked. And okay, so he felt a pulse of arousal at Enzo's words, surprising considering how little time had passed since he'd come his brains out.

Enzo laughed. "Oh, baby, to be twenty again."

"How old *are* you?" Will wondered.

Enzo turned to him, mischief twinkling in his eyes. "How old do you *think* I am?"

"I . . .uh . . ." Will hesitated awkwardly.

Reaching out, Enzo stroked his arm. "It's alright," he said, letting him off the hook. "I'm twenty-seven."

"Twenty-nine."

"Oh, I do like an older man," Enzo said. "But seriously, you're twenty-nine, and your parents still think you're at their beck and call?"

Will sighed. Flopped onto his back. "I know. Why do you think I came here? It wasn't just working for them or for their business. It was kinda what you had with your mom. They think they get to call the shots in *my* life, and they're annoyed when they can't. It's unfair."

"Well, I wish I could give you advice, but I only have two tactics: avoidance and apparently faking orgasms loudly in front of the town."

Will knew that Enzo had been trying to make him smile, and it had worked. "So you stay away from Indigo Bay and when you do come here . . ."

"I convince a very good-looking man to fake orgasms with me in an attempt to distract Giana enough that she'll forget all the ways I've disappointed her?" Enzo's voice was wry.

"Hey, the faking orgasms idea was mine," Will said, nudging.

"Not your most brilliant work." Enzo slipped closer and then he was only a breath away. Will felt the buzz building under his skin again. The wanting overwhelming everything else. "'Cause we could've been doing this for *real*."

Enzo kissed him sweetly. But it didn't matter how soft it was, it still fired him up. He told himself it was just that he was finally getting a taste of him, but deep down, he knew it was more than that.

It started sweet, but it didn't stay sweet. Enzo made a little groaning noise in the back of his throat, and it flamed the rest of Will's desire to life, and he tugged Enzo over, until he was draped across him.

"Maybe we *are* twenty again," Enzo mused, panting a little as he pulled his mouth from Will's, leaning against him, forehead to forehead.

"I feel twenty again." It was probably too much to say, but Will added, "*You* make me feel twenty again."

"I didn't feel like this even when I was twenty. Back then I thought I was in love with Oliver. And it sure wasn't like this."

Will felt a pulse of jealousy, but how could it last when Enzo was the one here with him now, the one who'd *run* to Cherry's, just so he could kiss him for real?

And Enzo had said it himself. It hadn't been like this.

As for Will, he didn't think he'd ever felt like this, not in all his twenty-nine years.

They were in new, uncharted territory. Both of them.

But it was easier to pull Enzo even closer and kiss him harder, lose himself and all his nagging worries about how was this going to *work*, to the passion that flared between them.

Less than five minutes later, Enzo was naked and on top of him, one beautiful hand wrapped around their hard cocks, arching as Will dug his fingertips into his ass, encouraging him.

"Fuck," Enzo groaned as he leaned in, sucking Will's bottom lip into his mouth, and Will was lost to little burst of pleasure-pain, to intoxicating slide of his cock through Enzo's fist, bumping up against his toned stomach.

Entranced by the vision of his precome smeared across Enzo's skin. Like he could mark him and *keep* him.

Enzo squeezed harder, flicking his wrist, and pleasure spiked.

"Oh yeah, that's good," Will panted. "Give me more, baby."

Will thought he might protest, draw it out longer, make it even hotter, even as Will's skin slicked with sweat. But he didn't, just as lost to it as Will was. Especially when Will tucked a finger between his ass cheeks, sliding it and pressing right into his hole, still a bit loose from earlier.

Enzo moaned and exploded, stripes of come painting Will's chest.

"Next time," he said, still panting as he came down from his orgasm, "I'm riding you."

And that was all it took for Will to tip over the edge, his own orgasm painting up Enzo's chest.

Enzo didn't seem particularly concerned about the mess though, because he collapsed onto Will, breathing heavily. "I think," he slurred, "that we're gonna *wish* we were twenty again."

Will shook his head. He didn't want to be any other age than the one he was right now. "I'm happy right here. Never been happier."

"Me neither," Enzo murmured, fingers digging into Will's shoulder. Like he'd fight to hang on to him. To never let him go.

Maybe that was the answer to the question Will didn't know how to ask.

They'd just have to hold on to each other.

Enzo knew he should be exhausted after last night's sex marathon, but instead he was the opposite. He was not only full of energy but wired, like he'd been plugged into the nearest electrical socket. Lit up from within with a hundred ideas, a *thousand*. He was painting as fast as he felt comfortable with, sloppier than he'd normally go, and his teachers back in San Francisco would have cautioned him, but Enzo thought they'd understand. Sometimes you were gripped by inspiration and you had to indulge it, not push it away.

He'd gone to work the same way he always did, but the moment he'd turned the corner, lugging the day's supplies, and seen his work in progress, it had started, and it hadn't let up in hours.

He set his brush down and stretched his hand, trying to keep it from cramping. Picked up the water bottle he'd brought up the scaffolding with him and sucked half it down, realizing as the water hit his tongue that it was lukewarm and no longer cold

Turning, Enzo glanced at the sun and from its position, he knew he'd been at this hours, with no break. He really *should* take one. At that thought, his stomach grumbled, and so, reluctantly, he headed down the ladder next to the scaffolding he'd set up.

On the ground he found more water and a little sticky note with a heart drawn on it and a "W."

His heartbeat accelerated, and for a minute, he seriously considered going into Cherry's and finding Will.

But no. You're gonna take a real break. Get cool somewhere. Get something to eat. Drink a lot of water.

If he sought out Will, he'd probably hit a few of those, but not all of them.

Besides, he'd made himself a promise that he wouldn't bother Will when he was working, just like Will had promised that he wouldn't bother *Enzo* when he was working.

Normally Enzo would've liked the bothering. Not today, probably, but any other day.

He craned his neck back and took in his work from the morning—well, it was clearly past morning, but his work of the last few hours. There was the cliff, perhaps bigger and with a hair more dramatic flair than real life, and Eliza's figure on top of it, her hair swirling around her.

But it was her face that caught him and held him. Her expression.

The naked yearning and the undeniable love written across it. It was more than just hope, because Eliza hadn't just hoped that Nathaniel would return to her. She'd believed.

He'd intended to capture as much as he could in her look as she stared out across the water.

Taking another swallow of warm water, Enzo decided he'd accomplished what he'd set out to do. But he couldn't deny, either, that this growing thing with Will and all his growing *feelings* had given him new perspective. He'd poured those into every brushstroke, wanting it to be good not only for him and for the town, but for Will. This was Will's building, his own legacy that he was creating, one delicious sundae and milkshake at a time, and Enzo wanted to do it justice.

Give him something concrete, when Enzo wasn't here. A reminder that he was more than just his parents' lackey.

Evidence that he was *Will*, and someone out there cared about him very much. The kind of way Eliza had cared about Nathaniel.

Except she was in love with him.

Enzo's fingers slipped on the bottle's condensation and he nearly dropped it.

He told himself it was just a figure of speech. It was just a way he'd used to connect to the story he was telling.

But the thought followed him anyway, down the street, to the deli.

Rocco was leaning against the front counter, a small laptop in front of him. He glanced up when the bell on the front door rang and Enzo walked in.

Above him was the menu board Enzo had painted when he was only nineteen. An art collector had come in last year and offered Giana and Luca twenty thousand dollars for it, and his mom had just laughed at him.

He'd felt a puff of undeniable pride at that. Both at the offer, and the rejection.

"Hey," Rocco said as he approached. "You look . . ." His gaze swept up and down Enzo's form. "You been working *all* day?"

Enzo glanced down at himself. Not just his tank, but his skin was generously flecked with paint and now that he was in the air-conditioning, he could feel just how damp with sweat he was. Well, there was something to be said for the fact this was his family's deli. They weren't exactly going to refuse him service. Maybe it was good he'd avoided Cherry's. Of course, it wasn't like Will had seemed particularly averse to the way he got when he was working.

"Yeah," he said. "And I'm starving."

"Whatcha want?" Rocco asked.

Enzo ordered. A big Italian chopped salad *and* a meatball sandwich.

"I've got one of Luca's Gatorades in the walk-in in the back," Rocco said. "You want me to steal it for you?"

"You think he'd mind?"

Rocco shot him a frank look. "No. Not if he saw you like this."

"Like what?" Enzo frowned.

But instead of answering, Rocco just stepped through the doorway to the back and a few moments later, he returned, carrying a neon green bottle of Gatorade. He handed it over and gave Enzo another one of those frank looks, along with a wave that indicated he should go to the dining room.

"Go wash up and sit down. I'll bring it out to you."

Enzo sighed. "Fine."

And okay, yes, now that he'd stopped painting and wasn't under the burning hot sun, the exhaustion was hitting him—along with a bit of shakiness that he had a feeling was low blood sugar.

He'd only grabbed a coffee and a danish on his way out of the Inn this morning and that really wasn't enough for the kind of work he'd put in today.

Of course when he'd headed to the mural this morning, he hadn't known that he'd do *this* much work. He'd had a loose plan to work on Eliza, but he hadn't really anticipated nearly finishing with her. There'd be some final details, but that would be at the end, when he'd go over the entire mural.

His face was more drawn than he'd realized, a white cast under his tan, and he knew he'd need to thank Rocco when he brought out his food out.

After washing up, he sat in the corner, his favorite table since forever, and a few minutes later, Rocco brought the food over, setting it front of him, along with another bottle of water.

"There's more where that came from, too," Rocco said. "Though you're already looking better. You were white as a sheet before, all clammy looking."

"Oh. Well. I guess I overdid it, a little," Enzo admitted. "Didn't realize it, until I looked in the mirror."

"Good. At the risk of sounding just like Giana, you gotta take better care of yourself when you're out there in the heat, painting."

"I will," Enzo promised, digging into the chopped salad. It was cool against his tongue, spicy and bursting with herbaceous flavor.

"I got an email today," Rocco said casually as Enzo continued to shovel salad into his face.

"Yeah?" he asked between bites.

"You know I'd been putting out feelers to buy a place. In a small town. Not *this* small town." Rocco shot him one of the patented Moretti smiles. "I love our cousin but I couldn't live with him looking over my shoulder the rest of my life."

Enzo considered telling Rocco that it wouldn't be *so* bad, but then he reconsidered. For Rocco it probably would be tougher, because he wanted to run a coffee shop. First, it was way too similar to Oliver's concept, and second, because it was food related, Luca would be unable to help himself.

He'd just want to help, and then he'd help Rocco right along into insanity.

"I get that," Enzo said.

"Well, yeah, there's a reason you don't live here, though . . ." Rocco gave him a sly look. "Maybe you'll be spending more time here in the future. Because of a certain ice cream guy . . ."

"Yeah," Enzo said. Because Rocco's insinuation wasn't untrue now. Not now, anyway.

"Anyway, I've been talking to some people. Hoping to find something close-ish. That's *like* here, but not here, you know? And I got an email today. Some ladies want to sell their coffee shop."

"Where's it at?" Enzo asked.

"Town in Illinois, outside Chicago. Get this," Rocco said, leaning forward, excitement gleaming in his dark eyes that felt so much like a mirror of Enzo's own, "it's a *Christmas themed town.* It's even named Christmas Falls. They do a big ass festival celebration there every year."

"Do you even like the holidays?" Enzo asked, a little skeptical. That seemed like a *lot* of Christmas.

"Well, yeah. Who doesn't?" Rocco waved his hand, dismissing Enzo's concern. "Anyway, I figure I'm familiar with that whole festival vibe, since I've been here for the Sweethearts Festival the last two years."

"And they want to sell it to you?"

"Yep. They told me to make an offer." Rocco looked so excited, and Enzo was genuinely thrilled for him. The guy worked his ass off, at what felt like a hundred part-time jobs, to save money and to get as much experience as possible. He knew Oliver spent hours with him every week, teaching him every baking secret he knew.

"That's so great, man. I'm happy for you." Enzo finished his salad and moved onto the meatball sub, using the knife Rocco had provided to cut it in half, picking up one side. A glob of marinara dropped on his hand and he licked it up.

"They say they want someone with an affinity for the business. They said they heard of the Morettis all the way out there. Isn't that cool?"

"So cool." It wasn't that Enzo wasn't thrilled for his cousin. It was the reminder that he *wasn't* part of that Moretti tradition. He was different. Just different enough that he'd never felt like he belonged.

Everyone was nice enough about it, but that didn't mean it didn't still suck.

"Luca said he'd look at the offer. Let me know his thoughts, but I'm gonna be honest. I want this." Rocco leaned over, dark eyes gleaming. "They got a little kitchen in the back—not as big as Oliver's of course, because they're more of a coffee shop than a bakery, and not nearly the size of Will's—but I'll be able to do a bit of baking. Maybe expand, in a few seasons. Make all the pastries in-house. Maybe add paninis and hot sandwiches. Soup. Salads."

"It sounds like the perfect spot for you. And the town's chill, yeah?"

Enzo would be remiss if he didn't ask. Some small towns, especially in the South and the Midwest, weren't. And he knew Rocco had been out of the closet, out-and-proud, since early high school.

He wouldn't want to go back in, just to own a business.

"Nah," Rocco said. "I did some research. It's friendly. Won't be a problem. Besides, the couple I'm buying it from? Two lesbian ladies."

"There you go." Enzo finished the first half of his sandwich, but before he picked up the other half, he swallowed down half the water. "It sounds like a perfect fit."

"Yeah." Rocco leaned back. "Kinda like you and Will."

Enzo rolled his eyes—even though it wasn't like he hadn't had that thought cross his mind more than once. "I'm only surprised it took you so long to drag the subject back around to him."

Rocco grinned. "That's 'cause I was so excited about the coffee shop I had to lead with that first."

"Of course."

"It's going good, then?" Rocco paused. "The other day, at the coffee shop, when he kissed you, you looked *floored*, then you ran out of there and forgot your muffin. And you know Oliver's muffins aren't very forgettable."

"They're . . .uh not. I just remembered something I had to do then," Enzo mumbled. He didn't think he'd even spat out an excuse before he'd gone running after Will.

"Your mom was a little worried you were upset with him."

Enzo knew a leading question when he heard it. He hummed under his breath as he finished the second half of his sandwich.

"I told her she was being paranoid," Rocco continued. "But I wondered."

"It's . . .it's fine. Everything's fine."

"So that wasn't your first kiss with him, then?"

Enzo didn't want to lie, but then he'd done it before, hadn't he? Out of necessity, not necessarily out of choice but . . .

"You were there, at our first date. What do *you* think?" It wasn't a lie. Of course it wasn't exactly the truth, either.

Rocco shot him a knowing look. "I think that was a farce. A total freaking farce. You weren't dating. But now . . .*now* I think you are."

"It's complicated." It wasn't, though. Not nearly as he'd convinced himself that it was, back then.

Of course that didn't mean it was simple, either. How could it be, when for the first time since coming back to Indigo Bay, he'd experienced that same ache that had always driven him away before?

He didn't want it to drive him away now. He wasn't going to let it. But that meant learning to live with it, too. If he'd been able to do that before, he'd have just *done* it.

But you're older. Wiser. You grew the fuck up. You can do this. If it means keeping Will.

"It would be," Rocco said calmly. "He lives here. You don't."

"I don't really live *anywhere*." It was true. He had some stuff in a storage unit in San Francisco, but otherwise, he traveled around from city to city, painting murals and building his reputation.

"True." Rocco gave him a speculative look. "So you're gonna change how you do things, huh? For him?"

He was booked a year out. There were breaks, of course, and during those he'd explored new places, visit Chiara and Ilaria, or even head down to LA and stay with Gabe and Ren for a few days. Occasionally, he'd even let his mother guilt him into coming here.

But now . . .well, what was stopping him from using Indigo Bay as his home base?

Nothing.

Except your own freaking sanity.

But how sane would he be if he didn't see Will again? If he came back to town and saw him sad and alone? Or even worse, if he saw him happy with someone else?

That was so much worse.

"For him. And . . ." Enzo trailed off. Realizing he was about to say, *for me, too*. Realized that it was actually true.

Rocco smiled, so knowingly, and patted him on the arm as he stood. "Told you he was hot."

Enzo scoffed at Rocco's back as he walked away.

Yeah, Will *was* hot. So hot it was a freaking miracle he hadn't kissed him on that first date. But it was so much more than Will being hot. That was what told him that no matter how tough it was to figure out how they were going to do this, he was worth it.

After finishing his lunch, Enzo took his time getting back to work.

Really, he'd already accomplished more than he'd intended to today, and he could admit the only reason he was headed back was to clean up a bit and to pop into Cherry's and see Will.

He skirted the edges of the sidewalks, keeping to the shade. When he made it to Cherry's, he ran a hand through his hair, gave it up for a lost cause, and stepped inside.

Will was at the counter helping someone—a mother with two young kids—but he glanced up and their eyes met. He tipped his head, indicating that Enzo could take a seat.

He did, sprawling out in the corner on the bench in one of the booths.

A few minutes and two ice cream cones and a confection that was coffee and ice cream blended up together that made the mother perk right up, Will made his way over to where Enzo sat.

"Hey," he said, reaching out and resting a hand on Enzo's shoulder.

There was a smear of chocolate on his arm, mirroring the paint streaking Enzo's, and not for the first time he thought, *in so many ways, we're so alike.*

"Hey." Enzo thought he could just sit here, basking in Will's gaze, in his touch, forever. They didn't even need to talk. He didn't need to say, *I worked my ass off today, but what kind of work it was*—because Will understood.

Every morning when he unlocked the door to Cherry's was like when Enzo picked up a brush.

"Thanks for the water," Enzo added. Because he *had* been out to see him, and Enzo had clearly been in too deep to even notice. He hoped Will wouldn't be pissed. He wouldn't be the first one to resent that sometimes Enzo lost himself in his art.

The warm look in his blue eyes told the whole story. He not only wasn't mad, he *understood.*

"You looked completely absorbed so I left you alone. But it was so hot I didn't want you to give yourself heat stroke . . ." Will trailed off.

"I was in a zone, for sure," Enzo agreed. "I got so much more done of Eliza than I anticipated. Sometimes you just *understand*, and it's a struggle to get the paint on the surface as fast as the ideas come."

Will smiled. "Well, she turned out incredible. Her face . . .I didn't think there'd be so much detail, so much *emotion*, in her, but you captured it, and well . . ." He flushed. "You know just how good you are."

"Yeah, but you're always free to tell me, baby," Enzo joked, nudging him with his shoulder. "It *is* a hot one, today. I'm probably done, except for some clean-up. But I stopped by to ask if you want to cool down with me later."

Will raised an eyebrow. "Is that what we're doing?"

It wasn't how Enzo would've described it either. But he'd been talking about something else. Well, *sort of* something else. "Skinny dipping. In the ocean. After you're off." He grinned. "Get your mind out of the gutter."

Will leaned down. "I can't," he admitted quietly, with a fire in his gaze. "Not after last night."

"Then come with me," Enzo said. But it was more, wasn't it? He was pleading. Nearly begging.

When was the last time he'd ever needed a man so much?

Never. That was when.

But he could sense Will hesitating. "It'll be late . . .I *want* to, but yeah it'll be late. It won't be a dusk swim, but a full night swim."

Sure, Enzo knew why he was saying it. Was it safe? Not exactly.

But taking the physical risk felt like nothing when he thought about the way he was risking his heart.

"But I'll have my big strong man there to protect me," Enzo teased. "My very own Stud Muffin."

Will smiled, the brightness breaking over his face like he couldn't even restrain it anymore. "You're ridiculous," he said, squeezing his shoulder again. It sounded exactly like *You're amazing.* Or maybe, *You're unbelievable.*

Or maybe even, *You're so sexy, I can't wait to have my way with you.*

"In the best kind of ways," Enzo said, grinning right back.

Will ducked his head, so much fondness in his eyes Enzo thought he was going to have to switch his name for the heart eyes emoji in his phone.

"Okay," he said. "If you want to do this crazy thing, the least I can do is participate."

Enzo raised an eyebrow. "That all you're gonna do?"

He was already imagining Will's bare skin, slick with the ocean, glowing under the moonlight. Could taste the salt on his lips as they kissed.

"Guess you're gonna have to wait and see. I gotta go help Kate, but I'll meet you at the Inn?"

Enzo nodded, Will tossed him one last hot look, and then walked away.

"Phew," Enzo said to nobody in particular. He waited a minute—for his erection to be less obvious—and then slipped out, feeling Will's eyes on him the whole way to the door.

Chapter Fifteen

It was a little bit nuts to do this. Will knew it, and Will didn't care.

It had been a really long afternoon—punctuated by a text message exchange with his mom that had made him briefly want to punch something—followed by an even longer evening.

Normally a day like that would've made him want to walk up the stairs to his room and fall face first into bed, but he'd known, even as busy and as crappy as things were, he had *this* to look forward to.

And he'd looked forward to it.

So much so that he'd actually had a spring in his step as he'd left Cherry's, Kate shaking her head in disbelief and muttering something about falling head over heels.

The thing was: as Will approached the Inn, spotting Enzo, leaning against the porch railing, he wasn't sure she was wrong.

It was nearly ten and already full dark, but it didn't matter. Will couldn't see anyone else; maybe it was the way Enzo looked so stunning in the moonlight, the shadows carving out his face like an old Italian painting.

Or maybe it was *just* Enzo.

"Hey," Will said. "I should—"

But before Will could suggest grabbing a sweatshirt—it could get chilly after they got out—or a God forbid, a towel—Enzo gave a dramatic hand wave to the items sitting on the porch swing next to him.

"Yes, I got you a towel, Mr. Overly Cautious," Enzo joked. "And I want you to know that you were not necessarily right before about the towel thing, but it *was* a cold walk home the other night, and I have a reputation to maintain, now."

"And you didn't before?"

Will came closer, then closer still, reaching out and tugging Enzo right into his arms.

"I did, but . . ." Enzo melted into him, like a popsicle left out in the sun.

Will kissed him then, because he couldn't stand here, looking at his gorgeous face anymore, and *not* kiss him.

Kissing him back with enthusiasm, Enzo groaned in the back of his throat.

If they kept going like this, they wouldn't make it past the property line of the Inn, and as much as Will craved Enzo, he craved more than the feeling of his hand on his dick.

"So, *Honey Bunny*, you ready for our swim?" Will asked, pulling back. It was amazing how much lighter he felt, when he shouldn't be feeling like this at all.

But he'd already miraculously shed all that guilt like a skin he didn't need anymore.

"I'm ready for something," Enzo muttered, taking a step back. "That was almost unfair. I say *almost*, 'cause it was real sweet, too. Just like you." He grinned, suddenly, and Will's heart beat even faster. He would never get used to the way this man looked. *Never*. He didn't even want to.

He wanted to feel this swoopy, butterflies-madly-fluttering-in-the-stomach, lavender haze way forever.

"Come on, then," Will said and took Enzo's hand and led him off the porch, towards the beach.

The waves were crashing along the coastline, loud in the silence, as they took the path through the dunes.

When they reached the strip of sand within easy reach of the water, Enzo stopped, depositing his bundle of towels on the ground and tugging his T-shirt up.

It was just as Will had imagined it, so many times, both long and fleeting thoughts all day. Enzo's skin, gleaming silver and gold under the light of the moon, the knowing look in his eyes as he tucked his fingers under his shorts and pulled them down, nothing underneath them.

Will felt the thrum of desire spike through him but ignored it, following Enzo's movements and shucking his own clothes.

Reaching out, Enzo set a palm against his chest, right where his heart was beating a hair too fast. "Rocco told me that you were hot," Enzo mused in a quiet voice. "But he was wrong."

Will laughed out loud. "Thanks? I think?"

"You're so much more than *hot*." Enzo said this very seriously. "You're so sweet and kind *and* gorgeous. Like you glow with all this inner light. Hot's just a guy on Grindr who spends too much money on the gym and fake tanner. You're . . ." He glanced up, eyes full of wonder and something else that Will *felt,* but was still afraid to name. It was too soon. It was too unexpected.

Yet he felt it, too, all the same.

Will kissed him, then, because he couldn't say any of that.

It *was* too soon. Didn't change a goddamn thing, but that didn't mean it wasn't floating around inside him unspoken, anyway.

Enzo pulled back a second later, eyes shining with mischief. "Race you to the water," he said, and then he was running, so quick, his legs flashing in the moonlight, and Will could only chase after him, laughing the whole way.

They crashed into the water, and it was cool, but not cold, refreshing in the best kind of way, and Will laughed, joy spilling out of him as he kicked his legs and swam out past the first few sets of waves.

Enzo was right there, laughing too, his eyes lit up. "I think I beat you," he teased as he floated close.

"Maybe you need a reminder that we're both winners," Will said, all faux seriousness.

"Do I?" Enzo grinned. "Then you'd better come over here and give it to me."

But before he could, Enzo was swimming over, determination in his gaze. He wrapped his limbs around Will, tucking a foot determinedly around his knee and pressing their bodies together.

"You didn't let me," Will murmured, tipping his head against Enzo's.

"I couldn't wait."

Will leaned in and kissed him again. And this time there was no reason to stop. Nothing but the stars above and the sea below, gently lapping at their skin.

Enzo's mouth, hot and wet against his own, and then his body, rubbing against Will's, the desire between them growing tougher to deny.

"Goddamn," Enzo breathed out, his breaths coming in ragged gasps when they finally broke apart, Will's mouth finding his neck, then drifting lower, to his collarbone.

Sucking a little hickey there, that would be hidden by his clothes, that only he would know was there.

"Remember the last time we did this?"

Will laughed. "I could hardly forget it. I think your naked body was permanently implanted in my brain. Every time I closed my eyes, I thought about you."

"It was kind of a stupid, reckless, insane thing to do."

"And it's not now?" Will raised an eyebrow. "It's full dark, now, Enzo."

"That's not why it was stupid, reckless, or insane. Getting naked with you was."

"Yeah." Will grinned. "It kinda was. We were playing with fire."

"And I enjoyed it too much to worry about getting burned."

Oh, they were in it now. Deep in the fire. And getting burned was the least of their worries. Enzo's dick was pressed hard and insistent against his stomach, and he was thrusting now, just little ones, rubbing it against Will's skin, like he couldn't even help himself.

Enzo tried to reach down, palm Will's dick, but their position and the slickness of the water helped a little, but it wasn't *quite* slick enough, and their skin kept catching.

"Come on," Enzo finally said, huffing in frustration, and he practically dragged Will out of the water, back to the towels. He flopped down and Will followed, bracketing his body with his own.

He wrapped a hand around Enzo's cock and gave it a stroke, just as Enzo reached for his. Their mouths met in a fury of a kiss, and it didn't take long at all for Will's orgasm to hit, Enzo shuddering beneath him only a moment later.

"Wow," Enzo breathed out, and Will rolled over, wet now with water and other fluids, onto his back.

"Yeah," he agreed.

Hands down, this was the most romantic night of his life. Romantic *and* sexy *and* fun. Every time he was with Enzo, it was *everything*, a unique combination that he hadn't ever found with anybody else.

"You know, our fake dates were fun. But nothing's better than this," Enzo said, a happy sigh accompanying his confession.

"Yeah," Will agreed. Then he glanced over, shooting Enzo a knowing look. "I'm honestly not sure how fake those were, really."

"Oh, so you *liked* me calling you Stud Muffin?" Enzo asked archly.

Will laughed. "I didn't hate it."

Reaching out and squeezing his bicep, Enzo said, "It felt true. Ridiculous, but also true, somehow."

That felt like the best explanation that Will could come up with, so he just lay back on the towels and stared up at the stars, quiet for a minute.

He hadn't intended to tell Enzo about the short conversation he'd had with his mom, hadn't wanted to drag that into this night and ruin its flawlessness. But he found himself saying, anyway, "My mom texted me today."

"Yeah?" Enzo rolled over and looked at him with concern. "Is everything okay?"

Was everything okay?

Was *he* okay?

He was frustrated, he was more than a little guilty, but he was holding firm. Will supposed that was the best he could do.

"Yeah, I guess so. She's still pushing me to help them out with this store opening on Tybee."

"They haven't found anybody?"

"Oh, they found someone. And then *they* quit. My brother, Brewer, is even out there. And if you know Brewer, he's not the kind of guy who likes to get his hands dirty."

"Can't they manage with him, then?"

"Not well."

"So she pushed you again."

"Guilted me, more like. And it wasn't even untrue. I'm sure the stories she told me *were* true. I knew I should tell her I'd drop everything but . . ."

"If you do it this time, there will always be a next time," Enzo said softly. He reached out and took Will's hand and squeezed it. "I get it. I had to do that with mine, too. When I first went away to California, to art school, she expected I'd come home for every single break. A long weekend? She'd book me a plane ticket. I finally had to tell her I couldn't do it. I was trying to build a new life. She cried for days. I felt worse than I've ever felt in my whole life. It felt awful, but it was still the right thing to do."

"You telling me that?" Will asked. "It helps. It really does. I wasn't going to talk to you about it. At least not tonight. Honestly, thinking about going skinny dipping out here with you was the only thing that got me through the day. It was busy, and I was stressed, worrying about how to replace Rocco, just when I've got him on board, and then her texts and . . .it all faded away, the moment I stepped out to go meet you."

Understanding and empathy shone in Enzo's eyes. "You know what? I've never been here this long and not wanted to turn around and run away before. It's been what . . .three weeks?"

Will nodded.

"I can't say I haven't felt anything bad, because *ugh*, just today Rocco was telling me about his new opportunity, that coffee shop he's gonna buy, and he was saying how they knew the Moretti name even there, in this little podunk town in Illinois, and I thought, but I'm not part of that. I'll never be part of that. Before? That shit would've sent me into a funk for days. Maybe even weeks. But . . .I don't know . . .it's easier, now. With you."

"Maybe they don't know you because of your cooking or your meatballs or the way you can run like fifty businesses without barely blinking, like Luca, but they *know* you, Enzo. They know your name. It would've been easier to just be a Moretti like all the other Moret-tis—"

"If you've ever eaten my cooking, probably not," Enzo inserted wryly, but Will kept going.

"Yeah, maybe, but it would've still been easier. Instead you did something different, you forged out on your own and made your own kind of reputation for yourself. That's special. *You're* special."

"You're just saying that so I stick around more." Enzo's words were teasing, but his dark eyes were so serious.

"I want you too, yeah, but only if *you* want to. The moment this town makes you miserable, I'm gonna be the first one to push you out of it." *And it might kill me, but I'd do it anyway, for you. 'Cause anyone like you deserves the best. Deserves their smile to always come that easily.*

"Aw, trying to get rid of me already!"

Will laughed then and rolled over on top of him, ignoring Enzo's faux protests. "I never want to get rid of you," he said and kissed him.

Trudging back to the Inn should've sucked. It wasn't exactly cold outside—they were in the thick of June now, every day reaching at least ninety, with some insane percentage of humidity—but they were wet and a little clammy.

Still, Enzo thought if he could smile with Will like *this*, he could do it anytime.

"I'm really looking forward to that warm shower," Will groaned a little as he unlocked the door to his room.

He hadn't asked Enzo to accompany him, and Enzo hadn't offered, they'd just done it. Like it only made sense.

And Enzo was beginning to think that maybe it did.

"I kinda can't believe you're still staying in the Inn," Enzo said, depositing the wet, sandy towels in the corner and beginning to strip his clothes off again. Will had ducked into the bathroom to start the shower, and he could hear it.

It wasn't a very *big* shower, but Enzo still had every intention of sharing it with him—and he didn't think Will was gonna push him away.

"I know." Will's voice echoed through the small bathroom. "I keep saying to myself I need to find a place. But I never seem to have time."

"You should just move into my apartment over the garage with me." Enzo said it easily, casually, without even thinking about it.

But yes, when Will's expression turned shocked, okay, it was probably a bigger deal than he'd considered it to be.

"You're serious," Will said.

"Well, yeah," Enzo replied. He approached where Will was leaning against the doorjamb to the bathroom. "I mean it. I don't know how this works, between us, exactly. I know I'm booked out through the next year. But I get breaks in between jobs, you know? I don't come back here for them, because I never had a reason to, before now. I can't say it'll be easy, but . . ."

"Easier than saying this isn't anything," Will continued solemnly. His big hand cradled Enzo's cheek. "Because it's something."

Enzo nodded. That was easier and perhaps a little more cowardly than saying, *I'm beginning to think it's everything*, but there'd be time for that, later. "And if I'm not home most of the time anyway, you might as well use it. I know Giana won't mind. And when I *am* home, I fully intend to not let you leave my sight," he said.

Will made a face. "You don't know you're gonna feel that way."

"Yeah, I do." *I already feel that way now.*

"Okay, well, I'll think about it."

"Just say yes." Enzo knew he was pushing and probably employing more persuasive powers than he should, pressing his naked, still damp body against Will's. "I know you want to. I know you're . . ." Enzo swallowed hard. "As crazy about me as I am about you."

The way Will's blue eyes went hazy and soft as he tipped his head down towards Enzo's told the whole story. The only story that mattered.

Without answering, he reached down and took Enzo's hand, pulling him into the hot steam of the shower, pressing him against the cool tile wall and kissing him firmly, leaving him gasping.

"I thought . . . I thought we were supposed to be getting clean," Enzo said as Will's hand trailed down his chest to his half-hard cock.

"Oh, we are. And then we're gonna get dirty all over again."

"I hope that's a promise," Enzo said, and Will grinned.

"Oh, Honey Bunny, it's a *guarantee.*"

He made good on it too. The shower took longer than it probably should have, because they couldn't stop kissing and every time they managed to wash something, one or both of them got distracted by the feel of their hands on the other.

By the time they were done, toweling off, Enzo's heart was beating irregularly, his cock as hard as it had ever been in his life, and he had zero compunction about walking Will right over to the bed and pushing him onto it.

"Now," he said breathlessly, "you're gonna finger me open and then I'm gonna ride this." He reached and trailed his fingertips down Will's hard length, making him groan in the back of his throat. "You want that?"

"I'm dying for it," Will said, and his gaze—flayed open and honest, full of unmistakable desire—made it clear that he meant it.

"Good," Enzo said and dropped his towel. "I'm on PrEP. So no need for a condom."

Will nodded. "Me too. Come 'ere, then," Will said in a low voice. He reached for the drawer next to the bed and pulled out lube, wetting two of those big, calloused fingers. Those hands were capable of everything: taking care of business and scooping up the most delicious ice cream, and also capable of making his man scream.

Enzo keened when he slid those fingers against him, swirling around the sensitive edges of his hole.

But as desperate as Will's face had proved he was, he took his time. Being careful, considerate. Shallowing thrusting only one finger in for a freaking eternity, making Enzo squirm on his lap and beg him to get on with it.

"I'm gonna fuck you when I'm good and ready," Will said firmly. "When *you're* good and ready."

"I'm ready right now," Enzo whined as another finger finally slid along the first. He tried to thrust them, but when he did, Will just shook his head and held them inside him. Not moving. Not letting *him* move.

"I'm only gonna get to do this for the first time *once*," Will said, "and this has been a pretty magical night, so . . .I'm gonna make it as good as I can."

"It's pretty amazing right now," Enzo huffed.

"Only pretty amazing huh?"

Will twisted his fingers and crooked them and Enzo nearly screamed as the pleasure soared through him. "Oh yeah, there, there, *there*." Then Will began to thrust them in earnest, Enzo's fingernails digging into his shoulders, trying to muffle his wails into his neck.

Mostly unsuccessfully.

Joy was going to hate them, forever. But maybe if she came and knocked on his door a *third* time, that would finally be the thing that convinced Will to move into his place.

"You want a third?" Will asked and Enzo was about to say *no, no way, I want your cock, now,* when he gave it to him anyway, Enzo's body stretching around it in an easy slide.

Will's other hand, latched around his thigh, slid around his waist and toyed with Enzo's cock. Enzo groaned. "You could come just like this, couldn't you?" he asked in wonder.

He began to thrust more urgently. Enzo bit his lip, hard. He didn't know if it was Will's astonished awe or the look in his eyes or the fingers moving inside him so goddamn perfectly, but suddenly, he *was* right on the edge.

"Yeah," Enzo said. "And I don't wanna. So *come on*. Lie back. Let me make you feel good."

Will gave a few last lazy thrusts and then finally removed his hand, slicking up his cock with the remaining lube on them.

"Come on, then," he said, a desperate twinkle in his eyes. "It's all yours."

Even with taking his time, Will's cock was still big, an inescapable intrusion as he began to sink down onto it.

Enzo hung onto his shoulders and onto the way Will's mouth dropped open in astonished surprise, his eyes fluttering shut with the pleasure of it.

Then he was bottoming out, his thighs hitting Will's, and he took a second to get used to it, to let that little bit of pain melt away until all he felt was pure bliss as he rose up and sank down again.

"Fuck you feel . . ." Will trailed off, his hands clamped onto Enzo's skin, one on his ass, one on his waist.

Enzo agreed. But didn't think he could trust any words that were about to come babbling out of his mouth, his brain-to-mouth filter completely fucking destroyed by how good it felt, and so he kissed him.

Poured everything he felt into the kiss, letting his lips say it all for him as he continued to bounce up and down on Will's lap, Will starting to thrust upwards.

Enzo groaned into the kiss as his cock brushed Will's abs, and he angled his body just enough to do it on every thrust, until he was pretty sure he was going to fly apart, just from that little bit of friction, and how Will's cock was hitting every single glorious spot inside him, like it had been *made* for him, to make him feel this good.

"I'm gonna—" Will broke off, murmuring against Enzo's lips, and then he gave one last thrust and he was coming hard, warmth flooding Enzo's body and that was the last little bit he needed to fall off the edge himself.

He swore and sank into his orgasm, clenching hard around Will's cock, loving how he could feel every twitch, every bit of his pleasure.

For a long moment, neither of them moved. Neither of them said a word.

They just gazed at each other. It felt momentous, like something between them that had been shifting from the first time Will had pressed his lips to Enzo's, settled finally into place.

Will reached up and stroked Enzo's cheek. "You're amazing," he said.

There was so much truth and completely unvarnished honesty in his blue eyes it was hard not to look away. But Enzo didn't. He forced himself to sit there and just look.

To understand that Will had meant every word he'd said earlier. That he'd never seen him as a lesser Moretti. To Will, he was the *greatest* Moretti.

If anything was ever going to convince him to come home, as frequently as he could, it was that look. That truth.

"You're not half bad yourself," Enzo said.

"That what I have to look forward to, when you swing into town?" Will teased. "*Not half bad* and you riding my cock like you were born to do it?"

"Yes," Enzo said.

He wasn't sure it was a good trade-off. He was afraid it wasn't. But he also knew he'd do everything in his power to guarantee it was.

"Alright, then," Will said lightly and helped Enzo slide off, grabbing his towel off the floor to help him do a cursory clean-up.

When Enzo finished in the bathroom and came back out, Will was spread out, still naked, on the bed, a quiet smile on his face. "I sent Joy an email, one I think she'll be very glad to receive," he said, as Enzo tucked himself into his side. Suddenly exhausted. It had been a long day. A glorious one, but *long*.

"Yeah?"

"I'll move my stuff out in a few days. You sure about this?" Will didn't look particularly apprehensive when he asked. Like *he* was sure. He just wanted Enzo to be sure.

"I've never been surer of anything in my whole life," Enzo said.

Chapter Sixteen

Kate was on her break, and it was a quiet afternoon, so Will grabbed his laptop from his office and was working his way through some of the resumes he'd gotten in response to his job posting a few days back.

Tonight, he and Enzo were going to cart over the last of his stuff to Enzo's place. Giana was over the moon, fluttering around like she'd just won the lottery. It didn't matter that Enzo had reminded her a dozen times over the last few days that their relationship was still new, that they didn't want any interference or "helpful advice," she kept walking around with stars in her eyes.

Stars that reminded Will a little of himself every time *he* looked in the mirror.

She *had* refrained from saying, "I told you so," but probably only because she still thought she'd set them up in the first place. That it was *her* matchmaking that had brought them together.

Will supposed that was technically accurate. If Giana hadn't been so pushy, he never would've suggested he and Enzo go on a fake date.

And that fake date had led to all those other, *real*, ones.

Last night, Enzo had said, leaning against the sink as Will had brushed his teeth, that maybe someday they'd need to come clean.

Will understood why he wanted to be honest, but *ugh,* that was going to be one can of worms once it was opened.

"She can't be pissed because what she wanted *still* happened," was Enzo's argument, and yeah, Will could see that logic.

He also thought Enzo was intentionally underestimating how peeved his mother might be by their deliberate lies.

Will pulled up another resume and, after scanning it, decided she would at least be worth an interview, and moved onto the next.

The bell jingled over the door, and he glanced up.

His "Welcome to Cherry's" was half out of his mouth before it died. Before he trailed off in utter surprise.

"Mom!" he exclaimed, shocked. "Dad!"

"Oh, honey, the pictures didn't do this place justice," Carla said as she wandered around, her bright blue eyes, the same color as his, taking in the bright white walls, the candy pink striped booth cushions, the comfortable but old-fashioned white enamel chairs he'd spend ages sourcing.

"Yeah, they really didn't." His father walked over to the counter and put a hand on his shoulder. "It's good to see you, son."

Will gazed at him, still shocked at their appearance. "It's . . .uh . . .good to see you too. Didn't expect you. At all."

Why are you here?

'Cause you're proud of me and wanted to finally see what I did?

Or because you want to convince me in person to do what you want?

"You've built something really nice," his mom said, giving him an approving smile.

"Yeah," Will said uneasily. He wasn't naive enough to believe that because the former was true, the latter wouldn't be either.

"Your mom said it was busier?" Patrick Johnson was all business.

"It's quiet in the early afternoons, but in a few hours, we'll be slammed," Will said. Disliking the fact that his parents had been here for less than five minutes and he was already trying to prove to them that he was doing good.

He'd been a good father, from the angle that he'd instilled responsibility and determination in his sons. But everything else . . .*yeah*. Will couldn't say his childhood had been shit. He knew he'd had a better one than a lot of kids out there, but sometimes he'd just wished for his dad to show some softness. Some love or approval that didn't come directly from whatever accomplishment they'd just achieved.

Will knew he'd been trying to gain his unconditional love forever, and that was one of the reasons he'd finally come to Indigo Bay and opened Cherry's.

The first thing he'd done *entirely* for him.

Because he'd wanted to. Because he'd wanted to carve himself a place that wasn't dependent on his family.

"I'm not surprised, you know how to run a good business . . ." Carla said, trailing off.

"It's a nice town, too. Busy downtown. Clean streets. Lots of tourists. Reminds me of a lot of places we've opened shops," Patrick said. "This was a good move, son. Diversification is everything. You know that."

Will did not roll his eyes. But he still considered it.

"Yeah, I do," he said instead. "Not that I'm not happy that you're here, but *why* are you here?"

"Can't we want to see you, see what you've created here?" His mother shot him a smile.

Will did not bring up that he'd been open for months now, which he thought was heroic levels of restraint on his part.

He did *not* bring up Tybee Island either, even though part of him just wanted to cut through all this crap and get to the bottom of why they were here, sooner rather than later.

"You want some ice cream?"

"Oh, just a taste," Carla said, when Patrick shook his head. "Come on, Pat. You gotta try it. It's homemade, right?"

"Yep."

Will's plastic sample spoons were the same bright cherry pink as the stripes on the walls. He *did* roll his eyes a little as he grabbed a handful and bent down into the ice cream case, picking a handful of different flavors before passing them to his parents.

"This is the dark chocolate espresso bean," he said as his father's face creased into pleasure at all the flavors exploding across his tongue.

There was nothing *wrong* with the ice cream they served at the Johnson's chain, but it wasn't made in-house with the best milk and cream and eggs he could get his hands on.

"Delicious," Carla said, as she sampled the brown butter cherry brickle he'd just finished perfecting. "You even make the vanilla here?"

Will swiped two more sample spoons into the bucket of Tahitian vanilla and watched as they both truly appreciated the complex flavor he'd accomplished.

Most vanilla was an absence of flavor, but he'd brought out the best in the beans he bought.

"It's all a bit pricey," Patrick said, "but the quality's there. That's some delicious ice cream, son."

"Thanks," Will said, genuinely pleased.

He'd been experimenting with homemade ice cream for years now, and there'd been a time when he'd tried to convince his father to swap out the ice cream they bought for his own, for the entire Johnson's chain.

Patrick never went for it, though, and in retrospect, Will could agree that he'd been right. They'd have had to raise prices, and that wasn't what Johnson's was.

It *was* what Cherry's was, though, and Will was proud of that.

He was just beginning to think, to actually *hope*, that they understood that, too, but then his mother said, "You seem like you're all settled in."

You know better than to expect things to be different.

"Yeah," Will said cautiously.

Patrick set his elbows on the counter and leveled that same stare at Will that he'd given him in little league and in high school debate and the first time he'd tried to resist uprooting his life for Johnson's. "Brewer's in over his head in Tybee," he said bluntly.

"Of course he is. That's not Brewer's skill set," Will said. If his dad could be blunt, then so could he.

"Because that's always been *yours*," Carla added persuasively.

It was true. But that didn't mean he wanted to spend his entire life using it for Johnson's.

"You said when you left and came here to start this place that you'd still help us out if we needed you."

He'd said that because he'd been trying to forestall any panicked freakouts.

Of course, he'd hoped it wouldn't come to this. But here they were, wanting to cash in on that promise.

"I know I did, but I'm still getting up and running here." Will shrugged, trying to keep himself calm. "Cherry's has to be my priority now."

His parents exchanged looks. Will didn't need a translator to understand what they weren't saying. *We didn't expect him to stick to his guns like this. We expected him to crumple, if we showed up.*

But Enzo had been right the other night when they'd talked at the beach. If he didn't stick to this line he'd drawn now, he'd never be able to get them to respect it.

"We're in a real bind," Carla said. "Surely you can help us for a week. Two, maybe."

"Tops," Patrick added.

But Will knew how that worked. One week would turn into two would turn into four. And he couldn't leave Kate for that kind of time. Not yet.

Even if he *wanted* to. And he didn't want to.

"I can't," Will said. "I'm sorry, but I really can't."

He was waiting for one of them to bring up his manager, and of course that was the moment Kate walked out of the back, a perplexed expression on her face.

"Everything alright, boss?"

Will winced, internally. Naturally she'd had to use *that* nickname just then.

"Uh, everything's fine," Will said. Introduced his parents as quickly and painlessly as he could.

Then Kate turned to him and said, "I thought you were gonna meet Enzo for lunch?"

Ugh. Enzo. He would be in here in a few minutes and they'd grab a late lunch together. That was the plan anyway.

But the last thing he wanted to spring on his brand-new boyfriend was his parents being here, unexpectedly. And not just to check out Cherry's, but to persuade him to come with them.

Enzo wasn't going to want to be around for *that* conversation.

"Who's Enzo?" Carla asked.

"Uh . . ." Will trailed off, shooting Kate a *Please help, please please please help* look. "He's painting the mural on the side of the building. Did you notice him when you came in?"

"Oh, we approached from the other side," Patrick said. "We'll have to check that out, when we leave."

Oh God, please don't.

"Can you . . ." Will motioned Kate closer. "Can you uh . . .go intercept him? Tell him I'm sorry but something came up and he'd be better off grabbing lunch on his own? And I'll take my parents to Oliver's for a sandwich?"

Kate nodded, but there were a hundred questions, barely restrained, in her gray eyes, as she turned and walked out the front door.

"When she's back, we'll go grab a sandwich at the local bakery," Will announced. "And we can . . .uh . . .discuss this further."

His mother's expression brightened, like she thought the discussion would entail something other than Will saying *no*, over and over again.

"I knew you'd see sense, son," Patrick said, patting him on the shoulder again. Will flinched. Not for the first time he wished he'd already moved to Enzo's apartment, which had a rudimentary kitchen. It wouldn't be much, but he could take them there for lunch and avoid a public scene.

Not that his parents ever made a scene. But he had a feeling that if he kept firm, it wasn't going to be particularly pretty.

Of course, if he *did* take them to Enzo's, he'd have to explain exactly who Enzo Moretti was to him. Like he wasn't just the guy painting the side of his building.

Enzo was just about down from the scaffolding, glancing up as he took in his work from the morning, pleased with the way the ship was coming together, when he spotted Kate approaching.

"Hey," he said, picking up a water bottle and draining the last of it. He was supposed to meet Will for a late lunch before he headed to Charleston to pick up a few things that would hopefully make Will's move later that night a little easier.

Another dresser was going to be necessary. More hangers. Something in the kitchen besides one pan and one sad half-melted plastic spatula.

"Will's parents are here," Kate said under her breath as she walked closer. "And he is freaking out."

Enzo's eyebrows went right up, nearly to his hairline. "What?"

"He told me to come out here and tell you to stay away but . . .he needs you, Enzo. He's going to fold, and he doesn't *want* to."

"He told you to tell me not to show up for lunch?" Enzo was a little baffled by this. "Does he not want me to meet his parents?"

Kate shot him a frank look. "He's not thinking clearly. But I think he's trying to save you from getting dragged into this mess."

"Maybe it's a mess, but isn't that what a partner's supposed to be around for? Making things a hell of a lot easier? Not only does he have a business here, he has a boyfriend. He said he wanted roots; he's got them now," Enzo said.

"You gonna go charging in there like a white knight and save him?" Kate sounded full of disbelief, which was totally unfair.

Enzo could do the right thing. He did the right thing all the freaking time.

"Yes," Enzo said firmly.

Kate smiled then, all that disbelief melting into approval. "Knew you would," she said, patting him on the shoulder. "You're a good guy, Enzo."

"Did you really do all that to convince me to do the right thing?" Enzo complained. He took off his bandana and ran his hand through his curls, damp with sweat. This was not how he'd hoped to meet Will's parents—not that he'd really spent a whole lot of brain power on that eventuality—but he also understood there wasn't time to waste.

Kate looked annoyingly smug. "Worked, didn't it?"

"It was going to work anyway," Enzo grumbled. He shoved his bandana into the pocket of his paint-stained shorts. "Come on, let's go deal with this."

When he walked into Cherry's, a tall man with the look of Will's build and a woman with Will's blue eyes turned to him.

Will didn't look particularly happy to see him, but he also didn't look particularly surprised either.

More resigned to the inevitable, if Enzo had to guess.

"Hi, I'm Enzo Moretti," Enzo said brightly, plastering on his best *I'm a good guy and I'm gonna be a good guy for your son* smile. It wasn't one he'd had much occasion to use, but he'd witnessed Luca utilizing it enough over the years with Oliver's mom.

He held out his hand and shook both their hands briskly. Wishing he'd had at least time to wash the paint off, but at least it wasn't wet anymore.

Probably.

"Patrick Johnson. And this is my wife, Carla. We're Will's parents. Thought we'd stop by on our way to Tybee, see him in person," the man said. He had a firm handshake, firm enough that even Luca probably approved.

"Nice to meet you."

"You must be the mural painter," Carla said, eyeing him speculatively.

"What gave it away?" Enzo winked, shifting from the *good guy* smile to the *I'm a handsome rogue* smile.

That one was a smile he was intimately familiar with and he knew he wore it well.

Carla melted as quickly as he'd expected.

"Oh, Will, is he *just* the mural painter?" she whispered, loudly enough that he could hear every single word.

Will met his eyes over her head. Yep. He was definitely resigned, but there was more too, now. He looked relieved that he wasn't in this alone anymore.

If Enzo had any say in it, he wasn't going to be alone, again.

Will had bailed him out with his mom, and now it was Enzo's turn.

"I hear we're all going to lunch," Enzo said casually, walking behind the counter and pressing a quick kiss against Will's mouth.

"I'd guess he's not *just* the mural painter," Patrick said dryly.

"I . . .it's still very new," Will said, by way of explanation. But he didn't move away. Instead, he slung an arm around Enzo's waist, like Enzo wasn't damp and sweaty.

Like they were a team now. A united front.

"Is it?" Patrick looked amused, not upset.

"Yes," Enzo said, "but serious."

Enzo wasn't surprised at all that Will hadn't told his parents about him. After all, it *was* new, and from everything Will had said, he wasn't necessarily going to tell them everything.

He was trying to set boundaries. Enzo understood all about that.

"Yeah," Will agreed, meeting Enzo's eyes. There were a bunch of questions lurking there, but also a lot of answers, too.

Yes, I'm glad you're here.

Sorry I tried to keep you away.

We're in this together, now.

"Well, let's go to lunch," Carla declared happily. "I would love to learn more about you, Enzo."

"And we'll talk more about you coming with us to Tybee," Patrick added.

Enzo didn't miss the determination in his expression as they walked out the door. Or the equally as certain look in Will's eyes that he wouldn't be going anywhere.

Phew. Enzo was going to have to be on his best dancing monkey behavior to distract Will's parents from what they'd come to Indigo Bay for.

"So, Enzo, tell us a little more about you," Carla asked as they walked down the sidewalk towards Sweetie Pie's. Will hadn't let go of him yet, which Enzo was taking as a very good sign. He'd hoped Will wouldn't be upset he'd ignored Kate's message, but this was even better than he'd envisioned.

Okay. He hadn't really envisioned *anything*.

It had been clear enough that Will had been trying to white-knuckle this situation alone, and Enzo just wasn't going to let him. He'd charged in, without really thinking it through at all.

"Mom," Will chided gently.

"I'm from here, originally," Enzo said. "My mom and I moved here when I was ten. Then five years ago I moved away, went to art school in San Francisco."

"And you're a full-time muralist?" This question was from Patrick.

Will hadn't said it explicitly that his father was a hard-ass business-man, but he didn't need to, now. Enzo could see it.

Will's dad was Luca, if he'd never met Oliver.

"Yep. Booked about a year in advance. All over the US. Even a few dates in Europe, now. Bless social media. It does all my marketing for me."

"You must have quite a reputation," Carla said approvingly.

"He's brilliant," Will said, his firm response making it clear he wouldn't tolerate any kind of argument on this point. Enzo flushed with pleasure.

He *knew* he was good, sure. People said it all the time. But hearing it from Will's lips meant something more.

"So you travel all over, but you're based here?" Carla asked as Patrick opened the door of Sweetie Pie's, ushering them all inside.

Enzo felt Will tense and knew they'd hit on the one potential wrinkle that worried both of them.

"Uh." Enzo hesitated. He didn't want to lie. Not to Will's parents. But what else could he say? "I wasn't before, but I am now." He glanced over at Will, meeting his eyes, full of sudden trepidation. "After meeting Will, it was a no-brainer. I want to be with him, as much as I can."

Carla melted again, but Patrick was a tougher nut to crack.

"That sounds awfully lonely for you, Will," Patrick said.

Yep, this guy was just as blunt as Luca had been. Before he'd been forced to learn how to be an actual human being with emotions and with *tact*.

Bless Oliver for all that work he'd put in, because Enzo had a feeling it hadn't been a particularly easy job.

"Not at all," Will said, his jaw jutting out with frustration and annoyance. "I'll have the business here."

"And I'll always make time for him," Enzo added, deciding that if Will was going to brazen this out, he could too.

"Let's order," Will said, turning towards the front counter.

They ordered sandwiches and iced coffees and then took a large table in the corner, Rocco eyeing their group with undeniable interest, but because Rocco had a brain in his head, at least he didn't offer any pointed comments.

Enzo was grateful for that, at least.

"I'm sure," Enzo said, after taking a sip of his iced coffee, eyeing Will's parents across from him, "that when Will's business is more established, he could even come with me to some projects. See the country."

"Will's business *is* established now," Carla argued.

It was pretty brazen for her to claim that now, when she'd just freaking arrived. Will tensed next to him, even though he'd hardly relaxed from the last time, and Enzo knew shit was about to hit the fan, no matter how public of a confrontation this might be.

At least there was nobody else in the bakery except for Rocco, who was not doing a very subtle job of listening in to the whole conversation.

Well, if that was *all* Rocco was doing, Enzo could hardly blame him for that.

Enzo's hand, lingering on Will's leg, squeezed his knee reassuringly. *I'm here. I got you.* He couldn't say it out loud, but he could tell Will in every other way that they were a team in this. Setting boundaries was hard and painful. Nobody would leave this conversation happy, but it had to be done.

"It's not," Will argued. "How would you even know? You've just showed up here for the first time. And only because you needed something."

"Well, it's good we did, or we might never know you were hiding a boyfriend," Carla said, amused.

"If Enzo's traveling all the time for work, then I don't see what the big deal is that Will travels, too," Patrick argued.

He *would* think that. Enzo was beginning to understand why Will had gotten frustrated arguing with his parents. They were pretty damn slippery.

"It's not about me traveling," Will argued. "It's about me setting down roots here. We're trying to make a life here."

"You just started dating," Carla said. Enzo had a feeling she wasn't trying to be dismissive but it came across dismissive anyway.

Enzo had been trying to not escalate the situation, but he wasn't sure he had a choice anymore.

Enzo squeezed Will's hand again. A warning. And something else too. A *prepare yourself.*

"Not just dating," he said, working hard at keeping his voice even. "Will's not just my boyfriend; he's my fiancé. We're getting married. Will can't leave, not now. Not just because of his business. *That's* the kind of life we're building together."

"*What*," Carla exclaimed.

"I thought you said this was new!" Patrick argued. "How could you be engaged?"

Enzo was afraid to see the look on Will's face when he turned to look at him, but there was no anger, no frustration, no anything except pure fucking relief.

He'd taken a risk, but he'd also known how it had felt, when he'd had to do this exact same thing with his mother. The guilt he'd endured.

Maybe if Will's parents didn't think that it was just a fleeting thing, if they *knew* it was serious between them, maybe they'd stop pushing so goddamned hard.

"We uh . . .we've been talking for a long time, before we met in person," Will improvised. "His mom thought we'd be a good match and gave me his phone number. When we met in person . . ." Will trailed off and gazed into Enzo's eyes, deeply. *He's really good at faking this. If he's faking it at all.* "I already knew he was the man for me. Seeing him in person, *being* with Enzo, it only confirmed what I already knew."

"Oh. Well. That does change things a bit." Carla appeared to have softened, considerably. "We're very happy for you two. Congratulations."

"A bit surprised," Patrick added, but he was smiling now, "but yes, very happy. We'll manage on Tybee."

Enzo could barely believe that had worked. He'd hoped it might, but he certainly hadn't expected it to.

"Thanks, Dad," Will said dryly.

No doubt he was thinking the same thing Enzo was: *they wouldn't accept me saying no when it was about my business, but I meet a man and that's all that matters.*

It was ridiculous but Enzo wasn't about to look a gift horse in the mouth.

"Good, 'cause I'm not ready to let go of him yet," Will said, and his voice wasn't quite steady.

"I'd hope not," Patrick said, "if you're going to marry him."

Enzo was insane.

Enzo was insane and wonderful and brilliant, and Will had never wanted to kiss him more than he did right now.

Or tell him he loved him. Because he'd thought he might, before, but when Enzo had walked in, cocky and confident and *so* sure, ready to face head-on the messiness of his parents even though Will had warned him off, he'd been sure.

It was the moment he knew.

Maybe not the moment he'd knew he'd marry Enzo, but the moment he knew this was serious for him.

Though . . .considering what Enzo had just announced to his parents . . .maybe there *would* be wedding bells sometime in their future.

But not now. No way. Will was crazy about this guy but not crazy enough to marry him after dating him for only a few weeks. No matter how good the dating was.

"When's the wedding?" his mom asked excitedly.

Of course, Rocco had just arrived at their table with his hands full of sandwiches, and his jaw dropped open at her question.

Shit. Shit, shit, shit.

Will was very certain Enzo had felt comfortable and safe making that declaration because his parents would be gone by tonight, and nobody else in town would know.

But now Rocco knew.

And if Rocco knew, Giana was sure to find out.

"Uh," Enzo said, very eloquently.

"Soon but it's going to be very small," Will said firmly.

"I just couldn't let another day go by without making him mine, forever," Enzo said, giving Will the gooiest smile in his repertoire. Will recognized it, because they'd exchanged quite a few of those looks on their fake dates.

And that was what this really was, wasn't it? Just another iteration of that.

"Wow," Rocco said.

Enzo shot his cousin a warning glare. "Not now, Rocco. *Later*."

Rocco seemingly got the message, because he left then. Hopefully not to text every single person he knew in Indigo Bay.

"I can give you a list of what I usually do during a store opening. Brewer might find that helpful," Will said, changing the subject.

He was grateful Enzo had intervened. Something had been needed and he'd provided it. But he also didn't want to spend the rest of his lunch break talking about non-existent wedding plans.

"He would for sure," Patrick said with a firm nod. "We've done this before, of course, but this is a big opening for us."

Will asked about the location then, and as he'd expected, once his dad was off and running talking about business, the subject took over the whole conversation.

After Enzo finished his sandwich, he excused himself, and when he came back a few minutes later, Will was pretty sure he'd talked to Rocco and contained the situation.

The way Enzo reached down and squeezed his knee again seemed to confirm it.

"Well, it's too bad we're not staying," Carla said, with true reluctance. "I'd love to spend more time with you, Enzo. You seem like an excellent young man, with true feelings for Will."

"I've never felt this way before, about anyone," Enzo said and for a moment, Will was almost sure there was the ring of truth in his voice. He'd heard Enzo fake it enough, after all, but nothing about how he sounded now felt fake.

"We'll have to swing back around, after the opening," his dad said firmly.

"Definitely. And you said your mother lives here, in town?" Carla asked, an innocent expression plastered across her face.

But Will didn't believe it.

And he could feel Enzo freeze next to him.

Yep. There was *no way* he was letting his mother meet Giana Moretti anytime soon. And when they did eventually meet, it was going to be under very, *very* controlled circumstances.

Not when Enzo had just brazenly told his parents they were engaged.

"Yes," Enzo said cautiously.

"Oh, next time we're in town, I'll definitely have to meet her." Carla smiled.

"Yes, next time," Will said, emphasizing the last part of his sentence.

"I've got to get back to work, but it was wonderful to meet you," Enzo said, deploying another one of those smiles that melted his mother and even seemed to ensnare his father.

Enzo was something else.

Will adored him. Every single part of him.

"We'll also have to stop by to see the mural, when it's done," Carla said.

"Definitely," Enzo agreed, a twinkle in his eye.

He leaned down and apparently was not at all averse to PDA, even in front of Will's parents, because he gave him a kiss that would leave him thinking about Enzo's lips on his—on every single part of him—the rest of the afternoon.

Then he was gone, waving to Rocco, as he headed out the door.

"Well, he's sure something else," Carla said, with an approving nod as the door closed behind him.

"Yes," Will agreed. He could hardly argue with that assessment. "I've got to get back, as well. But I'll make sure to email you over that opening list, and some tips for Brewer."

"We appreciate it," Patrick said, putting a hand on Will's arm as he stood. "I'm just sorry you weren't able to come yourself."

Will wasn't surprised his father had gotten one last guilt trip in. Enzo had worked him hard, but Patrick Johnson wasn't the kind of man who would ever put personal life above business. Mom might've been convinced, but Patrick wouldn't be. Not entirely.

"I am too, but not *that* sorry," she said, giving him a quick hug. "Not after we've met what's keeping you here."

"Cherry's is what's really keeping me here," Will emphasized. "Enzo is just an added bonus."

"But what a bonus," Carla teased.

She was right, again.

Still, he was unbelievably grateful when he finally waved goodbye to them, a few minutes later and returned to Cherry's, walking in the door feeling like he'd just gone through a war.

Kate looked up as he walked in, not even bothering to hide her curiosity. "How did it go?" she asked.

Will just laughed. "Good. I think."

I just upgraded from a boyfriend to a fiancé.

Chapter Seventeen

Enzo slipped into Cherry's right before Kate locked the door.

She looked tired. Enzo could only imagine how Will looked.

"Busy day?" he asked.

Kate nodded. "We were slammed from four on. Rocco stopped by to help out and we had Mari, but it was a lot." She paused, giving him a little smile and a gesture towards the back. "He's in his office."

Will was on his laptop when he sauntered in. He glanced up, meeting Enzo's eyes.

"They left?" Enzo asked.

Will nodded.

"And without you," Enzo said, feeling relief flow through him. The only problem with him declaring them engaged was the possibility that the Johnsons wouldn't leave, like they'd planned, and head to Tybee. He'd been pretty certain they would, considering the store opening situation, but if they'd stayed . . .well, that could've created some *serious* complications.

"Yes, thanks to you," Will said, the corner of his mouth quirking up. "That was a risk. But it paid off."

Enzo leaned over and kissed him, even more thoroughly than he'd done in the bakery earlier today.

He'd gone a bit overboard then, because he'd wanted to convince Will's parents they were as wild for each other as they claimed.

But it hadn't felt like too much. Actually the opposite. It had felt *right*.

"I figured you'd bailed me out, I could help you out right back?"

"Oh yeah?" Will asked in a teasing voice. "That's all it was? You helpin' me out?"

Enzo flushed. Caught out. "No," he admitted.

Yes, he did look tired, but he looked happy, too. And Enzo wondered what he'd have looked like if they hadn't sent his parents packing, together. If he'd been forced to internalize all that guilt.

"I thought so," Will said knowingly, leaning back in his chair.

"And I talked to Rocco too—like you probably thought I did. He understands." Enzo grimaced. "Okay, he *mostly* understands. But he won't say anything. I made sure of it."

"Good." Will seemed relieved to hear that. That was all Enzo had wanted. To take some of the burden off the guy, some the interminable guilt he was all too familiar with, but he was afraid

"If you're too tired to deal with the rest of the moving tonight—"

But before Enzo could even get his suggestion out, Will shook his head. "Nope. I've just got two duffel bags of clothes left. If you can help me, I'll be done. Besides, Joy told me she needed the room." He grinned. "I think the exact words were, *I need to sanitize and fumigate it from all the excess testosterone.*"

"Excess my ass. I think it was just the right amount," Enzo scoffed.

"That's your story and you should stick to it, Honey Bunny," Will joked, patting him on the arm, his grin widening. "Come on, let's get going."

They made quick work of heading over to the Inn, grabbing Will's duffels. On their way out, they spotted Joy and Giana on one end of the long wraparound porch and they waved but didn't come over.

"I want to say I'm glad about that," Enzo said as they walked the few blocks over to his mom's house—and the garage with his apartment above it. "I should be relieved she's giving me some room to breathe. But . . ." Enzo sighed heavily.

"How many times has your mom said *I told you so*?" Will asked casually. But it wasn't really a casual question.

Enzo glanced over at him, his handsome face shadowed as he unlocked the door. He'd already given Will a key, and he'd felt a whole lot of things as he'd watched him slide it onto his key ring, next to the bright pink keys Will had for Cherry's.

"Not many yet, but I'm sure there's more to come," he said, pushing the door open. "I can't believe this is all you've got."

Will looked up from where he was setting down his duffel next to where Enzo had dropped his own load. There were half a dozen boxes and the duffels, and that was it. Enzo thought *he* traveled light, but Will put him to shame.

"Eh, there's more stuff in my condo in Destin," Will said. "But I realized I haven't lived there in months and I've never missed any of it." He glanced over at Enzo. "I don't know what that says about me."

"That you know what really matters," Enzo said, coming up and putting his arms around him. It was so easy to tip his head back and meet his lips with his own. "Welcome home," he murmured against Will's mouth. Wondering if he was saying it to his boyfriend—or to himself.

Or maybe to both of them.

Will's eyes were a serious, contemplative blue, but then they blazed hot when he leaned in and kissed Enzo more firmly. Like he was taking Enzo's offer and accepting it with both hands.

They stumbled back, Enzo's butt hitting the little row of cupboards in the tiny kitchen, and for a minute it was enough just to kiss, Enzo's fingers gripping Will's shoulders, but the kiss evolved. Turned hot and slippery and passionate.

Will broke off, panting a little, probably because Enzo had found his erection in his shorts and was palming it. "I need to shower," he said. "I *stink*."

"I disagree with the latter and agree with the former," Enzo said and reached down, pulling his T-shirt over his head. "Come on."

Will followed him, both of them shedding clothes, and it was glorious to not worry for a minute about who would hear them or interrupt them. Glorious knowing that they would get to do this over and over and Enzo didn't have to hide his desire for it, anymore.

Didn't have to pretend to look away when Will lounged, naked, against the bathroom vanity, every inch of him gorgeous and every inch of him belonging to Enzo.

"This is a nice bathroom," Will said, glancing around. "And a nice big shower." He grinned as Enzo reached in and flipped the water on, nice and hot.

Not that they were going to have trouble with the *hot* part on their own.

"You saw it the other day," Enzo pointed out dryly. He'd given Will the full tour—not that it took all that long to tour the handful of rooms he'd "lived" in since he was eighteen. There was the big living room slash kitchen, then the bedroom, and the bathroom.

"Yeah, but you weren't naked in it," Will said, shooting him a hot look from those smoky blue eyes. "It's nicer now."

"Just how nice?" Enzo raised his eyebrow and slipped into the shower. Will followed like they were connected, and he couldn't help but stick close.

"I'm gonna show you just how nice," Will said in a deep, gruff voice, and then he was pressing him against the tile wall. Enzo gasped, the tile deliciously cool against his back, Will's skin hot against his front.

Enzo understood Will better than he'd thought he would. He didn't want to let him out of his sight, either.

What's gonna happen when you have to leave in a few weeks?

Yeah, Will would be waiting for him here, but it wouldn't be the same.

It would still suck.

But he shook that thought off. Maybe in a few weeks he'd feel differently. Feel less like his heart was in his throat every time they did this.

Enzo let himself sink into the sensations, Will cradling his face, kissing him fiercely, like he knew just what Enzo was thinking and wanted to dispel all his uncertainties and fears. Pressing his body insistently into the tile, Enzo gasping into his mouth as their cocks rubbed together.

"Want you," Will murmured against his mouth. "Want you all the time."

Enzo's heart throbbed and his cock twitched. It was a combination he was helpless to resist. He didn't even try. Just flipped their bodies and pressed Will back against the wall.

Slid his water-slick hand around Will's cock.

"God," Will groaned, "how do you keep being so goddamned sexy?"

"It's a gift," Enzo said. Then he slid to his knees, and Will made another of those half-restrained gruff groans that always made him weak in the knees. He'd brought this man to *his* knees.

"Not just a gift. A fucking miracle," Will revised, as Enzo teased the tip of his cock with his mouth. He tangled his fingers into Enzo's hair, gently tugging him forward, and Enzo went, easily. Wanting to give Will this probably as much as Will wanted it.

Will's cock was engorged and twitching against his tongue as he sucked him deep. Loving the way he groaned as he let even more of it slide into his mouth.

His own cock was heavy and aching, and as Will's hand caressed his head, fingers digging through his wet curls, gently coaxing him to take him even deeper, Enzo lost the last shred of his own self-control and wrapped his hand around it, giving a sharp twist that made him moan.

"You're so fucking amazing like this, your mouth full of my cock. You want to take it all? God, I think you do." Will was a surprisingly dirty talker. Was it any wonder that Enzo was wild for him? He looked like a gay porn wet dream—all those tanned, chiseled abs and thick thighs and even thicker biceps—and had those guileless blue eyes, still innocent as so much hotness spilled out of his mouth Enzo was surprised he hadn't spontaneously burst into flames.

"Come on, baby, take the rest, I know you can." Will's fingers were gentle on his skull but insistent as he tugged him the rest of the way, Enzo choking around the last bit of it. He risked a look up and yeah, it wasn't any wonder he loved this so much, because *Will* was in bliss, head tipped back against the shower wall. Then he looked down, and their eyes met and the fire inside Enzo stoked even hotter, until he wasn't sure he could take it anymore.

"Oh, yeah, that's so good. So fucking good," Will continued. He'd let Enzo pull out a little enough that he could use his tongue the way he knew he was best at, curling around the head. Relishing the taste of him. Sucking him hard.

Enzo reached up, wanting to send Will over the edge, and Will's groan when Enzo palmed his balls and then slid a finger back farther, just grazing his hole, was enough.

Will muttered an oath and a second later Enzo's mouth was empty and Will was jacking his own cock, come landing on Enzo's face and his shoulders.

"Fuck. So hot like that," Will muttered.

Enzo caught a little of his come with his tongue and savored it as he twisted his hand harder around his cock, pushing himself easily into his own orgasm.

It blasted through him, making it easy to ignore his aching knees and his tired back and his probably roughed-up throat.

He gave himself up to the pleasure, wringing the last of it out of him, and then sinking back on his heels.

"That was something else." Will's voice was rough, too, and he hadn't just been deep throating a cock.

"Yeah?" Yep, Enzo's voice came out as a croak, but he didn't mind. He'd do it again, in a heartbeat. Will reached down and helped him up, Enzo slumping against the tile wall.

"A perfect way to christen this shower properly," Will said, eyes twinkling.

"You'd think so," Enzo retorted. But he'd loved it too. Undeniably. He'd barely had to touch himself to come.

Will raised an eyebrow. And okay, clearly he'd noticed that too. "I was gonna help you out, give you some of what you gave me, but you didn't even need it."

"What can I say? You inspire me," Enzo said casually. But it was more than that, and he knew Will believed it, too.

"I said it, and I meant it, you're a miracle, Enzo Moretti," Will said, and then he was kissing him again, fierce and wild.

Will had just wrapped a towel around his waist, believing that nothing could possibly ruin his mood, when his phone dinged in the bedroom.

"I don't think that's mine?" Enzo said, leaning over the vanity and spitting in the sink as he finished brushing his teeth.

"I'm gonna order some pizza," Will said. "And I'll check when I do that."

"There's only Leonardo's, and his pies are only mediocre. But then you probably already know that," Enzo said. He ran a hand through his wet curls. It was amazing how gorgeous he looked, even like that. Wet, Will always thought he looked a bit like a soaked golden retriever, but Enzo never did.

Will detoured into the bedroom, and when he grabbed his phone, his jaw dropped at the handful of texts.

One was from Rocco, accompanied by a picture. It clearly had been surreptitiously snapped, the interior of Rudy's restaurant unmistakable, and sitting in the booth were Will's parents.

Not sure what you had in mind, but I don't think it was this, Rocco's text said. **They told everyone in the restaurant. Loudly. Multiple times.**

"Shit," Will exclaimed to himself in a low voice.

The second text was from his mom.

We were halfway to Tybee when we decided the store can wait another day. Grabbed a room in town, and spending the night here. Would love to see you for breakfast, with your fiancé! his mom had sent.

Will's knees gave out and he collapsed to the edge of the bed.

"What is it?" Enzo said, walking in. "Is everything okay? Did Leonardo's already close? I keep telling Luca he needs to open a *decent* pizza place, that stays open later. Some of us aren't seventy years old and want to eat dinner after five."

"I . . . you . . . us . . ." Will stammered in a strangled voice.

Enzo frowned. "What?"

Will couldn't find his words, still, so he held out the phone. Let Enzo look at the damning evidence for himself.

"Shit," Enzo said.

"Exactly what I said," Will said heavily. "Your mom knows now."

"Oh, Stud Muffin," Enzo said mournfully, "the *whole* town knows now."

Will's knees felt even shakier. He'd been so on board with Enzo's declaration, imagining that nobody else would find out and it would be easy enough, if things worked out, to eventually make his assertion a reality. And if they didn't . . .well, that fact would speak for itself.

But he'd never imagined that anyone else would discover the little white lie Enzo had told.

"Has your mom called you yet?" Will asked.

Enzo glanced over at where his phone sat on the charger. It was innocuous, but his look was full of trepidation. "Once she finds out, it's gonna blow up," he said. Will noticed he didn't go over to check it yet. Maybe he wasn't ready to.

"Not just that." Will hesitated. Realizing, in real time, that the lie he'd told his parents was not going to hold up. "She's not going to buy the whole 'we've been texting for months and I knew you were the man for me before we even met,' because she *tried* that, and it didn't work."

That was true. That story had sufficed for Will's parents, because they hadn't known any differently. But Giana had been trying to force-feed Will Enzo's phone number, and he'd never taken it.

Except. He had.

Once.

"Ugh," Enzo said. He collapsed on the bed next to him. "I'm sorry. If I'd known they'd be staying . . ."

"You couldn't have known," Will said. Reaching out, he patted Enzo's knee and then squeezed it reassuringly. He'd put on a pair of tight black boxer briefs, and even though he'd *just* sucked Will's brain out of his dick, Will still felt a pulse of desire for him. Even panicking, face unsurprisingly pale, he was still so freaking gorgeous.

And he was all Will's.

"What are we gonna do?"

"Well . . .I realized that I didn't speak *entirely* accurately just now. Your mom did try to give me your phone number a bunch of times—"

"Ugh, please don't remind me of that. I'm *still* embarrassed," Enzo interrupted.

"But," Will added pointedly, "I did take it. The last time. And I didn't tell my parents how long we'd been texting."

"You said a *long* time," Enzo said. Then he smacked him in the chest. "You actually took my phone number and *didn't* text me?"

Will laughed. How did he know he wanted Enzo? Because even in the middle of this situation—admittedly a situation they'd created for themselves—Enzo could still make him laugh. He wasn't just a work of art and he didn't just suck cock like he'd been born to do it, he was so funny, too. Irreverent and snarky, and always full of surprises.

Will was looking forward to Enzo keeping him on his toes for a long time to come.

"In my defense, I thought you must be ugly and weird if you needed your mom to try so hard to get you a date."

"Ahhhhh," Enzo exclaimed in mock frustration, smacking him again. "Embarrassed *and* humiliated."

"Good news, Honey Bunny. You're not ugly *or* weird," Will teased. "Okay, maybe a little weird, considering you declared we were engaged and we've been dating what . . .a week?"

Enzo buried his face in his hands. "Ugh," he cried, the word muffled, "what are we going to *do*?"

"I'm trying to tell you. We brazen it out. Your mom *did* give me your phone number. Admittedly, only a few weeks before you came to town, but it *did* happen. I guess we can say that counts as a long time."

Enzo looked up, skepticism written across his face. "And what, you thought that it was 'long' because you'd never talked to anyone else you wanted to meet more?"

"Uh, sure?"

Enzo smacked him a third time, but Will had learned and he caught his hand, cradling it in his.

"You'll need to sound a whole lot more convincing," Enzo said.

"I can do it." Will didn't want to admit that it wouldn't even be that hard. It wouldn't even be that far from the truth.

Maybe if he *had* texted Enzo when he'd finally taken his number, none of this subterfuge would've been necessary. Maybe it would've been the truth from day one.

"Alright." Enzo sprang up and began pacing. "We can deal with this. We can contain this. It's entirely possible my mother is going to show up here sometime in the next twelve hours and drag us to city hall—but *no*, she won't. She'll want a big wedding, the whole town invited. That takes planning, *time*. She wouldn't be able to pull that off right away. We'll be able to buy some time, some time to make sure . . ." Enzo trailed off and looked at Will, surprised like he hadn't even realized he'd been speaking out loud.

Will realized, a second too late, what he'd been saying. That he'd be *willing* to get married to Will, with only a little more time to make sure.

Suddenly it seemed very stupid that they were actually contemplating going through with this, and he'd not told Enzo how he really felt.

Because he did love him. He was sure now. Not one-hundred-percent sure he wanted to spend the rest of his life with him, but then, if he *had* believed that, after only knowing the man for a month, then Will wasn't sure it would've been true.

Not really. Not deep down.

The fact that he wanted to be sure, wanted to know that Enzo was the man for him *in his bones*, made him believe even more that they needed to be.

That they needed the time.

That they didn't need to rush anything.

"Or," Will said slowly, "we could just tell them the truth."

Enzo's eyebrows skidded upwards. "Are you serious?"

"Completely. It's . . .I'm not just . . ." Will trailed off, clearing his throat. Enzo was still looking at him *that way*, almost the way he'd been staring at him from their first date onwards, when he'd supposedly been trying to prove he was head over heels for Will, and honestly, that realization was the reason he kept pushing forward. Kept talking. Because it seemed very likely that Enzo *was* actually crazy about him, that none of it had been an act, not from the beginning. "I'm serious about this. About you. I want this to work out. And it's going to be challenging. I'm going to miss you, like a limb, when you go. And I hope you're gonna miss me too—"

"Undeniably," Enzo said quietly, seriously, reaching and squeezing Will's hands.

"It's going to be hard. I knew that when we made this thing between us real. I'm going to have to juggle my business and you. I hope that in a few months, I *can* come with you to jobs. And I hope you'll take more, when you can, around this area. I want this so badly to work, because I . . ." *You can do this, Will. It's just three words. Admittedly, three words you've never said to anyone else before, but this is* Enzo. "I love you. If I loved you less . . .maybe I'd be willing to play around more. To keep up this insane charade. But I don't think I am. This matters too much to me. *You* matter too much to me."

Enzo's face softened, his dark eyes glowing. He leaned in, and his forehead touched Will's. "And here," he said in a wondrous voice, "I was worried you wouldn't be able to convince anyone."

"It's easy because it's not an act," Will said.

"I know," Enzo said and kissed him. Sweet and firm, like they had all the time in the world. And maybe, now, they did. After a moment, he pulled back. "I love you, too. Of course. I wouldn't do *any* of this for *anything* less."

Will had suspected it, but it was even more amazing than he'd imagined to hear Enzo say it. Wrapping his arms around his waist, he pulled Enzo in close, resting his cheek against his bare skin. Feeling the beat of his heart. The heart that belonged to him now. That he'd fight any battle to keep.

Including coming clean with both his parents and Enzo's mom.

And no two ways around it, it was going to be a battle, but he'd do it, he'd face them, because he had Enzo by his side.

"So we're decided then?" Will asked softly.

"Yes," Enzo murmured. "Telling the truth is almost crazier than continuing the lie, but yes. You're right. I don't want to get married only because I told your parents we were engaged, same as I didn't want to date you just because you'd told my mom that we were. I want to do it for real. I want to do *everything* for real."

"You keep saying stuff like that and I'm gonna . . ." Will trailed off, eyeing Enzo again. All those tanned slender limbs. The hint of muscle that turned him merely attractive to a work of freaking art.

"You *just* came," Enzo squawked in outrage. "I know, I was there. But you know, it's a good sign that even at twenty-nine, you've got a decent recovery window. Maybe that means in fifteen years you're still gonna—"

Before Enzo could finish that sentence, it was Will's turn to smack *him* in the chest. Enzo laughed. "Okay, fine, *fine.* I guess we need to talk about how we're going to be honest."

"We should do it together. My parents. Your mother. Oliver. Luca. Rocco, even, if he's not running around like a chicken with its head chopped off."

Enzo shot him a doubtful look. "Are you serious? You want to tell everyone, *together*? You know what that means."

Will knew. But he was also counting on the fact they *were* together and actually pretty goddamn happy about it to smooth over any hurt feelings or disappointment that they wouldn't be heading down the aisle any time soon.

And if his parents met Giana, well . . .that was inevitable, anyway. Maybe it was better to do it on *their* terms.

"Your mom is gonna freak out."

Enzo stood and started pacing again.

"And your parents won't?" he questioned. "We just told them *yesterday* that we were engaged. We're going to have to tell them *why*."

Will winced. Yes, he was. And no, he was not looking forward to that conversation. Sure, the fact they were together now might placate all three of them, but the fact they'd felt the need to lie in the first place? Both times? That was going to be a much tougher part of the conversation.

"Yeah," Will agreed. "We both will."

Enzo flopped down on the bed, groaning. And not in the fun kind of way. "I know it's the right thing to do, but it's gonna suck."

"Yeah, but in the end?" Will reached out and smoothed a curl back from his forehead. "I can't be angry at myself that we're in this spot, because we wouldn't have gotten *here*, if we hadn't been very stupid in the first place."

"And desperate," Enzo added hopefully. "We were stupid *and* desperate."

Will laughed. "I'm not sure how that helps."

"It doesn't. Thought it might, but no." Enzo sat up. "We need to formulate a plan. And to do that, I need pizza. After I call Leonardo's,

I'm gonna text Luca and tell him again that he needs to open a late night pizza place."

"You want your cousin to start another business?"

"Well, he didn't get to open his gelateria," Enzo joked. "Because someone else opened up an ice cream parlor."

"Too bad for him," Will said, with mock seriousness.

"But not for me. Turns out that guy's hot and sweet and I'm absolutely wild about him," Enzo said. Pressed a kiss to the corner of Will's mouth and slid off the bed.

He approached his phone like it was a poisonous snake about to strike.

"Well?" Will asked after a moment. "Did she text you?"

Enzo glanced over at him, making a face. "She called twice and sent several text messages. Most of which consist of *I can't believe you didn't tell me* and *Please let me plan the wedding* and *I bet Will's parents are so sweet, just like him.* And a lot of exclamation points. A *lot* of exclamation points."

"She does love her exclamation points."

"Don't say because she's a Moretti," Enzo said grumpily. "I'll admit we *can* be overdramatic but I know how to practice restrained punctuation usage."

Will laughed; couldn't keep the sound in. "Actually, I was gonna say it's *just* a Giana thing. Can you imagine Luca using too many exclamation points?"

"No," Enzo said morosely. "Never. Not even in relation to Oliver."

"There you go. When it comes to punctuation, you're the best of the Morettis," Will teased.

Enzo shot him a look that promised retribution for that remark later—the *fun* kind of retribution, too. But instead of replying, he dialed Leonardo's and put in an order for two large pizzas. One a pepperoni and pineapple. The other a supreme with everything on it.

"Don't tell me *you*, a good Italian boy, like pineapple on your pizza," Will said after he hung up, Enzo still bent over his phone as he no doubt did as he'd promised and texted Luca about opening a pizza place of his own.

Enzo glanced up. "Guilty as charged. But actually it's a *Moretti* thing. Most of us like it, actually. We just won't publicly admit to it."

"See?" Will stood and wrapped his arms around Enzo, pressing a kiss against his cheek. "You *are* a good Moretti."

"Pineapple and all," Enzo said, but he was smiling, no trace of that shadow lingering in his eyes. "Pizza will be here in thirty." He waggled his eyebrows, gaze falling on the towel still wrapped around Will's waist. "What should we do until then?"

"*I'm* gonna get dressed," Will said, with mock sternness. "And you should too."

"Ugh, no fun."

"You love me," Will said. Then flushed, because Enzo *did*.

"Yeah." Enzo leaned over and kissed him once, firmly. "I sure do."

Thirty minutes later, they were both clothed and on the couch, munching on Leonardo's mediocre pizza. "Maybe Luca could just buy him out," Enzo said.

They had done a lot of chatting since hitting the couch, but almost none of it had been about what they were going to do tomorrow. Will knew they needed to, but it felt so good to just sit here like this, talking about nothing important at all.

He could imagine them doing this in six months and in six years, and he wanted it so strongly his heart ached with the desire.

"And what? Change everything?" Will snagged another piece and took a big bite. "It's not *bad*. It's just not good, either."

Enzo leaned over, head drooping down onto Will's shoulder, snuggling him into him in what felt like a perfect fit. "I have it on good authority," he said in a hushed whisper, "that they use *frozen* pizza dough."

"I'm surprised Luca hasn't marched in there already and demanded changes, ownership or no," Will joked.

"Oh, he's thought about it. You know exactly what's stopped him."

"Probably *who*," Will said. "Oliver."

Enzo nodded. "His better half."

Will thought about this as he finished his pizza. "You ever think we'll end up like them? Like Luca and Oliver?"

"Married and still wildly in love, running three businesses like they never want to do anything else?" Enzo's voice was drowsy. "Yeah, I hope so. Which is why . . .I hate to say it, but I think you were right. There's nothing else to do but come clean. With my mom. With your parents."

"I thought we already decided that?"

Enzo nodded and glanced up at Will. His dark eyes were as serious as Will had ever seen them. "Not just that. Not just a partial truth but the whole truth."

It was what Will had been rolling around in his head, too, and he'd come to the same conclusion as Enzo.

"It's going to really suck," Will said. "But I think you're right."

"And, I do think it should be just my mom and your parents. Not Luca, not Oliver, definitely not Rocco."

"What did Rocco ever do to you?" Will asked, giving him a playful nudge.

"Was very snotty when I asked him to not tell everyone yesterday," Enzo complained. "He basically knows, anyway. And Luca and Oliver must, too, but I think we should still tell them. Just not with our parents."

"Agreed."

Enzo pulled his phone out of his pocket. "No time like the present," he said and dialed, setting it on his knee as he hit speaker phone.

Luca answered in a clipped voice. "I'm busy," he said in lieu of a greeting.

"We got something to tell you," Enzo said.

"I meant it. I'm on the line, at the restaurant, and I've got half a dozen tickets. What is it?"

Will realized that Luca was *that* busy and yet had still answered Enzo's phone call. He hoped Enzo realized how meaningful that was.

"Will and I are dating," Enzo said.

"Yes, and?" Luca still sounded impatient.

"Remember how you told me something seemed off?"

"How could I forget?" Luca asked wryly.

"You weren't wrong. It *was* a scheme. Sort of. Kinda. But it's not now. It's hundred percent not fake. We're together. We're in love."

"I know," Luca said.

"But I—"

"I know what you *said*," Luca interrupted. "But that doesn't mean I actually believed you. You went on a few dates, pretending to get Giana to quit matchmaking. And I guess it worked—or it didn't?"

"It worked," Enzo said, chuckling. "A little too well. You'll tell Oliver? And that we're sorry we lied to both of you?"

"Enzo. The only person you were really lying to was yourself," Luca's voice went from impatient to empathetic in a second. Will watched as Enzo heard it, the look on his face as he absorbed the change. He realized then that maybe Enzo hadn't completely comprehended how much Luca cared about him before, but he was beginning to realize now.

"I was lying to myself, too," Will added in. "A lot."

Luca chuckled under his breath. "Yeah. I know. But it's alright. You got there in the end. So you're coming clean, then? Both of you? 'Cause I have to say I heard an even *crazier* rumor that you two were already getting married."

"We're not. Well, not now. Not *yet*." Enzo paused. "And yes, we're telling the truth. Tomorrow morning. If you see a crater in the middle of Main Street, you'll know why."

"Nah," Luca said. "Giana's gonna be upset, sure, especially when you tell her why, but I think she'll ultimately understand. And be happy, of course, because she gets to say *I told you so*."

"Thanks for that," Enzo retorted.

"Hey, I'm just the messenger. Now I gotta get back to cooking. But you don't have to worry about us. Let's have dinner next week, all four of us, alright? We'll go to Charleston. Make a real evening of it. Celebrate your sort-of-new relationship."

"Sounds good," Enzo said and then in a quieter voice added, "Thanks, Luca."

"Anytime," Luca said, and Will could tell he meant it.

Enzo hung up and Will could tell *he* knew Luca meant it, too.

Will didn't say anything. Let Enzo think for a minute.

"I . . .I hated him when he came here, you know?" Enzo sounded like he'd never regretted anything in his life more.

"I bet you did."

"Really? *Saint Luca*?" Enzo's tone was wry.

"He isn't a saint, and I bet he wasn't a saint back then, either. But yeah, I can imagine how it felt when he showed up here, and even though your mom had asked him to come and help you guys, I bet it sucked when he told you everything you had to change. Everything you were doing wrong. And you didn't even want to be here."

"I didn't," Enzo said. "And you know how he paid back all my bullshit? He intervened. He stood up for what I wanted, with my mom. He saw my dreams, when I'd given up on them. I wouldn't have anything I have now, if it wasn't for him." Enzo was quiet for another moment. "I don't know if he even understands that."

"He does," Will said firmly. He pressed a kiss to Enzo's shoulder. "I promise you, he does."

Enzo sighed. "I shouldn't have lied to him."

"You heard him. You lied to yourself, not him." Will nudged him. "After all, you couldn't have known you couldn't ultimately resist this *stud muffin*."

Enzo laughed, and Will knew he wanted to make Enzo sound *exactly* like that for the rest of his life. Was it still too early to say so? Absolutely—which was why they were gonna have to come clean tomorrow morning.

"I have one piece of good news for you," Enzo said.

"What's that?"

"Tomorrow night," Enzo said, leaning in and brushing a kiss across his lips, "it'll be over and they'll know everything and we'll still have each other."

Chapter Eighteen

To say Enzo was nervous was an understatement.

Already he'd guzzled down two cappuccinos and every time he eyed Rocco, standing at the counter, by the espresso machine, Rocco eyed him right back, like *No way am I giving you another one.*

"You ready?" Will said, spotting his parents approaching from one side through the windows that lined the street side of Sweetie Pie's. They'd taken the same table they had the other day, when they'd all had lunch.

They'd debated having this conversation somewhere private, like Cherry's before it opened, but Enzo had staunchly argued that they needed to do it in public—hopefully to contain the fallout. Besides, Enzo barely considered Oliver's bakery *public*, because he'd spent so much time in it over the years.

"As ready as I'll ever be," Enzo said and watched as his mom approached from the other side. Enzo realized he was holding his breath—not from anticipation, but sheer, unadulterated dread—as they met at the Sweetie Pie's front door, exchanging what seemed to be basic pleasantries.

Okay. So they *hadn't* met yet. But as they walked into the bakery, Enzo could see they were eyeing each other, and when they all ended up walking towards the same table, Carla Johnson turned to his mom and said, "I'm sorry, but are you Enzo's mother? You look so much like him."

Giana beamed. "Do you think so? Everyone always says so, but I always wonder, if he'll turn out to be just like his father."

"And who's his father?"

Ugh, Enzo really didn't want to go down *this* road. Not now. Not today. He liked Will, and he liked Will's parents, and they seemed reasonable but it never seemed to go over well when he mentioned that his father had probably been part of *the* family and was probably lying dead somewhere, which was why he'd never met the man.

Just because he was okay with it didn't mean other people were.

"Mom," he said, walking over and wrapping an arm around her shoulders, "meet Will's parents. This is my mom, Giana Moretti."

"Oh! *Oh!*" Giana looked thrilled. "Of course you are Will's parents! You look just like him."

Carla put out a hand and said, "Carla and Patrick Johnson. It's so nice to meet you. We had a chance to talk to Enzo yesterday and he's *wonderful*. And the mural! So beautiful, already."

Giana, not surprisingly, bypassed her outstretched hand and pulled her into a big hug, instead. Carla looked surprised but pleased. Next she hugged Patrick, who seemed equally as surprised, but a hair less pleased.

"We will be *family* now," Giana said firmly. She glanced over at Enzo. "Now that our sons are family."

"Oh, they told you too?" Carla said. "Were you surprised? We were surprised they were so serious, so quickly."

Will's eyes went wide. Enzo considered interjecting, before their mothers could go into more raptures about how they were about to get married. But Will put a hand on his arm, and okay, they could let this play out. For at least a minute or two. But that was it.

Giana smiled. "Oh, I wasn't surprised at all. I knew they'd be serious about each other. A perfect match if I may say so myself."

"Hardly perfect, if they're in a long-distance relationship much of the time." Patrick's voice was calm, but there was a sternness in his eyes that worried Enzo.

"Patrick, we talked about this," Carla said under her breath.

"We're gonna work this out," Will interjected. "I know it seems sudden and soon, and a lot, but it's gonna work out."

"Honey, you have to understand. We don't want you to be *married* to someone who's never around!" Carla exclaimed.

"Good news," Enzo said, unable to help himself for one more minute, "he won't be."

"*What*," Giana exclaimed.

"Let's sit down," Will said hurriedly and gestured towards the table.

His mother slid in next to Carla. Patrick sat next to Will. Enzo didn't move. Maybe if he didn't sit down, he could still run away.

Avoid that betrayed look in his mother's eyes.

"Does anybody want any coffee?" Enzo asked.

"Coffee! *Coffee!* He asks about coffee right now. You need to tell me what's going on," his mom demanded. "Explain what you meant."

But before he could, she turned to Carla, dark eyes wide and upset. "See what you just did! You put all these doubts in them, when they were *perfect* before! I made sure of it! And now they're going to break up!"

"Mom, you didn't do anything. In fact," Enzo winced a little as the truth came out, "you did *less* than nothing. We didn't even start dating because you suggested it."

Well, Enzo supposed you could make the argument that they *had*. Because they'd fake-dated because of Giana, and they'd *real*-dated because of the fake dating.

"But you said you did! I showed you what you could be! I'm the one who suggested you date *in the first place.*"

Will was right; Giana was the queen of exclamation marks. Even if they weren't written down, they were right there anyway, in her dramatic delivery.

"When we first started dating," Will said hesitantly, "we weren't *actually* dating for real. We just thought if you . . .if you thought we were, you might . . .uh . . .get off our cases, a bit. But uh . . .no worries? 'Cause we're actually dating now."

Her jaw dropped.

Carla and Patrick looked equally as stunned.

"And," Enzo added, because they were in for a penny now, might as well be in for a pound, "we aren't engaged either. We're dating, yes, but we're not going to get married anytime soon. Sorry. It seemed the easiest way to convince you that Will couldn't leave town, right now."

"But *you* can," Patrick said a little bitterly.

And okay, that was fair. Sort of.

"Enzo has a job that isn't in town, that he's *very* good at, that he's *famous* for," Will said, and he put an arm around Enzo's waist.

Showing a united front. "And yes, maybe I will go with him. When my own business hasn't been open for only a few months. When my manager isn't brand-new on the job."

"And because he wants to. He's spent all these years working for you. He wants to work for himself now. It's time," Enzo retorted.

It was Patrick's turn for his jaw to drop.

For a moment, everyone was stone still and silent.

Absorbing what they'd just said, no doubt.

"Your first date," Giana said hesitantly, "it wasn't at Rudy's? The first week you came to town?"

Enzo shrugged awkwardly. "We *did* go out to dinner that night." He looked over at Will. "What do you think? Should that count?"

"I don't think it matters when it happened, for real. Only that it did," Will said steadily, meeting Giana's dismayed gaze straight on.

"I suppose I can accept that," Giana said. "But Patrick is right! You can't leave Will here all the time. You don't even *live* here, Enzo! You don't live anywhere. How can you be together if you're not together!"

"And uh, that's the second part of it," Enzo said, rubbing the back of his neck. A few people had come in to order coffee and if he wasn't mistaken they were all listening to the family drama play out. He supposed he couldn't blame them, really. It would've been entertaining, if he hadn't been a part of it.

"I moved into Enzo's apartment," Will said. "And he's going to be coming back to Indigo Bay more."

"Between every job," Enzo added.

Will's parents only looked partially mollified at that. But clearly, they wanted the best for Will, even if, just like Giana, they were apparently the ones who decided what that was.

"It's not going to be easy for sure," Will said, glancing down at Enzo, and it was so easy to fall into the resolute certainty in his eyes. The steadiness. The ride-or-die loyalty. Everything he loved about the man—though it wasn't like his gorgeous body wasn't a good enough reason on its own. "But I don't care. I love him. That's all that matters, in the end."

There was chaos then.

Giana cried.

Carla hugged him, then Patrick shook his hand—and that was slightly awkward; Enzo hadn't made it a habit to meet his hookups' parents, for exactly this reason—and then Giana embraced him over and over.

"It's alright," she said, right before she pulled away the final time. "I know you'll marry him someday."

"Mom," Enzo groaned.

"I mean it," she said. "And we're going to talk more about the fact that you felt like you needed to lie to me."

He'd already known that was the case. And that wouldn't be a conversation that would happen around Will or his parents. He nodded.

"I'm working today, or *trying* to anyway, but I'll find you later tonight, alright?"

Giana just waved a hand. "Of course."

"You'll be at home?" Enzo pressed. It seemed like she was *never* at home anymore.

"Naturally, where else would I be?" He knew she was lying. He could see it in her eyes. And that baffled him more than anything else. *He'd* been honest; what was holding her back?

Well, he'd be sure to find out.

They didn't need any more secrets between them.

"Alright," Enzo said.

"I'm just gonna grab a coffee to go. Maybe two. I'm meeting Joy," she said, as Enzo watched Will saying goodbye to his parents out of the corner of his eye. He was hoping they would *actually* leave and go to Tybee Island this time around.

"Have fun," Enzo said. He turned to say goodbye to Will's parents, too, because that was a thing he had to do now. Being in a relationship was sure an adjustment. A *good* one, but an adjustment nonetheless.

"Enzo," she said, and he turned back. She cupped his cheeks with her palms and looked him deep in the eye. "I'm so proud of you, you know?"

Enzo swallowed hard. He *did* know it. Or he *mostly* did. But sometimes he forgot, or that feeling got consumed by all the other bullshit.

But he knew it right now and whenever he got frustrated with her or sick of her bullshit—and that *would* happen, because even though they loved each other, they were family, and it was inevitable—he'd remember this moment.

"Thanks, Mom."

She gave him one last squeeze. "Of course. And I'm sorry *you* didn't know it."

"I do now," he said.

Smiling, she turned towards Rocco at the counter, and after he'd hugged Carla and shaken Patrick's hand one last time and they were gone, along with Giana and her two coffees, Will looked at him.

"Well, that's done," he said.

"You look relieved," Enzo said. "Did you talk to them about it?"

"A little," Will said. "But we'll have to talk more, later. They're off to Tybee, finally. But I do know it's not over. They're still getting used to the idea that I'm not a doormat or an employee they can order around. When they do . . .we'll talk. But for now, I gotta go to work. Kate came in early to do the prep instead of me, but . . ."

Enzo didn't need Will to explain. He understood. "I get it. I have work to do, too. I told my mom I'd find her later, tonight, and we'll talk too."

"Alright." Will looked even more relieved then. He tucked a hand around Enzo's waist, and he tilted his face up towards Will's. "You okay?"

"Happy the truth's out, to be honest," Enzo said. "I didn't realize it was bothering me, until it was, until . . ."

"Yeah," Will agreed. He leaned in and brushed a lingering kiss against Enzo's mouth. "I guess I'll see you later tonight, at home?" He flushed, like he wasn't used to saying it, and Enzo had to admit that he wasn't used to *hearing* it.

"Yeah," he said. "At home."

Will smiled. "That's gonna take some getting used to, isn't it?"

"In the best kinda way." Enzo kissed him again, a little longer this time, ignoring Rocco's semi-outraged squawk across the bakery.

"Yeah." Will looked bashful and sweet about it, and Enzo didn't think he'd ever get tired of that look. Like he couldn't quite believe that he'd be coming home to Enzo—or that Enzo would be coming home to him.

Once upon a time, Enzo had imagined that feeling would be the death of a relationship. But instead, with Will, it felt like the beginning.

Enzo was going to see a thousand shades of blue in his dreams, tonight.

His hands were splattered with royal and indigo and sky and every color in-between, but when he finally climbed down from the scaffolding, the swirling sea between Eliza's perch and the town was almost done.

When he gazed up at it, the colors still vibrant even in the growing dusk, pride swamped him. This never got old, seeing his vision come to life. The story in his mind taking solid form, hopefully lighting up the imagination of everyone who walked by this and saw it.

Tomorrow, he'd just need to add a few final touches, and he'd get to move on to the tall-masted sailing ship, and Nathaniel, floating on a broken-off spar.

Enzo leaned back, stretching out his back and then his hands, beginning to pack up his supplies.

A few minutes later, he stuck his head into Cherry's, saw the long line nearly reaching the door and stepped right back out. He'd talk to Will later, when he wasn't slammed.

After he walked home and he ducked into his own apartment for a shower, he glanced over at the main house, which was, as it often seemed to be these days, dark.

"Ugh," Enzo muttered. He shed his paint-stained clothes, throwing them right into the washer before heading to the shower. Right before he got in, he texted his mom, but sure enough, when he was done and dressed, he'd gotten no response.

"Fine," he said out loud. "Fine, I can go find her." He needed to find some food anyway, so he'd cross two things off his list while he was at it.

She'd mentioned seeing Joy earlier—admittedly, *hours* and *hours* earlier, but Enzo decided, after swinging by the deli and picking up a sub, that was probably the best place to start.

But tonight, the wraparound porch was empty. No Giana. No Joy. Enzo was about to turn and leave, maybe eat his sub in the park, when he heard voices inside.

He pushed the door open, and stopped, right there in his tracks.

Because just inside, in the dim light of the reception area, was his mom.

And Joy.

And they were kissing.

Splat.

His sub fell out of his suddenly numb fingers, and they both looked up, surprise and trepidation written across both their faces.

Enzo didn't know what to say, so he didn't say anything at all.

Just stared.

At where Joy's arm was still wrapped around his mother's waist.

Giana spoke first, but not before doing the opposite of what Enzo expected. Instead of disentangling herself from Joy's embrace, she leaned in closer. Like she didn't want to let her go. Like they were partners, a *team*.

Enzo had felt that way with Will, just this morning.

"Enzo, darling," she said softly, "I wanted to tell you the truth. I was going to tell you, actually, tonight, but we got . . ." She hesitated. Clammed up.

Enzo swallowed hard. "Please don't say you got carried away, Mom," he said.

It was easier to banter with her like he always did than face head-on the truths that were currently, blatantly, in front of his face.

His mom was *not* straight.

Oliver's mom was *not* straight.

And they were *not straight* together.

"I won't then," Giana said. She glanced up at Joy. "I do need to talk to him, though, and you said—"

"Yes," Joy agreed, nodding. "I'll talk to Oliver. Tonight."

They kissed again, briefly, but thoroughly enough Enzo felt his whole world re-aligning around him. He swallowed hard. "I'll just be . . .uh . . .outside then." He turned, nearly tripped over his sandwich, picking it up in its paper-wrapped bundle at the last second, and managed to get outside, to the far end of the patio, with no more accidents.

Because he really wasn't thinking right now.

If he thought . . .*well*.

He just wasn't going to think about it. No good could come from him doing any thinking whatsoever right now.

Of course, with the way his mom approached, wringing her hands and looking like she wanted to bare her soul, Enzo had a feeling the opposite was in the cards for him.

He settled down on one of the long couches and she sat, right next to him.

"I'm sorry you had to find out that way," she said quietly.

Enzo had seen his mother a whole lot of ways. Since his dad had never been around, he'd only known her. He thought he'd witnessed every possible mood she possessed but he didn't think he'd ever seen this one before. Almost like she was diminished.

Ashamed.

And holy hell, that was not going to work. Not now, not ever.

"Mom, you *know* I don't care right? I don't care if you go around kissing a hundred women. A thousand. Or . . ." *Don't think, don't think.* "Whatever you want to do with them." *I only care that you didn't care enough to tell me.*

"I know you don't, but it's . . .it's a huge adjustment," Giana said. "And it's new. So we're still working our way through it. It's why we didn't tell you or Oliver yet. Or anyone. But it's one of the reasons I pushed so hard to have you come home. When I did tell you, I wanted to do it in person."

And not only why she'd pushed so hard to get him home, Enzo realized.

Why she'd pushed so hard with Will.

She was happy; she wanted *him* happy.

It was hard to be so frustrated and hurt, after that particular realization crossed his mind.

"You're happy?" Enzo reached out and grasped her hand, squeezed
it. "That's all I care about. You happy."

"I am. Happier than I've been . . ." Giana sighed then, and there
were those Moretti heart-eyes, the ones he liked to tease Luca about all
the time. The ones he probably shared with them now, whenever he
looked at Will. "Probably in forever." She paused. "No, *the* happiest
I've been, period."

"That's all that matters."

"Your father . . ." Giana trailed off.

But they didn't need to talk about him. He'd never been present in
their lives. Giana had raised him entirely on her own, and whenever
he'd asked, as a precocious and inquisitive kid, where *that* half of the
family was, she'd told him firmly that they were better off not knowing
them.

He'd always believed her—and he believed her now.

"You don't need to explain to me," Enzo said.

She looked surprised. "No?"

Enzo had always known that things might've been a lot different
if he hadn't grown up in his idyllic town—admittedly a town that
had driven him nuts, but *still,* he couldn't complain about his childhood—if she'd allowed his dad's family to be a part of their lives.

"No," Enzo said firmly.

Some of the anxiety in her eyes dissipated. "So you're not upset."

"How could I be? What did you say to me when I came out to you?
I was, what, twelve? Thirteen?"

"I said *okay, I love you no matter what*."

"Exactly," Enzo said. Paused. "Okay, I love you no matter what."

She beamed, and there was the woman he knew.

"I mean, it's going to be a little weird," Enzo continued, giving her a wry grin. "Did you *have* to date Oliver's mother?"

Giana laughed then. "I suppose it's good you didn't end up with him."

"For many, many reasons," Enzo said.

She patted his sandwich. "Eat your dinner. You're practically wasting away in front of me."

He hadn't thought he'd want to, but his stomach was grumbling so he unwrapped half and began to eat. Between bites he said, "You know, Mom, just because you're happy doesn't mean you get to dictate other people's happiness."

"I didn't," she said, all false bravado. "You're the one who fell for him."

"I did, and I probably would've no matter what. But. *But.* You got lucky, Mom. You interfered and it could've been a total disaster."

"But it wasn't!" she interjected.

"But it could have been. And we could've been running around town, pretending to be in love but not even *liking* each other, because you wouldn't quit hounding us about it."

Enzo hated being so harsh with her, but he was going to be around Indigo Bay more. Around *her* more. He needed to re-establish their boundaries. Because he couldn't risk her meddling in his relationship again. Not when Will meant so much to him. Not when he wanted it to work out so badly with him.

"I suppose . . ." Giana trailed off and sighed. "Joy told me I should leave you alone, that *she* left Oliver alone and he found Luca and it all turned out. I just *worried* that you wouldn't find someone. Or you'd find someone and they'd be three thousand miles away and I'd never see you."

"It could've happened that way," Enzo agreed. "But it didn't. You can't always force things to happen the way you want. You've got to let me figure things out on my own. When you don't—that's when I stay away, Mom. You know that. We've talked about it." He said it gently, but he could feel the words hit her and her gaze grow solemn as she absorbed them.

"I know. I'm sorry. I got carried away. I shouldn't have, but . . .*ugh*, he *was* perfect for you, Enzo, darling. He *is* perfect for you."

Well, he'd known he probably wasn't getting out of this conversation without a little *I told you so,* but he'd take that, as long as she understood the boundaries he was setting.

"Yes, he is," Enzo agreed.

She sighed again, but happier this time. "All's well that ends well. I shouldn't have pushed, I know. I *am* sorry. Well." She laughed. "Mostly sorry. Also happy to be right."

"You know what?" Enzo wiped his hands on a napkin and wrapped his arms around her, hugging her tight. "I'm really happy you were, too. And one more thing. I'm happy you were going to tell me about you and Joy. That you *wanted* to tell me about you two."

"Well, of course." Giana beamed at him. "You're my beloved son. I just wish I'd managed to say it before you saw."

"Well, how about we just . . .make sure there's no more seeing," Enzo said.

Giana batted her eyelashes innocently. "And I'm sure you and Will won't be engaging in *any* PDA whatsoever."

Enzo groaned. "I take it back. I don't approve at all."

Giana just laughed though. "Oh, you can't take that back. Any of it, actually."

And he knew then that they'd be okay.

❧❧❧❧❧❧ ❧❧❧❧❧❧

"And *then*," Enzo continued, "I walked inside the Inn and there was my mom and Joy. Kissing."

Inside the shower, Will made a gratifyingly surprised noise. "What?" he exclaimed. He dropped the soap as punctuation, just like how Enzo had dropped his sub sandwich. At another time, Enzo might've made a joke about how if he'd been in there, he'd have taken advantage of that fact, but he was too occupied telling Will what had happened next.

"They were kissing. And then, thank God, they *stopped* kissing."

"What happened after that? Did they tell you what's going on?"

"Apparently they're in love. Or dating. Or whatever." Enzo wiped a hand across his face. He didn't want to think about the *whatever*. Giana wasn't old; she still deserved happiness and companionship. He just didn't want to *think* about it. "My mom told me she'd wanted to tell me about it, she just didn't have time before I walked in on them."

"But she *did* talk to you," Will said. He flipped the shower off and Enzo reached over, handing him his towel.

He'd meant to tell him all about their talk. But then Will stepped out, towel wrapped around his waist, chest still damp, droplets of water snaking their way down his tanned chest. Enzo wasn't proud of it, but okay, he *still* got a little distracted whenever Will was naked around him. Even when Will was *partially* naked around him. Just a little flash of skin and his blood went hot and his brain power slowed to a sluggish crawl.

"Enzo? You okay there?" Will asked, chuckling under his breath.

"Sorry, you're just . . .you're just really distracting."

Will laughed out loud. "I've finally figured out the secret for shutting up a Moretti. Get naked."

"This Moretti isn't going to argue with that technique. Not in the least."

Will ran a hand through his hair, shaking droplets all over Enzo, even though he hadn't moved from his perch on the counter. "But you did talk to her?"

"Yeah." Enzo hesitated. "It does make sense that she was working overtime to find someone for me, if she was happy and worried that I wasn't."

"It doesn't excuse it, but it *does* explain it," Will agreed.

"I told her she can't interfere anymore. She promised she wouldn't. I didn't say this, but next time, if she breaks her word, you know who I'm going to tell." Enzo waggled his eyebrows.

Will laughed again. "Your cousin?"

"Luca's disappointed face could make anyone regret their choices," Enzo said, nodding. "Ask me how I know."

"You didn't change your life because he disapproved of you," Will argued loyally.

"No. Not entirely, anyway." Enzo pressed a kiss to Will's damp cheek. "But thank you for believing the best of me."

"Of course."

Enzo leaned in, and there was that butterfly-fluttering, blood-moving-hot-and-slow, feeling again. But this time he tipped his head closer and was angling for more than just a peck when the sound of someone knocking on the front door echoed through the bathroom.

"Who's that?" Will wondered.

"No clue," Enzo said. "It better not be my mother. I made her promise she would leave us alone. Apparently she's in a bit of honeymoon phase of her own. You'd think she'd have a lot more respect for ours."

"You'd think," Will said dryly.

Reluctantly, Enzo jumped down off the counter, forgoing what had been shaping up to be a very promising makeout session, and maybe even more, considering that all he'd have to do to strip Will bare was tug on a corner of his towel.

"I'll get dressed," Will said as the knock echoed again.

Enzo walked to the front door, thinking that he was going to have to have a peephole put in, so he could decide if he actually wanted to talk to the person on the other side. It had never been an issue before; but now that Will was living here and Enzo was going to be around a lot more . . .well, he was going to do whatever he could to protect their hard-won privacy.

Maybe if this worked out for the next year or so, they could buy a house together. Away from his mother. On the other side of town, preferably.

But when Enzo pulled the door open, it wasn't Giana.

It was Oliver.

His tanned cheeks were ruddy and his eyes were narrowed, upset.

It took Enzo a moment to realize why.

"She told you, didn't she?" he asked, pulling the door open wider.

"You look pretty calm about it," Oliver said, striding in, hands shoved in the pockets of his jean shorts, a frown marring his expression.

Enzo shrugged, following him into the living room.

The bedroom door stayed closed, and Enzo supposed he couldn't blame Will for staying out of this mess. It was *their* mess to deal with—his and Oliver's.

If he hadn't already been involved, he'd have avoided it, too.

"I guess I am," Enzo said, sitting down on the couch. But Oliver continued to pace. Clearly *he* was not calm about it.

"I couldn't believe it, when she told me."

"At least she *told* you," Enzo pointed out dryly. "I found out because I saw them kissing."

"*What*," Oliver exclaimed.

"Yep." Enzo nodded. "You definitely had the better revelation."

His confession seemed to have taken the wind right out of Oliver's sails. He dropped down onto the other side of the couch.

"I just don't . . ." Oliver took a deep breath. "I don't understand."

"Don't you?" Enzo said as kindly as he could manage.

"She *never*, not before my dad, not with my dad, not . . ." Oliver took a deep breath.

Then Enzo realized what the issue was. Unlike Oliver, he'd never known his father. He'd likely been dead before Enzo was even born. But Oliver's dad had been a presence in his life, for *most* of his life. He'd only died ten years ago, from a quick-moving cancer that had claimed him almost as soon as it had been discovered.

"Doesn't mean this isn't legit, that her feelings aren't legit," Enzo said gently. "You know that. Queerness isn't a thing that always goes in a straight line. It doesn't always make sense."

"I know. I *know*," Oliver said. "But she's my *mom.*" He paused. "With *your* mom."

"Believe me, nobody was more surprised than me. And if you want my advice, just don't . . .*think* about that part very hard."

Oliver barked a laugh. "Probably easier for me, since I found out different than you."

"Probably. But I got the impression they're not wanting to hide it anymore. So I can't guarantee what you're going to see in the future."

"I know," Oliver said with a short groan. Then he smiled and glanced over at Enzo. "I guess it's good we didn't end up together."

It was good—*so* good, finally—that they could both joke about this. It had taken a lot of years and two happy relationships. Though it wasn't like Enzo had been pining after him, before he'd met Will. He'd long since acknowledged that he and Oliver had been doomed from that first date. Probably even before.

"Yeah," Enzo agreed. "You talk to Luca about this?"

Oliver shot him a look. "What do you think?"

"I think if you have the kind of relationship I wanna have with Will, then yeah, you told him."

"He actually told me to come talk to you about it," Oliver admitted.

"Yeah?" Enzo was more pleased about that than he'd thought he would be.

"He said you'd get it. And I guess you would. I think he probably knew that I was overreacting."

"If there's one thing a Moretti knows about, it's overreacting," Enzo said.

Oliver laughed, lighter than he'd sounded since he'd arrived.

"Listen," Enzo continued, "it's easier for me. My dad never really existed for me. My mom never dated anyone else. Not that I knew about anyway."

"Might've been good for her—and you—if she had," Oliver observed.

And yeah, that was true. Enzo nodded. "It's not like I told her not to. You don't tell a Moretti to *do* anything," he said.

Oliver smiled. "Being married to one, I'm intimately aware of that. And I told Joy that she could date, of course. Dad's been gone for ten years. I don't want her to be alone forever, that's not it at all. It's just . . .an adjustment."

"Yeah, it is. But a good one." Enzo hadn't realized that he thought so until he said it. Until he was worried that Oliver would say the opposite.

"You really mean that."

"Yeah. I do."

"Ugh." Oliver wiped a hand across his face. "I'm being very stupid, aren't I?"

"I don't know. I think you're allowed to be once in a while. And you basically never were, before."

"You're saying it's my turn, Moretti?" Oliver asked wryly.

"Sure."

"I can agree with that. But I do think yeah, it's the way I have to think of it differently. Think of her differently."

"She's still your mother. She's never gonna *stop* being your mother," Enzo reminded him firmly.

"Oh, no, *no*. I know that. I just . . .with *your* mother." Oliver shuddered a little. "I guess I didn't think of her like . . .like a *sexual* being."

"Please don't. I'm begging you not to keep going down that road. I keep trying to stop myself from doing it."

"Alright. I think that's fair."

"They're happy. *She's* happy. You know what? That's all that matters." Enzo paused. "What did your mom say to you when you came out to her? Did she think you were a different kind of person?"

Oliver let out a sharp sigh. "No. No, she didn't. Which you know."

"I do. Joy's a great mom. A great person. And she deserves to be happy. However that happens."

"I know you're right," Oliver said with a sigh. "This is a *me* thing. I'll adjust, and I'm sure in a few months it'll be like they've always been together."

"You think they're serious?"

Oliver shot him a look. "Do you think they're *not* serious?"

"Point taken," Enzo said wryly.

"Exactly. At least I won't be the only one around to witness it," Oliver teased. "You're gonna be around a lot more, enjoying your *own* relationship."

"That's the plan."

Oliver reached over and gave him a quick hug. "Well, if I had to be a stepbrother with anyone, I'm happy it's you," he said.

And that wasn't something that Enzo had ever thought he'd hear, but he realized he agreed.

"Yeah. Me too."

Oliver smiled. "That settles it then. I . . ." He trailed off as he stood. "I'm glad I came. Luca said it would make me feel better talking to you, and I thought he was full of shit, but I'm happy that I was wrong."

"And he will be too. Happy enough he probably won't even say *I told you so*," Enzo pointed out.

"Probably," Oliver said, smiling now. "Well. Thanks for listening to me rant."

"Anytime."

A minute later, the front door was closing behind him, and almost immediately, the bedroom door opened and Will walked out, wearing only a pair of navy blue boxer briefs. "He okay?" Will asked, putting his arms around Enzo and tugging him close.

"Yeah," Enzo said. "Or he will be. It's a bigger adjustment for him. He knew his dad."

"Right." Will looked like he wanted to say something else, but then he smiled, slowly. "You wanna come to bed?"

Enzo didn't need to have it suggested even twice.

"Yes," he said and lifted his head to kiss Will's mouth.

Chapter Nineteen

"It's really coming along," Will said, shading his eyes as he looked up at Enzo's figure, perched on the highest corner of the scaffolding.

Enzo had a cap on, turned backwards, the edges of a maroon bandana peeking out from under it. He'd lost his shirt sometime in the first few hours of work, the tail of it tucked into the back of his paint-stained shorts.

"Yeah, it really is," Enzo said, leaning back a fraction and taking in the semi-finished mural. He was working on the fine details now, the white crests of the waves and the surprisingly evocative expression on Nathaniel's face, even buried under his thick beard, as he hung onto a loose spar, desperately trying not to be sucked under the swells.

"Come take a break," Will called up again. "I've got water and some food."

"I can take a few minutes," Enzo said, wiping his face and beginning to climb down. "But Joy just told me they were hoping to do a little ceremony during the Fourth of July festivities. I'd like to be almost done by then."

"Will you be ready for that?" Will wondered. From his perspective, he thought the mural was probably almost done. But every time he said so, Enzo would roll his eyes and list off a dozen or so things he still needed to work on.

"I think so," Enzo said. "At least the bulk of it will be ready anyway. Joy and Mom are already talking about having a big-deal dedication during the Sweethearts Festival next year. I'll have to make sure I'm around for that. But for this, yeah, I think so."

He leaned against Will, tilting his head for a kiss, which Will was happy to give him. He didn't mind he was damp and sweaty. Frankly he'd have pressed him to the wall he'd just finished painting and kissed him thoroughly, if they'd had time. But Enzo had only said he had a few minutes, and his priority had to be to get some water and some food into him.

"I got water and some chicken salad inside. Come in and cool down—"

Enzo opened his mouth, no doubt to argue about how little time he had for a break, but Will took his hand and began to tug him towards Cherry's door. "I know," he said. "You only have a few minutes. But you gotta take care of yourself in this heat."

"How can I?" Enzo asked. "When you do such a good job of it for me?"

Will rolled his eyes but led him through the empty room and behind the counter.

Kate was working on prep for the day, slowly pouring ice cream mix into the big industrial ice cream machine. "Hey," she said. "I'm finished with the chocolate and the vanilla, and then I'll work on the cheesecake next, for the Fourth of July specials."

Will nodded, distracted by his boyfriend next to him. "Sure thing. I'll be done in a few."

"Right." Kate shot him a knowing look. "You just take your time."

"Do you think," Enzo said, slipping into the desk chair with a happy sigh as Will closed the door behind them, "that she really thinks we're going to christen your desk?"

"I don't know. Maybe." Will flushed a little, just thinking about it. Remembering how many times he'd *seriously* considered it. Before they'd even had sex. The very first time Enzo had even been in here and he'd said, *maybe we should go on a fake date.*

He'd wanted him bad even back then.

"So you are gonna do some Fourth of July specials?" Enzo asked as Will pulled out two bottles of water and an ice-cold Gatorade, blue raspberry flavor, because one of the things he'd learned about Enzo was the faker the flavor, the more into it he was.

Made Will shake his head.

Made him love Enzo even more. Because now he *knew* those things about him.

"Yeah. The berry cheesecake, we're testing that today. I was working on how to top the shake and I thought, what if I did a little cheesecake wedge, dipped in chocolate, nestled right on top of the glass? Right along with the other fresh berries?"

"You're not one to go the easy route, are you?" Enzo asked, brown eyes twinkling as he took a long sip of water. Then picked up the fork and dug into the container of chicken salad that Will had slid in front of him.

"Not really," Will admitted. "I fell for you, didn't I?"

Enzo's grin was blinding, and Will wanted to see it every day for the rest of his life.

Maybe it was early, but he *knew* Enzo was the man for him, deep down, in the same place where he'd known this was the right building for Cherry's. That the tuxedo milkshake would be a bestseller. That the cherry brown butter brickle would be a special flavor he'd want to keep.

That the Fourth of July special—the glass striped with different berry compotes and filled with a cheesecake milkshake and topped with the little chocolate covered wedge of cheesecake—would mean they'd be busy every single moment of the long holiday weekend to come.

"You sure did. That does sound delicious, though. Not that you were really worried that it wouldn't be."

"True," Will said. He rested a hip against the edge of the desk. "We're going to be packed, with all the extra tourists, but you let me know when Joy's celebration is, and I'll make sure I'm available."

"You're sure?"

"Kate's capable. She should be able to handle things for an hour or two."

"Probably she could handle things for longer than that," Enzo said cautiously.

Will looked over at him in surprise. "You think so?"

"She's pretty good, Will. You hired her. Then you trained her. She couldn't be anything less." Enzo had looked worried when he'd pointed it out, like he hadn't wanted to interfere with Will's business. Will understood his concern; after all he'd just got done telling his parents to stop telling him how to run his business.

Was Enzo different?

Well, *sort of*. He did trust that Enzo wouldn't say something if he didn't believe it. If he didn't believe Will needed to hear it.

He wasn't saying it because he had ulterior motives either. Though Will supposed, he *could*. Because Enzo would want him to come along to his jobs sometimes. Frankly, *Will* wanted to come along to his jobs sometimes. He didn't want to be what his dad said—only hanging around Indigo Bay, waiting for Enzo to come home.

"You have a good point," Will agreed. "I'll definitely be relying on her more."

"Yeah?" Enzo tucked his free hand around Will's waist, pulled him in close.

"Yeah," Will agreed. "Can't let you have all this mural fun by yourself, anymore. Besides . . .I'm getting too used to sleeping beside you to stop now."

Enzo smiled, sweet and devastatingly sexy, both at the same time. "Even with how my hair looks in the morning?"

"*Especially* with how your hair looks in the morning." Will meant it, too. Every time he woke up and looked over, Enzo's dark curls spread out across the pillow, he felt an unexpected surge of joy and peace.

"I guess you're stuck with me, then," Enzo said, grinning, and yeah, he sure was, and there was no denying how happy he was about it.

Will leaned in farther. "Yeah, I guess I am. You know what? Thanks for saying something. Sometimes I get . . .I get too possessive of this business. Too worried about it."

"Well, it's *yours*," Enzo said matter-of-factly, like he understood. And maybe, more than anyone else, he would. "You worked for it and planned for it and made it happen. *Just* you. I don't blame you for not wanting to let it go. Even to someone as capable as Kate."

He'd thought he'd have to explain all that and hope that Enzo might understand, but he hadn't needed to, at all.

"Told you, I get it," Enzo continued. He pressed a kiss to Will's shoulder. He picked up the Gatorade. "I gotta get back to work. Sadly this mural isn't gonna paint itself."

"Alright. Me too. I gotta bake some cheesecake."

"Don't stop overachieving, yeah?" Enzo teased.

"I won't."

Enzo gave him one last brief kiss, and then he was gone.

Will finished his chicken salad at a bit more of a leisurely pace, checking his phone for email. He was just about to put it away when it rang.

Before, every time he'd looked at the screen and seen it was his mom, he'd dreaded answering. But he did feel like before they'd left, he and his parents had finally gotten to a better place.

"Hey, Mom," he said, setting his phone on the desk, flipping it on speaker. "Great timing. You caught me grabbing a quick lunch."

"Oh, honey, you work too hard. It's almost two in the afternoon."

"Yeah, and these Fourth of July specials don't make themselves," he said. "How's it going on Tybee?"

"I just called to tell you, actually." Carla hesitated and Will tensed, suddenly worried what that might mean. What was she going to ask him for now? But instead of asking for anything, she continued, "It's actually going well. Brewer's really stepped up."

"Brewer lives to step up," Will pointed out, but he meant it well. Brewer was great at everything he'd ever set his mind to, so it didn't really surprise him that he'd figure out how to be great at the nitty-gritty realities of opening a store, too.

"He does, but I was afraid this was too much for him. He was . . .well, things were a bit chaotic," Carla said diplomatically. Will didn't miss how she'd said that *things* were a bit chaotic, not Brewer himself.

Will didn't think Brewer had been chaotic a day in his entire freaking life.

"But they're not now?"

"Oh, there was a guy he hired to work at the store, who ended up teaching him a lot of things. I was impressed. And Brewer was *very* impressed."

"He must be something, if even Brewer was impressed. And if Brewer managed to listen to him."

"Brewer isn't *that* difficult."

"Mom," Will chided.

"Okay, he *can* be. Only because he doesn't usually get his hands dirty."

"Exactly."

"Well, I just wanted you to know that I'm glad you didn't come. You have Cherry's—and Enzo—and it's right. You should focus on those, right now."

"Thanks, Mom." He hadn't expected this phone call. Hadn't even imagined that he'd get it. But getting it meant more than he could put into words.

It was *You were right.* And *You're right where you need to be. Where you should be.* But most importantly he heard what else she wasn't saying: *And we're proud of you.*

"Of course." Carla cleared her throat. "It's a great life you're building for yourself there, Will. Don't forget to live it."

"Is that an admonition to not work too much?" he joked.

"You know it is. You have that handsome man in your life now, you need to *enjoy* him."

"Don't worry, Mom. Even if I was very stupid and forgot, I think he'd be first in line to remind me."

"He would. It's one of the reasons both me and your father liked him so much. He's going to be so good for you." She paused. "Whether you get married or not."

"About that, Mom—"

"No," she interrupted. "We don't have to talk about it. I know you and Enzo were only trying to do the right thing. We were just a little slow on the uptake."

"And I wasn't very good at telling you the truth," Will said wryly. He'd gotten better at the end, but there'd been so many years when he'd avoided the truth or not wanted to address anything directly. By the time he'd finally started, it had almost been too late, and his parents were so entrenched in the normal way of doing things that they hadn't known to really listen to what he was trying to say.

But now, hopefully, they were listening again.

Will wanted to believe that this phone call was his mom's way of saying they were.

"Maybe. Maybe not. In any case, we're aware now. You've got your own life. Your own business. And we're so proud of you for both, Will."

Will smiled. She hadn't need to say the words—he'd felt them nonetheless—but it sure helped to hear them.

"Thanks, Mom. Enzo was telling me today they're gonna have a big dedication of the mural next year, during the Sweethearts Festival. I'll text you the dates so you can pencil them into your calendar."

"Pencil? I'll be writing them in with pen," she said firmly. "Though I'm sure we'll see you before that."

"I'm sure," Will said. He'd never wanted to be a stranger from his family; he'd only wanted his own corner of his own life.

And now he did.

"Take care of yourself, honey."

"Good luck at the store opening."

"And you too, during the Fourth. I'm sure you'll be slammed."

"That's the hope and the worry," Will joked weakly.

"You've got this," she said confidently.

There was a brisk knock on the door. Sounded just like Kate. And yeah, Will really needed to help her with the prep, or else they'd never get done. "Hey, I gotta go. But, Mom? Thanks for calling."

"Of course, honey. Anytime."

When he opened the door though, it wasn't Kate standing on the other side, but Enzo, grinning madly.

"Do you have a minute?" he asked.

Will raised an eyebrow. He tossed the empty takeout container in the trash. "I've got at least one. Maybe a few, for you."

"What about for your building?"

"What do you mean?"

Enzo whipped out a paint brush. "Come on," he said. "Let's paint your mural."

Will held up his hands. "No way. I've not got an artistic bone in my body. I'll ruin it and then you'll hate me."

"Not possible. Either one. Seriously, it's on *your* building, and it was *your* idea."

"Do you ask the owners of every building you paint a mural on to contribute?"

Enzo shook his head. "No. But you're special. Makes sense that I should."

"If you're sure . . ." Will trailed off, dubiously.

"I *am* sure. Come on," Enzo straight up ordered this time, wrapping a hand around his forearm and tugging. "We got this. I wouldn't let you do something to ruin it. I promise."

"Alright," Will finally agreed. Let Enzo lead him outside.

He was working on the current generation of buildings surrounding the story of Eliza and Nathaniel. "This should look familiar," Enzo said, pointing with the brush to a building that had Cherry's signature white and bright pink striped awning.

"Yeah, sure does."

"I just want you to take this brush and paint the rest of the building. It's just white. I'll be adding the fine details later so no worries about that."

"Okay." Will took the brush and gingerly dipped it into the paint and even more carefully dabbed it onto the wall, right where Enzo had sketched out the outline of the building.

"How's that?" Will asked apprehensively, but Enzo just laughed.

"You're barely doing anything. Come on, *paint it.*"

So Will did, Enzo standing behind him coaching him through it with easy, judgment-free suggestions.

"See?" he asked. "Just like this." He moved behind Will, mirroring his body with his own, and reaching out cupping his hand, guiding the brush. "Yeah, you've got it. Just keep going like that. Fill in the outline, and I'll do the rest."

Will kept going, and the more he did, the more confident he felt. There was a stray stroke or two that went out of the outline, but Enzo just brushed off Will's worries. "Oh, I'm a *much* messier painter than you," he said breezily, but Will wasn't entirely sure.

Still, when he finally stepped back and the building was finally filled in, he felt an unexpected surge of satisfaction and accomplishment. *He'd* done that—and Enzo had been the one to suggest it in the first place, which was something he certainly hadn't needed to do.

"Thank you," he said, turning to Enzo, who was standing there grinning like he knew exactly the kind of gift he'd given Will.

"Of course. It's your building. It's your business. It made sense for *you* to do it." He leaned in, dropping his voice a little. "But don't tell anyone else. I wanted this to be special, just for you. Because I love you."

Will met his kiss with one of his own, fierce and passionate, and ending way too quickly. "I love you too. Seriously. Thank you for this. It means a lot. More than I'd imagined."

"I've got a few ideas how much," Enzo mused, his gaze flicking up as he took a step back, looking over the entirety of what he'd created. "I didn't know that I'd care so much about creating a mural in my hometown. I kinda wanted to forget my hometown existed at all—but you gave it back to me. All the good things, and none of the bad."

"It's both of ours, now," Will said.

Enzo's hope was by the time Fourth of July rolled around and the impromptu ceremony that Joy had talked him into, the mural would be done enough he'd be proud to stand next to it and take credit.

But as he did, Joy's voice raising to carry to the small crowd that had gathered in front of the mural, he realized he was feeling even more than the normal amount of pride at his work being admired and displayed.

He hadn't been exaggerating a few days ago when he'd told Will that this one was special.

Enzo glanced in the back of the crowd and met Will's eyes. He looked stressed—but undeniably proud—as he stood in the back and gave Enzo a smile that told him exactly how much this meant to him.

How much *Enzo* meant to him.

There was Giana next to him. Beaming up at him like he'd done so much more than paint a wall. Or maybe that was Joy she was beaming at.

Or . . .maybe it was both of them getting that look.

Their relationship was still taking a bit of getting used to, but Enzo had meant everything he'd said to Oliver the other night. He was thrilled they'd found happiness, and in some way, it made total and complete sense they'd discovered it with each other.

On the other side, Luca and Oliver must've taken time out from their busy schedules, because they were there, not holding hands, but with such an air of possession around them, an air of *belonging*, that you'd never believe they weren't still madly in love with each other.

Oliver was even looking at his mother with fondness in his gaze—making Enzo hope that any wrinkles from the fallout of Joy and Giana's relationship coming to light had been smoothed over already.

"And now, a big round of applause for our local artist, who came back to his hometown to paint this incredible representation of Eliza and Nathaniel's story. Ladies and gentlemen, Enzo Moretti."

Enzo waved and stepped up to the makeshift podium. He tucked his sunglasses into the open collar of his shirt and lifted his voice. "Thanks for that welcome, Joy. I'm going to be honest. I was not all that grateful to come back to Indigo Bay. For as long as I could remember, what I wanted most wasn't to stay here, but to leave. To learn to paint. To show people from all over what I knew I was capable of. I wasn't looking for an opportunity to come back, and give back, but I am so happy that I was gifted one, anyway.

"Growing up here in Indigo Bay, I never really understood Eliza and Nathaniel's story. I knew love existed, but I had never experienced it, so I couldn't understand it. But now . . .I've fallen in love and it was not only my pleasure to paint this mural, to give this town a visual representation of its history, but it's been my joy. I'm honored that I was the artist selected to do it. Even more, the artist *trusted* with this commission."

Joy went to shake his hand, amongst the applause, but he hugged her instead, tightly. "We're family now," he said to her, and she smiled wide, clearly pleased at his words.

After their speeches, the crowd milled around, many of them approaching Enzo to tell them how much they loved the mural.

By the time he was finally finished shaking hands, making polite small talk, and taking compliments, he looked around and realized Will had gone back inside Cherry's.

Well, that was fair. The town, festooned with red, white, and blue banners all down Main Street, was full of tourists and as a result, *Cherry's* was probably full of tourists.

Enzo turned the corner and yep, he could see through the big picture windows that the interior was packed. Will was working hard behind the counter, along with Kate, Rocco, and Mari.

Enzo hesitated only for a moment, then pulled the door open, working his way around the crowds inside, until he stepped around the counter.

Rolling up the sleeves of his dark blue button-up, he slid into place next to Mari. "Can you make ice cream stuff?" he asked her under his breath.

She looked over at him in surprise. "Yes?" she asked uncertainly.

"Okay. Then you do that. I can't, but I *can* take orders."

"You're sure?"

"If Will's unhappy about it, he can take me into his office later and punish me," Enzo said, giving her a wink. "Promise. I can handle this crowd."

"Alright." She looked relieved, and she stepped away to help Kate with an order.

Will met his gaze for a second and Enzo was pretty sure he was saying *thank you.*

Enzo straightened, taking in the fairly straightforward screen. He could figure this out. He could *do* this, for Will.

For himself.

"Hi, welcome to Cherry's," he said as the next family stepped up. "I'm Enzo. What can I get for you today?"

Every muscle in Will's body ached—except one.

Well, it *did* ache, but in a deliciously sweet way.

His heart felt like it kept expanding more and more, giving him an infinite capacity for love.

"I just flipped the sign off," Enzo said as he came back around the counter.

Rocco was in the back, washing dishes. Kate and Mari were in the seating area, cleaning up tables and sweeping up abandoned napkins and cherry stems on the floor before they went back over and mopped every inch.

It meant that for now, it was just him and Enzo.

Enzo, who'd taken one look at the crowd inside Cherry's and hadn't even hesitated for a second. He'd come in, Will's very own knight in shining armor, rolling up his sleeves, gently pushing Mari off to help them make ice cream, and had taken every order. Had figured out his point-of-sale system on the fly and soothed impatient tempers at the long wait and did it all with an easy, charming, *very* Moretti smile on his face.

"I don't think I had time to say, but thank you. *Thank you*." Will pulled him in, not worrying about the smears of ice cream and caramel and chocolate and strawberry streaked across his T-shirt and apron, because Enzo's shirt had hardly been clean before this.

Enzo had scooped ice cream too, even though he'd never done it before.

He'd been exactly what Will had needed, when he hadn't even realized he needed it.

"I'd say it was nothing, but it was hard work. Still, I was happy to do it." Enzo dropped his voice, and love was shining so unmistakably in his brown eyes. "For you. I love you, and this is part of you, so I love it, too."

"Really?" Will didn't even think he loved it, right now. He was so exhausted he didn't think he could make another sundae or milkshake or scoop another cone, not even if someone wanted to pay him a million bucks for it.

"Really." Enzo paused. "But maybe it's time to hire some extra help. I think you're a hit, Stud Muffin."

"Honey Bunny, I think you might be right." Will grinned. "But that's a problem for tomorrow. Tonight . . ."

"Yeah? I think we gotta get clean, first," Enzo asked, and even though his eyes were drooping, he still looked hopeful, like Will might press him against the cold tile in the shower and leave him panting with pleasure.

And Will? He'd do it, too. Use the very last of his energy to lavish it on the man he loved.

"Anything for you," Will said and meant it. "Let's go home."

Epilogue

A year later

Enzo was halfway up the scaffolding, the early breeze coming off the coast of Oregon ruffling his hair, when his phone rang.

"Hey, Mom," he said, answering without hesitating.

There'd been a time when he'd have put it off. Let her call go to voicemail. Call her back days—maybe even a week—later. Until his guilt was so overwhelming he couldn't do anything else but listen to it.

He'd become semi-permanently tied to that uncomfortable feeling that pressed up against his breastbone.

But no longer.

Now, she called and he answered, gladly, actually excited to talk to his mom, again.

"Enzo! I'm so glad I caught you. You aren't working, are you?"

The re-establishment of their relationship hadn't just been about healthier boundaries—but about mutual respect.

He'd learn to respect more what she'd sacrificed, and she'd learned how to respect his choices. It hadn't been immediate, a flip of the switch, but a developing process. They'd both had to grow. Had to learn.

"Nope, not quite yet. You caught me right before I went up."

"The pictures you sent me yesterday were gorgeous. And Will showed me a bunch more when I stopped by to pick up some ice cream for Joy and me."

"How's that going?" Enzo asked. He knew that a week ago, Giana had finally moved in with Joy, to the apartment she had in the Inn.

"The place is small but . . ." Giana paused, and Enzo heard a hundred emotions in that pause. Happiness and joy and frustration and angst at the inevitable change.

"I bet it is," Enzo said. "I couldn't believe it when it felt like my apartment was too small for us."

"It *was* too small. It barely had a kitchen, which was fine for you, but for Will . . ."

"Yeah," Enzo agreed.

"But no, it's good. We've both lived on our own for so long it is a bit of an adjustment to have someone underfoot. But in the end, it's good to have someone to share a life with, now."

"I'm really glad for you, Mom."

"And now the house is empty. I had it cleaned. You and Will can move in next week when you come home."

"You didn't have to do that for us, but I know both Will and I are appreciative."

Enzo had fully expected that they'd have to do some house hunting a few months back during one of his breaks. He and Will had started talking about it only a few weeks after he'd moved in. They'd realized pretty quickly that his apartment, while cozy, was really too small for two.

The lack of a real kitchen had been hard, too.

But then Giana had suggested over the holidays that she and Joy were talking about her moving into the Inn—leaving the house Enzo had grown up in empty.

"It seemed like the best idea," Giana said, sounding pleased, too. "You two deserve the ability to build a real life together."

"Thanks, Mom. You too."

"Anyway, it's all set to move in when you come home. You're going to be finished with your mural on time, then?"

"Yep." Enzo smiled at the mural, thinking of the excited call he'd gotten to make to Will last night, telling him that he'd bought his ticket to fly home.

This had been a short-ish job on the Oregon coast—only a few weeks—but it was the last one he'd done in several months where Will hadn't come with him.

He'd missed him even more than he'd thought possible.

"I bet Will's thrilled. What day are you coming home, then? We should do a big family dinner the night you're home—since you two will probably be too busy moving, after?" Giana asked slyly.

Enzo laughed. "If that's what you want to call it. But yeah. Wednesday. We could do that."

"I'll set it up," Giana said.

"You mean you'll ask Luca to set it up," Enzo teased.

"Well, *yes*, your cousin does love planning these sorts of things. Why should I deprive him of that joy?"

"Why should you?" Enzo mused. "Well, Mom, I gotta go. If I'm gonna go home next Wednesday, I've got work to do."

"Send more pictures! And good luck, darling. Love you!"

"Love you too," Enzo said and slipped his phone into his pocket.

He'd never imagined that he'd be *happy* to be going back to Indigo Bay, happy to be moving into his childhood home, wildly in love and ready to settle down.

But even settling down looked different to him and Will than it looked to others. He'd always be traveling, painting all over the country, though he was trying to prioritize jobs that were closer, these days. Will always told him not to do it—to take the jobs he wanted to take—but he knew now that their relationship was all about give and take.

He pulled his phone back and snapped a quick selfie, texting it to his boyfriend.

Love you. Miss you. Can't wait to move in with you, again.

Will texted back almost instantly. **Love you more. Miss you more. Can't wait to christen every room in the new house.**

When Enzo finally headed up to the mural, climbing up the scaffolding, he couldn't stop smiling.

It had only been a year, but it was amazing how much had changed.

And even more amazing, how goddamned happy he was about those changes.

Will didn't think he'd ever get tired of the surge of happiness he felt on the days Enzo came home to Indigo Bay.

To *him*.

He experienced them less frequently than he used to, because these days he often traveled with Enzo more often than not—but this time around, he'd been helping Kate finalize the summer specials, and the mural had been a smaller one, so he'd stayed.

Plus, he'd wanted to make sure that if Giana needed any help moving, he was around for her.

Oliver and Luca had volunteered of course. It felt like Giana had a whole town of people she could call on to help, but Will and Enzo had talked about him being around to offer his assistance, and Will had been happy to do it.

He didn't think, even after only a few weeks of separation, that he'd ever get used to this thrill racing through him. Didn't think he'd ever get tired of it, and how he knew, more than ever, that he was in love with Enzo. And he knew he'd feel like this every day of the rest of his life.

"Enzo coming home today?" Kate asked as he packed up his laptop, getting ready to meet him at the empty house they'd be moving into together tomorrow.

"Yep," Will said, grinning before he could stop himself.

"Aw, you two are too dang cute," Kate cooed. "A year in and still wildly in love."

"I think I'll probably feel this way forever," Will confided.

"Seems likely. But hey, good news, he gets that same look on his face whenever he walks in and sees you again."

"Yeah? God, I hope so."

"Were you worried?" Kate wondered.

"No. No, of course not." He never worried about Enzo. Enzo was a sure thing, his love always right there on the surface, written across his whole face, brimming in his beautiful eyes, always right about to spill over. Will would have to be blind to miss it, and he still wouldn't, even then. Because it was plain, too, every time Enzo touched him.

"You shouldn't be. Gonna have to make an honest man of him someday," Kate suggested, a smile on her face.

"Someday."

Will had bought the ring two months ago, a simple, classy platinum band, engraved on the inside with their initials and the date they'd met, and he knew he'd give it to him sometime soon. Maybe in the kitchen of their new house together.

But he wasn't in any huge hurry. They'd get there. And they'd enjoy every single moment and every single step.

Will heard the bell over the door tinkle, and Kate perked up, hearing it too. "I've got it," she said. "Have a nice night, boss."

Finishing packing up his laptop, Will slung the bag over his shoulder and headed out through the front, flashing Kate one last smile before he disappeared out the front door.

It was a nice short walk to the house.

Will knew he'd left earlier than he needed to, far earlier than he could hope Enzo would be there, but he'd been too eager.

He typed in the front door code to the house, the keypad he'd just installed on Monday, and when he swung the door open—he gave a surprised yelp, because there was Enzo, sitting on the kitchen island, grinning at him like he'd just given him the gift of his life.

And maybe he had.

He dropped his bag and practically ran over to him, hugging him as Enzo's legs wrapped around him, pulling him right into his embrace.

"You're home early," he said, breathing out unsteadily into Enzo's T-shirt-clad shoulder.

"Couldn't wait to get home to you so I took an earlier flight. Surprise," Enzo said, his voice filled with happiness. Will recognized it because he felt it too. Then he kissed him, because he couldn't stop himself any longer.

The kiss dragged on and on and Will was just about to suggest that they christen the kitchen *now*, when Enzo pulled back, resting his head on Will's shoulder.

"What do you think?" Enzo murmured. "Think we could be happy here?"

"I think…" The truth was staring at him in the face. "I think I could be happy with you anywhere, Honey Bunny."

"Yeah? You gonna be my Stud Muffin forever?"

Will thought about the ring, buried in his sock drawer. Thought about dropping to one knee—but there'd be so much time for that later. Right now was perfect, just as it was.

"Yeah," Will said. "If you'll be mine."

Don't miss the bonus scene where Enzo and Will debate a *very* important question.
To check it out, visit www.bethbolden.com/bonus

And if you haven't read *Sweet as Pie*, Luca & Oliver's book and the sweetest, spiciest grumpy/sunshine romance,
visit www.bethbolden.com/indigobay

To see a beautifully rendered version of Enzo's mural created by Loyal Hound Art,
visit www.bethbolden.com/cherry-mural

INTERESTED IN READING MORE OF
BETH'S BOOKS?

CHECK OUT A FULL LIST OF TILES
BY SCANNING THE QR CODE
OR VISITING HER WEBSITE

WWW.BETHBOLDEN.COM/BOOKLIST

WANT TO FOLLOW BETH?

MAKE SURE YOU NEVER
MISS A RELEASE?

SCAN THE QR CODE BELOW
OR VISIT HER WEBSITE
FOR A SOCIAL MEDIA LIST,
NEWSLETTER SIGNUP,
AND SO MUCH MORE!

WWW.BETHBOLDEN.COM/ABOUT